WOMBS

Ark *Rhapsody* and Ark *Amadeus*

CLIFF PARIS

Acknowledgments

Many thanks to Michael Carr, Editor; Karen Paris; Margaret Benjamin; Henry and Charlotte Paris; Amanda Turner; and everyone who helped bring this story to light, and those who read it.

Copyright © 2011 Cliff Paris

ISBN-10: 1456547763
EAN-13: 9781456547769
Library of Congress Control Number: 2011900883

This is a work of fiction. Names, characters, places and incidents are products of the author's imagination or are used fictitiously and are not to be construed as real. Any resemblance to actual events, locales, organizations, or persons, living or dead, is entirely coincidental.

All rights reserved. No part of this book may be used or reproduced in any manner what so ever without written permission, except in the case of brief quotations embodied in critical articles and reviews. To obtain permissions or for information contact
permissions@imaginaryearth.com

Material Registered with The Writers Guild.

For information regarding bulk purchases.

Please contact Sales@ImaginaryEarth.com, or call (703) 366-3854

To Mom and Dad

We are not skin and water as presumed, but a tango born into the sky.
—Brittany Morris, Maggie Argenon's fifth-grade gifted class, 2027

Ark *Rhapsody* and Ark *Amadeus*

ACT I

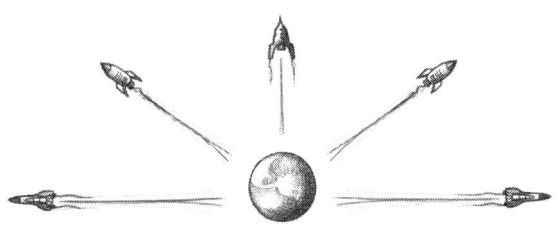

CHAPTER ONE

As I walked, leather briefcase in one hand, suit coat dangling by its loop in the other, I began to see how the sun runs everything down in this land of spiny plants and poisonous creatures and unreliable visions. This place could be anywhere: the Sonora Desert, Israel's Negev, even another planet. And down here the sun taunts me by quietly dry-rotting my spare tire. Welcome to the outskirts of Odessa, Texas, mile marker 81 on the two-lane toward Pecos, three hundred miles from home where the silence, the isolation, and the blunt force of the sun have me convinced that nature has no idea anyone's out here, or it would never have turned the heat up this high. I hope this was all worth it: the fourteen day shifts, the glitches and outright failures, not to mention the enormous expense to the government.— Sometimes the dream isn't worth all that.

I had left the car a few miles back with a rag on the door handle, and my useless phone on the front seat and just walked. I would have left the briefcase, too, but it had the B58 vial, and that stuff can't be left in extreme heat. What a find, though! A miracle vitamin, and set to be available to the general public in a year or so. A little rivulet of sweat was tickling its way down my calf when I recognized a particular thicket of cholla cactus, gracefully symmetrical but with a single broken offshoot spoiling the symmetry. That meant the abandoned insurance building was maybe two miles ahead—a short distance astronomically speaking, but on foot in this heat, with no water, well . . .

Hovering over the road ahead was the usual mirage: a wavy, buckling blanket of misshapen air from which I expected to see a car or a bus or a camel materialize at any moment. Or maybe this mirage would produce a passerby—a person with whom a bond might form, as when eyes meet, voices engage, or skin touches and a connection is felt and relished and travels like music through the air.

The space between two points instantly fills with this rare nonsubstance, so that you can almost run your fingers through its thick, soft, peaceful, long, radiant locks. Life's physical connections are so easily severed, ending abruptly to drop us alone onto a park bench, like a child being punished. I wish evolution would take charge, grab hold. I wish it would notice our struggle and help us adapt to this difficult world. I hope there's something like this to be found, out there to be discovered and brought to life. I hope I'm the one to find it. But that sounds like delirium brought on by the heat.

The mirage remained cautiously ahead of me, and the fragrance of the catclaw blossoms reached me in dry wafts, sometimes tangy, often sweet. Suddenly I realized how seldom I had caught a scent so reminiscent of Maggie as I did just then. I thought of how she was probably pacing back and forth at home, waiting for me to make my usual call upon arriving at work.

"Jason," Maggie said, pacing the kitchen floor. She leaned the shovel against the vacuum cleaner and sat down to stare at the papers poking out from the satchel hung on the empty chair across the breakfast table. Beneath the lazy ceiling fan, she nibbled her fingernail and pulled the stack out, removing some of the loose spiral shreds and brushing away the eraser remnants from the first page. She was more than prepared to correct all the *y'all*'s and *could of went*'s that she typically encountered from her ten-year-olds, but as she read the first paper, her hand lowered to the page and lifted the corner, and her soft summer moss–colored eyes savored the child's words.

"Wow," she said, leaning back and bringing the page with her. "Why, Brittany, this poem is quite good!"

Maybe he'd let me send these up in a ship, for the astronauts to read. She shook her head and sighed softly. Maggie, emotional Maggie. Sure, her emotions took hold sometimes, and to most she might seem pot-roast basic with her clipped hair and flowery dress, but she made sense— solid, rational sense—and she made me feel as loved as ice cream. She knew that right now I was all about the mission and didn't like distractions from it—sending a poem up would not be a big priority for me.

She lifted the next paper. "Another good one . . . Annette," she said to the name on the top of the page. Then, pushing the papers away, she walked out the kitchen door to the garage.

She pulled the chain of the fluorescent fixture to reveal my unfinished workshop, which she had not set foot in for a year and half. She had been almost afraid of it, I thought—afraid of what she might find. This was where I spent most of my nights, while she did the dishes and watched TV in the living room with our three year old golden retriever Duncan and an old Siamese stray she named Haiku. She looked down onto the workbench and stared at the complexities before her: odd-looking mechanisms of unfamiliar purpose. Silvery metals on disks, gold-colored gears and glides, fogged plastic tubes and bright-green circuit boards, motors lashed to batteries by zip ties, hard drives strapped to laptops by sticky black loops of electrical tape—these were the things of the mission, a mission of such grandeur that, as she often said, it took over the whole house.

She bumped into a long gold metal arm suspended from a rafter; when it moved, a tiny LED attached to the bench winked on. She studied the arm: six rods with pivots, each pivot sprouting a new wire that ran up to join the next, wires accumulating, gathering, twisting into a tight, colorful bundle that led to the socket of the LED on the bench. Carefully strapping the Velcro band to her wrist, she moved her arm in a broad circle, making a soft smile when the light shone brighter. It shone longer than seemed possible for her movement to create. Power created from human motion, energy drawn to its fullest extent: energy arms, known to us engineering types simply as EAs.

"Jason," she said. She spoke with the most adorable Texan in her words—just this subtle little twang. She also had this trick, this way of saying my name, much the way a poet would carve out a character for her own use, all with just those five letters. "Jason," she said, this time artfully adding admiration.

On the wall were photos and notes and the first sketch of an ark ship, tacked with a pushpin to a bare wall stud. The spacecraft was rounded and simple, about the length and width of a school bus—a '57 school bus, maybe, what with the three fins at the rear. A window and a door in the center, and solar panels encased under a layer of glass, took up most of the rest of the hull. Two long glass capsules extended from the sides of the ship and were attached by a retractable rail. From this rail, a drawn arrow pointed to a paragraph of notes that read, "Ship to spin from retro boosts during deployment of centrifuge capsules." Another sketch detailed the inner hull, whose strange mechanisms where tightly nestled inside like clockworks.

Maggie ran her finger along the thin penciled lines and studied the gear: the navigational telescope, nursery cradles, centrifuges, and Petri dish freezers, the main cabin's three monitors and a console, the sleeping accommodations. She knew of my childhood.

"Jason, honey," she said when she saw the bunk bed drawn on the inner hull.

She knew I had spent much of my early childhood in the basement of the nearby hospital, where, along with another boy, I was raised by the staff, parented part-time by shifts of doctors and nurses and groundskeepers. Some of the staff would take their time to tutor us, because doctors and nurses love to teach people things, but then they would go—they were tired at night and wanted to go home to their families, to turn off the lights and leave. The groundskeepers had the funniest stories, Mexican tales of sultry beauties and faraway places with snakes and one-eyed dogs, forests to play in and caverns to swim in, fields to work in and small towns to run away from.

The boy in the bottom bunk and I, in the top, would listen to the stories and daydream about adventure. This boy and I dreamed together. The most memorable features of the boy in the bottom bunk were his thick black eyebrows and big black eyes. Those eyes would stare up at me between the side rail and the mattress, and he would politely ask me not to bounce around and not to cover the air-conditioning vent. He was so polite. I used to drop Lego pieces on him. I think I generally annoyed him very much.

This boy and I, of about the same age—ten or so—lived, played, and wrestled with each other in this room in the basement of the old hospital outside Henrietta. I must point out, though, this wasn't a family life. There was not one photograph of us. We didn't go on trips to the park or to a restaurant, but we played on the grounds in the huge magnolias, ate routine food in the cafeteria, and learned from the boring books in the library.

One day, this boy was gone. He simply disappeared. At the time, I thought he was my brother, though he looked nothing like me. But he just left—adopted out, I think. No brother would just leave like that. What brother would do that?

For another year, I stayed in the basement, where the isolation seemed to grow and feed on itself, until a fat, drunk couple took me in for the government payment—"the check," they actually called me at times. I despised them and their lazy, haphazard drawl, deep and slow as molasses on a cold day, and I avoided adopting their manner of speech the best I could. I turned to admiring the long words and intricate phrases of the doctors and surgeons, and I longed to acquire my own elegant, oversize parchment with a mahogany frame. I wanted a diploma—but not in medicine, I decided. I wanted something of my own, a mixture of mechanical and biological, and I had always loved rocket ships. That was what I wanted to do, who I wanted to be.

During my sophomore year in high school, I was lucky enough to find Maggie; the smartest girl with the prettiest eyes and a can't-miss smile. Our first date was a vivid event to me, and it spoke of her nature like no other time I can recall. I had a photo of her then, torn and wrinkled but now lost like so many other things. This date, this wonderful life, started with just coffee. I was so taken with her exotic adventures to California—the ocean and Knott's Berry Farm that we walked inside a little bubble all the way to dinner. Our timing was perfect—we got the best table at the Elm Fire Grill, right under the huge stuffed bear. We had salads and steaks and the best conversation I had ever had with a girl. Maggie and I made it to the football game by halftime, and I was in my element. To me, football was dirt and pain. I loved watching it, but it was never team versus team to me, not athlete versus athlete, but enemy against friend.

Just for me, Maggie pretended to enjoy it: the quarterback forcing his way past three linemen and outrunning their best safety, ending the night with a glorious twenty-seven–twenty-six win. When Maggie tapped the bottom of the popcorn cup to get the last pieces out, the wind blew some into her hair and they fell around her like snow. She looked at me so adoringly when I brushed some of them away. It was a night to remember until I realized that sometimes the night can turn things around on you.

We walked from the gates, talking and laughing, when three drunk seniors from the rival school jumped out of the bed of a pickup parked beside my car.

They said some things about her and me, and after I shoved one of them, the other two threw me against the car and punched me in the stomach until I fell to the ground. The bottom of a boot kicked the side of my face. I remember that most of all: the tread, the smell of Neolite, and the coarse feel of the individual pebbles of asphalt against my forehead and cheek.

Just then I heard, in a deep voice, "Any room in there for lil' ol' me?"

I couldn't speak. I tightened my stomach muscles, expecting another kick to my gut. In science class, they always made you sit in the smallest desks—Tex could barely fit in one at all. He always carried a Bible and rarely spoke to anyone other than his little sister, and now, in between the punches—muffled *thunks* of fists against my jacket—I heard him growl.

"Jace, I got ya, hoss," he said.

My right eye was swollen all the way shut, but through my bloody left one I saw Tex haul those seniors off me, one at a time, like pulling overcoats from a pile.

I rose to my feet, staggered a bit, but managed to land a decent punch to an attacker's jaw. As blue lights approached, they ran off, and Maggie serenely approached me in the flashing colors. With my torn shirt, blood-ruined tie, and swelling face, she tried to button my shirt for me, but all the buttons had popped off and were scattered on the ground. As I leaned against the car, holding my ribs and trying not to breathe too deep, I watched her pick the buttons up, ever so carefully. I had never seen her in high heels before, but she was good at wearing them. When she rose, there was disappointment in her eyes. She counted the buttons again in her delicate hand, gave a quick frown and a sigh, and I knew one was missing. It wasn't important to me, but to her, she had failed.

"Jason, are you okay?" she asked—worry and pity stirred in with a motherly tone.

I nodded and looked around for Tex.

"Is he a buddy of yours?" she asked, sliding the buttons into my breast pocket.

"My science partner. We did a report together." He was gone.

"That musta' been a good one."

"Yeah, A-minus."

"Can I drive?" she said with a twinkle in her eyes, watching me hold in my winces.

I threw the keys to her and said, "Test-tube babies . . . Our report was on birthing children"—I coughed and grimaced—"in different environments." She nodded and cast me an impressed look. Or maybe it was a look of worry—I couldn't tell; women's looks often perplex me.

She drove me to the hospital, where I was able to sneak away long enough to buy the last sparse bunch of flowers left in the gift shop. Estelle still worked the register. She was always nice to me when I lived here; she didn't charge me for the flowers, on the condition that she could poke her head around the corner to see what my date looked like. She did and giggled in her Bette Davis way. While Maggie and I waited for my prescription, we batted a rubber glove back and forth over the daisy arrangement and talked about school, bullies, dogs and cats, and how she wanted to be a writer.

There she was, my date, my future writer, pretty as a pink slipper and filled with all kinds of dreams. I could feel them, static, waiting. I came out with no more than a few bandages, a finger splint, and a temporary limp, only to find out that young Tex, in his brown Carhartt work jacket and jeans smelling of ninety-weight oil, had been sitting in the waiting room the whole time.

"Nothing better to do 'round here," he said, and handed me my missing button. *Friends for life,* I thought then.

I aced the SATs and was plucked from high school early, graduated from MIT at nineteen, and married Maggie. Tex and I joined the Army and shipped off to another desert war, this one vastly more necessary than the last two. And even though I wasn't overseas very long, I missed Maggie, thought of her constantly.

Maggie stepped to the far right of my workbench, and behind some tall metal columns, her eyes fixed on something. It wasn't the bedsheet she had been missing from the linen closet, but what lay beneath it. She slowly pulled it back to reveal a clear plastic ball the size of the floor globe in the school library. This sphere contained a tight bundle of contorted pipes and rugged-looking clamps, all floating in a thick blue fluid the color of an airline toilet flush.

"A plastic womb" she said,

She then noticed that there were small EAs inside.

"To collect even the energy from an embryo." She closed her eyes tight. "Jason," she said with a slight but unmistakable tremble of fear.

Maggie stepped over to the tall metal storage cabinet, reached up and felt inside the top lip, and fished out an old pack of Marlboros she had stuck there when we first moved in. With an unlit cigarette between her lips, she inhaled, sat down at the bench, and sifted through a stack of unopened mail to find a large brown envelope.

The title read, "Manifest of accepted donors for the Wombs project." She unwound the string, broke the seal, and slid out a piece of paper with a long list of names. Her eyes darted in contemplation as she discovered a name familiar to her. "Jason Griffith Argenon." She whispered it. "On the ark *Rhapsody.*" She exhaled. "Jason, what are you doing?" She put down the cigarette, pulled out her cell phone, and dialed. Voice mail came on, and she sadly cleared her throat. "Jason, it's me. I just wanted to talk. . . Well, I guess I'll talk, then. I know you say you're not ready . . . not ready for a baby . . . but I see you're on this . .

. this list. What kind of thing is this? I don't know what to think. I don't know what's happening to us." She paused for a very long time, and a tear filled the corner of her eye. She bit down on her lip while looking up at a photo of me beside a huge telescope and left these chilling words on the message: "A ship called *Rhapsody*. A ship instead of me—are you really going to do this?" She wept. "Do this thing . . . 'I feel like your . . . well, do you really want to do this to us?"

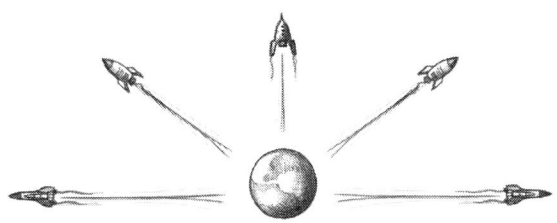

CHAPTER TWO

Mile marker 59 approached, and I looked back—still only desert. Not one car had passed by, but then, that was the reason we chose this location: desolate, isolated, secretive—well, as secretive as one can be with satellites above. We mostly bused people in to avoid stacks of cars. A few steps farther, and I saw the outline of the abandoned brick building as it birthed itself from the road. The little, lone structure had a flat roof, the sign brackets were pulling away from the cracked mortar between the old bricks, and the loose doorknob turned easily and the glass rattled in the door frame as I pushed the sand away—many footprints inside—and shut the door behind me.

Under the sink in the cleaning supply cabinet was a large combination lock. I spun the dial left, then right, then left again, and it clicked. With a sound like a desk drawer opening, the wall beside me split open, and I stepped into a brightly lit steel elevator. I pulled my badge from my briefcase and waved it across the sensor pad, pressed "M" for "mezzanine" and rode down twenty flights.

While I was at war in the Middle East, the awards I got for best aerospace design—a self-contained long-distance spacecraft—were sparking the interest of the U.S. government. My inventions were here, gaining attention without me. The concept was to build ships that would launch unoccupied, travel extreme distances, locate a habitable planet by use of optical comparisons of prebiotic chemical signatures, and then birth children inside the shipboard nursery. Onboard computers would raise and tutor them within the ship during deceleration and the last fourteen years of the journey. They were to land on a newly found planet to create a foothold for humankind. This was the idea. On paper it sounded grandiose—okay, impossible—but *I knew* it could be done, by combining existing technology with breakthroughs in a newly formulated xenon fuel accelerant. I always sensed an urgency to putting these things in place, but I was still overseas and in a war. From there, I heard news that a dear college friend, Dr. Hidetaki Yimosu, and several of my MIT professors spoke on my behalf. They encouraged the pursuit of my ideas, and the U.S. government began to engage my concept, and the theories began to take hold for the scientific community. Surprisingly and abruptly, the military ended my tour overseas and called me in to do this work. I had a mission; I had a project: Wombs. I am Jason Griffith Argenon.

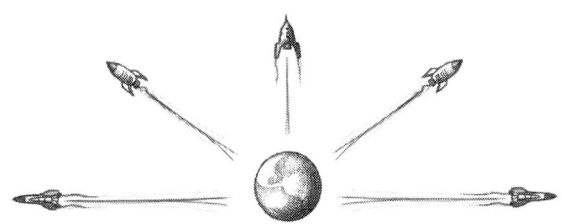

CHAPTER THREE

When the elevator door opened—in fact, every time it opened—I was in awe of the bright white of it all, of the vastness, the machinery, the people. Stepping toward the railing on the grated metal platform, I gazed at the progress since only two days ago. Engines were being lifted into place, ships' hulls lashed to overhead lifts, forklifts speeding in tight aisles with sheets of metal and framework. And I was excited to get back to work. Small groups of white-coated scientist gathered at their marker boards surrounded by the sounds of loud rivet guns and the pop of welding torches. Some of the workers looked up and waved.

I took a drink from the water fountain.

"You okay, Mr Argenon?" a scientist, Starghard, asked.

I nodded.

He continued over the sounds of the factory. "I've been working on the media library and the photo archives. Do you want photos of the parents of the astronauts included in the records?"

"I don't know," I said. "With everything else going on, everything to keep track of, it seems like too much can go wrong."

"You might be right about that," he said. Someone yelled up to him, and he said, "I'll work on it," before heading down the stairs.

From the glass offices along the platform, Veronica approached in jeans, tight blue Wombs shirt, and ponytail. She had the mien of a surly waitress and the body of a fitness instructor.

"Hi, dear," she said, pushing her tongue into her gum. "It's been a long two days withoutcha." She had a clipboard with a stack of papers. I avoided looking at them.

"I was told to give you this when you got in." She handed me a folded fax and popped her gum.

I read it. "Budgetary issuances are on a mandatory hold until further notice. More outside funding is required to be secured by your office no later than one week from today." I looked up at her.

"They're kidding?" I said.

"You didn't catch the prez's speech? Cutbacks, sweatheart—they're squeezin' everybody."

I folded up the fax and put it in my briefcase.

"They want *me* to find more funds—right," I said over the rail, exhaustion setting in.

Veronica leaned over the rail, too. "Also, they sent out the embryo list. You're on it; you get to have your specimens on one of the ships."

"Hell, that's the *last* thing I need," I grumped. "I've got to get these things off the ground!"

Veronica smiled and said, "You'll do fine," and went into the office. I looked across the floor and held my head down. I heard an alarm go off in a ship. It sounded like a British siren. It was loud.

I exhaled. "Money." This project had been showing signs of sputtering out. I was constantly altering the scope to direct what little funds were left into the most critical systems, but now this fax sounded as though they were trying to pull the plug on it completely. I thought about it—for about a second. *Money.* In this devastated world economy, there was only one place to get it. I didn't want to bring more cooks into the kitchen, but more cooks beat shutting the whole diner down. I had no choice.

I picked up the phone and dialed the comptroller's number. He picked up on the first ring.

"Skid."

"Yeah, Jason?"

"Do me a favor. I need a jet. Don't ask me why, either. I got problems, gotta sort 'em out."

"Yes, sir," he said. "Fifteen minutes."

"Thanks, buddy." I hung up and hoped no drivers or pilots knew of the project's money shutdown. If they did, I wouldn't be going anywhere. I dialed Maggie at home.

"Honey?" she answered. I could hear pain there.

"I had a flat tire. Sorry, I left the phone in the car."

"As long as you're okay." Her voice caught. "Did you get my message?"

"No . . ." I looked across the floor of the factory. But I noticed something was wrong; something was missing.

"When will you be home again? Is this a double-ten day this time?"

I only half listened because my attention was on the factory floor. Something was definitely out of place—something big. I felt dizzy, and my stomach lurched. It was ships. Ships were missing.

"Hold on, Maggie," I said. With my hand over the mouthpiece, I tapped on the glass. Veronica came out of the office. "Where are the ships that where over there?" I said.

Her face soured, and with a deep frown, she mouthed the words, "Bertrum took 'em."

"Colonel Bertrum, God damn it! That guy has always been a pain in my ass. Where is he?"

"He's gone, too—reassigned, they say."

"Shit."

I looked across the floor and saw Tex climbing down a ladder from the hatch of one of the ships. "Maggie, I gotta call you back." Hanging up the phone, I walked toward Tex, searching the plant floor for evidence—remnants, clues to where the ships might have gone. Some scientists stopped and watched me, and a few tried to get my attention. "Mr. Argenon, we believe these Embryo storage containers are too big, too heavy."

Over my shoulder, I replied, "Make them smaller and lighter," and kept walking.

Tex, surrounded by his usual ragtag accumulation of old-school wrenches and sockets, was breathing heavily while ratcheting in one of the retro-rocket flanges.

"How's it going?" I said.

"It's goin'," he said. Tex seemed to be three people: this cowboy, an unsettled veteran, and an altar boy who tried his best but sometimes flashed the girls after getting into the communion wine.

"Look, seven, maybe eight ships have been moved from here. Veronica says Bertrum took 'em. Did you hear anything?"

He finished seating the next gasket into the side fitting of the ship and looked up. "Not sure. I've been testin' the retro programs—been inside o' this ship comin' on two days. Those bunks are cozy, dude." He got a quizzical look on his face while pushing closed the cover for the rocket. "These rockets, I dunno—they seem to just mosey along into the turns."

"We don't want tight turns. Besides, it's a little late to change anything that integral now. Look, Tex," I said, looking up at the platform, "did you know the guvvies are here?" Two guys in ties and white shirts, with black briefcases, were staring down at me. They went into an office.

"Probably about your missin' ships, right?" Tex picked up a robotic arm and went up the ladder, and I put my briefcase on the bench and followed him.

Above the hatch was a plate that read, "Ark *Rhapsody*." Inside, the cool air hit me, and when I leaned on a bulkhead, the thin white aluminum gave a little. Tex lined up and slid the gold arm into its socket and snapped together its wire connectors. He bumped into one of the EAs, which dangled by springs from the ceiling. "This place is a death trap, dude."

"I told you, the computers keep them out of the way," I said, gathering the arms together and sliding them on their tracks back into the corner. "They won't tangle up." Looking around, I had to admire the elegant simplicity: three monitors mounted in front of two command chairs, no gauges or astronaut controls except for a biolock and some manual video controls on the nursery wall—but what was this? Between the door and the window, a glass tube, three inches in diameter, with wooden caps on both ends and what looked like a paper scroll inside.

"What's this?" I asked Tex, and he looked up at it.

"That? It's the Brit's idea. The boy to be born in this ship is the son of a parliament man or somethin' like that. It's some fancy birth certificate. Takes up a lot of space, if you ask me. Prob'ly cost a hundred grand in fuel right there—what, maybe ten drops of that fancy accelerant of yours?" He smiled at me.

"We had to agree to all kinds of things to get the British money. A scroll on the wall might not be the worst of it, either. How's the nursery coming along?"

"The white coats are finishing up the itty-bitty centrifuges now." He was adjusting the robot arm. "Doc, raise your arm." The arm rose.

I stared into the nursery. It was cramped with mechanical devices, gels in tubes, silver platforms, and even smaller robotic arms. Attached to the ceiling on a six-foot circular track were the plastic globes—the wombs—half filled with the thick blue fluid. I listened to them filling and emptying, being robotically tested for leaks.

"Maggie wants a baby," I said out of the blue.

"Yeah, she seems like the kind who would." Tex climbed under the computer console to hook up some more wires. "I got so many sisters, we got babies everywhere—in the yard, the kitchen, peein' on the sofa . . ."

"Yeah, I can't wait," I muttered.

I started back down the ladder, but I'd forgotten to tell Tex I was leaving town, so I climbed back up. When I poked my head through the doorway, he started and dropped something wrapped in a plastic bag.

"Oh . . . ," he said, bumping his head and shoulders against the bulkhead. "Don't worry, Jace, I'm keepin' my eyes peeled for ship snatchers." I noticed that his eyes were red and darted back and forth. "Where you goin', anyway?"

"Going?" I stepped all the way in.

"You have your coat and briefcase like you're taking off for the moon."

"Oh . . . China."

"Ah," he said. "You hate China."

"No, I don't."

"Yeah, you do."

"Well, maybe, but not all of it."

"You seeing Jing?"

"No."

"Yeah, y'are."

"Well, she'll be there . . . coincidentally. We're just friends."

Tex looked out the ship's hatch at the elevated platform. Veronica was leaning against the rail. "Just friends," he said, staring out.

"Seriously, you know I love my Mags." We both stared out at Veronica.

"I know. I'm just saying, Jing's hot"

"Tex, you never even met Jing."

"I know. She just *sounds* hot. Her name, Jing . . . like 'Jackpot'—the sound, y'know?"

"Yeah, I guess," I said, ready to change the subject. "You know, last week Veronica said you were like a tractor-trailer on a midnight run, whatever that means."

I started back down and felt Tex peering down at me through the doorway. He said, "I think that means she wants my body." As my feet hit the floor, I heard the sound of duct tape peeling from a roll, and the faint rustle of a plastic bag.

Tex, I said to myself as I grabbed my coat and bag, *I hope you're not screwing up again.*

From the warehouse floor I heard the phone on the wall ring. "Oh, shit," I breathed. Jogging, I made it up the stairs by the fifth ring. "Maggie . . ."

"No, it's your pilot, sir. The plane is ready. A car will be topside for you in five minutes."

The two guvvies came out of the office and stared at me. I put my back to them.

"On my way," I said, and hung up.

One of the guvvies tapped me on the shoulder. "So Veronica told you about Bertrum removing the ships for testing." The other one was eyeballing me. "Don't think of making an incident out of this. Just be grateful for the ships you have—take care of those."

I came close to decking him right there, but I just nodded. I could see the remaining ships in the corner of my eye. Like a father of a troubled child, I knew they needed me—my ships needed me to protect them, to keep them safe, and to be rational about my approach with these pricks. The guvvies went back into the office, and I got on the elevator.

Halfway up, I gritted my teeth and lightly punched the elevator wall, pulling my fist back. I'd forgotten to call her *again*.

The airport car pulled up, and I got inside and leaned back in the seat. I asked the driver if he got a signal here. He handed me his phone.

Maggie picked up on the first ring. She'd been crying.

"What's the matter?" I said.

"Jason, we have to talk about this thing. I went into the garage. . . . I saw the list."

"The *list*? What list?"

"The names of the specimen donors . . . you know, for the embryos on your ships. Your name is on it."

I was silent, unsure what to say.

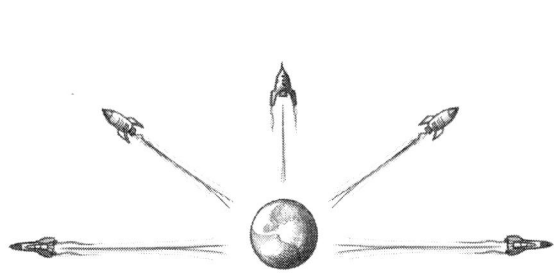

CHAPTER FOUR

"Oh, Jason, at first I thought, this seems so scientific, so impersonal . . . but now you're sending your own specimens up." I heard her sniffle. "It's personal."

When Maggie got excited, her words came out like river rapids, beginning slow and easy, but then drawing you into the center where it becomes fast and real and a fight for your life.

"Instead of some unreal, unlikely thing, this has turned real," she said. "I really can't believe you expect to launch these ships and never, ever care about the children inside. I know we've had this discussion, but now one of those children is going to be *yours*. You're going to regret this, all of it. And since I'm with you, I'll regret it, too. You and some other unknown woman, making a baby." I heard her chopping vegetables.

I paced on the platform, stretching the phone cord. Two scientists were waiting to talk to me. Turning toward the wall, I whispered, "Why'd you let me do it from the start, then?"

23

"When you told me about it, I didn't think it would ever happen. You know, like the tabloids: 'Women discovered on Mars.' 'Moon men found living in Graceland.' Well, try this one: 'Babies to fly spaceships to unknown planets.' How's that? Jason, I've tried and tried to think what it's like for you, to do your dream. It seemed so harmless, doing your dream, but it's *not* harmless, Jason—not harmless at all." I heard the knife slam down on the cutting board with each syllable. "I lived in Henrietta all my life, and I try not to let this damn dusty desert dry me up and blow me away."

Now I heard her pacing on the wood floor. "These last two years married to you have been good, but this place is no dream of mine. I swear, there's a ghost in the warsher. I broke in the shovel today. Yeah, used it on a baby rattler under the tawlit. Beyond the random reptile, the television has nothin' on it but preachin', and the dog hasn't seen a blade of grass in its whole miserable tick-ridden life."

I heard Maggie struggling to open the kitchen window.

"This is no dream of mine. What about *my* dreams? Swear to me— swear to me, Jason—when this project is over, we're moving north. I always wanted to be near the capital. We'll love it: rain, a little snow, trees you don't have to water . . . Why, I might even lose . . . well, this accent. Mom always hated it. She corrected me every day, but a lot of damn good it did Henrietta gets in your words like a virus. How 'bout Georgetown? How 'bout that—a nice row house like you had in Boston? Ivy on the bricks, finished wood floors, and maybe a court-yard—Duncan would love peein' in a courtyard. I'd put some flowers out there—real ones."

"We can think about it," I hedged. But she read through my stall tactic and kept rolling, harder and faster, more swirling water gaining on me and pulling me down.

"Seriously, Jason, I invite the women around for tea, and they show up in their nice doily-fringed dresses, their hair done just right, and when I let 'em in, they start spreadin' newspaper on the coffee table and pulling out their gun-cleaning kits. I thought, here we go, Henrietta strikes again. We sat there cleanin' our guns and chattin' about caps and calibers and reloads and how they watch the vet neuter their cats. I'm going crazy, Jason! And now what's happening? Your gonna have children, without me . . . *in space.* Yes, I'll tell the ladies of the Henrietta gun-toting and -shooting and -cleaning society, my husband's gonna have kids in space. That'll be good for a hoot."

"Maggie, stop. Maggie . . ." I waited to say it, yet couldn't believe I was about to. I found a warmth in the idea, like the first thought of getting a puppy, but then the reality set in, and the instant I actually said it, I felt a brick of solid reality smack me on the head. "We should have a baby. We'll have one." I exhaled. "Just make it a boy—please, a boy."

"For real? For *real,* Jason?"

"For real, Mags." I heard her cover the phone and yell a big woohoo. I smiled a little; she was happy. "Mom's coming to stay next week. She'll be so excited!" I heard her kiss her palm and blow it to me. "I blew you a kiss."

"I know, Mags." I closed the phone and settled back into the seat. I bought her that shovel. We were going to dig a garden together, grow peas and squash and okra, but there was so little time these days for gardens or television or hobbies. But now a child of my own . . . *I only hope I'm a better dad than my critics are making me out to be. Their concerns are overblown, I think. How is earth possibly going to miss some frozen samples? Maggie worries too much.*

She gets that from her mother. Her mother projects all kinds of things onto Maggie, things to worry about. She wants her to stay a child, to remain needful, suspicious of the world's intentions. Maggie's mother, Mrs. Crumwell, will spoil this child—our child—and torture it, the way she does Maggie and me when she comes to stay. Mrs. Crumwell reminds me of the entire cast of The Wizard of Oz: *the sound of straw when she moves about in her trusty red raincoat, the good, the wicked, the long whippy tail, the generously applied oils and lotions, the front basket on her bicycle for picking flowers or stealing dogs, the gracious gifts handed gently to us, things only a wizard could bring, two crated hissing cats, which she releases like those apocalyptic flying monkeys, and then, of coarse, coming from her car and up the walk, through the ornately etched oval glass window of our front door, Maggie and I see the single-fisted-elbow march of the Lollipop Guild in full regalia. Mrs. Crumwell. Her husband's been gone almost a year now. He would teach and help and slap you on the back and mean it. Weeds in his lawn were his only enemy; everyone who knew him was his friend. Maggie was her mother and father, and our child would be all three.*

I awoke as the car drove over the gate threshold and onto the tarmac, toward the private jet that would take me to the San Antonio airport, where I would board the next flight. I looked the silver aviator's watch given to me by Maggie's mom. I had been known to make rash decisions, to give in when it came to Maggie, but this, I think, was not giving in; it was necessity. Nearing the anniversary of her father's passing away, she needed something, and I knew she would do anything to regain the pleasant ambience of a complete family—anything to have a child. She'd make a great mother.

I was headed to China, to see Yimosu. His mind was mysterious, one that delved into the abstract, the ethereal, and the biological all at once. He often gave me glimpses of concepts I found unrealsitic. Oh, I embraced Hawking, Sagan, and others of our time, but Yimosu studied *mysterious* things. Rarely explaining them in detail during our frequent phone conversations, he would ask me about my progress and give me a general statement of what he was doing. I was headed to him because I was desperate and he was my friend. And because he knew people—people with money.

Twenty-nine hours later, I got out of a cab at the Puning-tse Monastery outside Beijing.

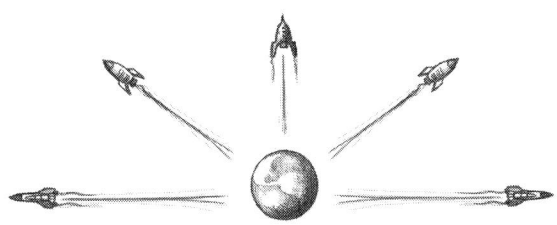

CHAPTER FIVE

I walked up the steps to the big wooden doors and lifted the weathered bronze knocker, letting it slam against the wrought-iron plate. I looked back down to the street to see the cab drive away to merge with the vendor carts and bicycles that swarmed beneath layers of laundry lines. A dark green car was parked facing me a bit farther down the street. It had two men inside, and the engine was running.

The doors of the monastery scraped the ground, making a narrow opening, and I turned and went through them. Two monks in red robes leaned in with palms and strong legs to heave them shut again. Swaying bamboo stalks let dappled sunlight down to the stone walk of the courtyard as the morning dew evaporated into a scent that reminded me of a forest floor—heavy and thick and with an occasional waft of white wax. I saw a shadow, yet I heard no footsteps. Then I saw him. The light-brown face, dark eyebrows, and smooth, confident features brought back my days at MIT. But here, instead of jeans and an Oxford shirt, he wore a golden robe with a rope belt. Standing before me was, to others, a wise and well-respected visionary of China—a prophet, some would say. To me he was Yimosu, my friend. I always kept our secret, which few knew: that his father was an anguish-ridden Japanese drug smuggler, captured and executed when Yimosu was ten. Yimosu's mother went to work under draconian conditions at a fluorochemical factory named China Auto Ice, near Shanghai. On her way there, she would walk her son through the vacant property next to the factory and leave him alone in the gray-planked wooden shed across the rice field for days at a time. She would return with books and newspapers and what food she was given, and they would eat together and read, then venture home to their little corner of a crowded sublet apartment. Her health declined, and one day he felt her struggle, smelled the treacherous chemicals within his own senses, as if they were in him, not her. She never emerged from the factory doors again after that day. He knew she was gone.

On a brisk winter day four years later, the new factory owner, Eddie Genji, took his daily walk into the north field this time. And there he found the shed, and young Yimosu inside, writing diligently and happily at a workbench. Weeds and kudzu were sprouting through the floor, and deer antlers and snake bones lay in little piles along the walls. Yimosu had not seen another living person in all of this time. Stacks of pages torn from biology and psychology books were weighted with rocks and bookmarked with fluttering rice leaves. Yimosu later told me he had clipped out particular terms, such as "neurons of the first order," "chiasma," "midbrain," and "sterognosis." Above these he had wedged, under a wooden splinter, a word that encompassed them all: "evolution". He was obsessed with finding the secret within human sensory faculties, not of what was or what had been, but of what was going to be.

Handwritten formulas and sketches filled the blank front and back pages of books with asterisked notes referring to the words above his bench. On one full page that his mother had brought him—the back of a blank form—he had written what he believed was his significant breakthrough. He kept it, and I saw it later in his dorm room in Boston: "The dormant olfactory receptor genes within a dolphin prove that these mammals once occupied land—a sense of smell deactivated. There are dormant areas within the brain of man, as well. I question whether they are from the past, or, quite possibly, for our future selves—what we intend to be.

Genji spoke with Yimosu for many days and was dismayed by the youth's solitude since his mother's death. Genji felt ashamed that his newly acquired factory held such a profound stigma of tragedy for this young man. But Yimosu told me he was not bitter. He believed everything happens for a reason—even death—and this time spent alone, thinking, learning, was productive and rewarding and could lead to something good, *should* lead to something real and right. This struck Genji as an extraordinary perspective, and he magnanimously sent Yimosu to America, to enroll in Harvard with frequent classes and symposium visits at MIT, where I first met him. Completely alone for eight years of his young life, he had raised himself up from those pale beginnings and stood proudly before me now. The wrinkles below his smooth pate gathered at the corners of his eyes, pointing to that flourishing smile, and I could tell that the sight of me touched a fondness within him. He reached out his hand, at the same moment giving me a questioning gaze.

I looked at him, and something kept me at bay, kept me from speaking—something unusual and pressing and contained in his left eye. At first it appeared to be a physical defect, but as he bowed, giving me a few more seconds to observe, I saw that it was, more precisely, a geometrically perfect feature: a split to the center right of his pupil—a horizontal divide with the complexity and angular form of a freshly carved ice sculpture. Anyone could easily have mistaken it for a reflection, but I knew the difference between reflection and reality, fact and fiction, and this was real. It was specific, and it moved within him.

He seemed unbothered by it, and he hadn't mentioned any health issues. Nor did I want to ask him, since some people and cultures were sensitive about their physical injuries, scars, and other "defects," so I let it go.

"I often believe you and I are brothers." His deep voice brought a slight echo, then a hush, to the courtyard. "And that we are closer because of our distance."

I smiled and said, "The farther I am from somebody, the more they seem to like me."

His face warmed. "Maggie—how is she?" The barest hesitation of my facial muscles gave me away, let him know that my love for her had become, well, less than it was only a short time ago. Maybe it was the war or, more likely, the project, slowly diluting the intimate things about me. "She's not as happy as I'd like her to be," I said, "about this whole thing."

He looked at the ground. "Yes, we are men of dreams, and these dreams affect those nearest us."

He reached into his pocket and pulled out a stone. "While on this subject, I think of you with great concern."

"Tell me," I said.

"My concern is for the children of this project, Jason." When I just blinked, he added, "A great concern."

"I do as much as I can to keep that section of the program one of the top priorities," I said. "I'm still fighting for new studies, new computer speculation programs, but I'm also under the gun to get them off the ground."

He casually flicked his hand upward, and the stone flew into the pond.

"I hear you, but I don't see it in your actions. Basic compassion is before you, Jason—compassion for those in the ships." He put his hand on my shoulder. "What one's life means to the person living it . . . it is everything. Not just to that person but to everyone. If one suffers, is it not on all of us for letting this occur?"

He pulled two of three wicker chairs out from a table. We sat down, and a redheaded boy—*odd, that*—placed cups and a teapot in front of us. My host poured, and steam rolled over my fingers.

"My government has made things difficult," I pointed out. "They've cut my funding. Before that, they were engaging inexpensive contractors, taking over some elements—which seriously rubs me the wrong way. The worst thing is—and this is unfathomable to me—they removed eight ships from the facility. *Eight ships* are missing. I have no idea how I'm going to test the systems on them. I feel I am losing control of this whole thing. If we start up again, they'll be rushing me, leaving things wide open for mistakes." I then spoke more softly. "But if we *don't* start up again—and soon—the mission will become rusty and lie down to die. Yimosu, this thing may already be over."

As the swirling tea leaf particles in my cup slowed their swirling, I said, "That's why I came to you. I was hoping you might know someone . . . who could bring this to your government. China is my only hope. In this economy, they're the only ones who can pull this thing back together."

Yimosu looked a hell of a lot calmer than I felt with my project hanging in the balance. "I must tell you, he said, there are reasons why your entry into our country was so effortless. China and the U.S. aren't getting along, as you know. And yet, they let you in—an American soldier, an ex-officer—about as easily as if you were going to Canada. Why do you think that is?"

I rubbed my neck.

"From the day you showed me your plans—the gold-and-glass ships, the nursery—ever since that day, I've been fascinated by you. In college, you were always playing inventor; now you are one in real life. But it doesn't stop there."

He looked up at me as if to display the splinter of light in his eye, its deep, reflecting facets moving and morphing like molten silver. "There's something more," he said. "I took the liberty of furthering your invention—much further, in fact—and I've found something. Something quite beyond the mechanical things you devise." I read triumph in his face. I waited. "I found the answer that trumps the moral issues I was concerned about. It supersedes and sets aside the insanity—*your* insanity of birthing parentless children in space, with nothing going for them. Because in there, Jason, in *there*"—he pointed at my forehead—"lies the secret. The secret within all of us." He reached across the table and gripped my forearm. "There is something visible within the invisible." The beam in his eye glinted like gold turning in the sun.

"Scientists with their expensive accelerators have discovered the Higgs proton, but they don't know what it truly is they have discovered. And they haven't a clue what to do with it. You, Jason, may think that because we are here in this place, a monastery, that we are foolish seekers after a higher power." His eye calmed.

I shook my head slowly.

He said, "Is everything untouchable also unreal? Do you not think thoughts or miss someone? Is longing not as strong as an iron blade?" His eyes grew distant. "Does loneliness not hurt more than cut flesh?" As he spoke, I recollected my years of working in the underground Wombs facility while, only a few miles away, my wife learned to live without me, and the dog stood chained to bark all day in the bare backyard.

We heard quick barefoot steps on sandy brick—a woman moving spectrally across the arched hallway. I caught a glimpse of her passing between the pillars. Both of us rose from the table.

"Jing," I said. I looked at Yimosu, then to her. I thought of her porcelain-smooth skin, soft as gardenia petals, and of her disappearing, without a word, so long ago.

"Welcome, Jason," she said. "I am glad you could come. How is your . . . Maggie—well, I hope?" Schooled in America, she used better English than I. She reminded me of an actress: calm and careful, knowing and beautiful. She wore the subtlest smile ever seen, and walked with an air of righteousness—not pompous or pretentious, but as if she owned and cared deeply for every root and ant and grain of sand beneath her every footstep. When she asked about Maggie, I felt like a regular guy, looking for a scintilla of jealousy inside her question, as any guy would.

"Maggie is fine," I said. I offered her a chair at the table. More monks gathered silently. The tallest patted the eager redheaded boy on the head, and the boy took off to swing a heavy plank down into the door's large iron hooks.

After the plank thumped into place, Jing said, "We have worked very hard for this day." The monks nodded. Intricate shadows of bamboo leaves moved across her face.

Yimosu stretched a wrinkle from his robe by running his palm down his side and said, "China needs to show a new face to the world. Our government feels that it is viewed as inferior to other governments, even though it is much larger, richer, and has more traditional values than all the others combined." He looked down, and Jing continued for him.

"We are still less to everyone," she said. "It may come as a surprise to you, but we knew that you would come to us, Jason. We have already made arrangements for our government to supply financing and scientists to you—whatever it is that you need."

Reining in the impulse to whoop with joy, I asked, "How in God's name did you do that?"

"Well," she said, leaning away to run her fingers along a smooth bamboo stalk, "I am now positioned as one of the delegates of the Chinese National People's Congress. And Genji—you know of him—is now the vice minister of commerce."

"Genji . . . yes," I said. "The factory owner."

Jing nodded. "But there is something more important." She let go of the bamboo. "I am also Dr. Yimosu's partner in something extraordinary that we have prepared for the ships."

I felt my face darken. "There's always a catch, isn't there? And just what is this extraordinary thing you speak of?" I raised one brow.

A yellow bird flitted down to the table, took a crumb, and flew away. "Yes, of course," Jing said. "But before we talk about the experiment, I need to know more about the project. She sat slightly more upright, listening.

"Okay, but this is secret stuff, so I can't give specific details." I peered in turn at Yimosu, Jing, the monks, and the boy.

"I may be oversimplifying this, but I can say that there will be over forty ships. Each ship will navigate space in a completely different direction, to spread out the odds of finding a habitable planet or planets. The ships will travel a very long time. Perhaps they will never find anything at all and, thus, never start the birthing sequence. The closest stars are reachable with our new xenon fuel accelerant, but still they are very far away." I took a deep breath. "If a ship somehow manages to find a habitable planet, the birthing of two astronauts will occur. But know this: these astronauts will be so far from earth, we will never see or hear from them ever again. Communication over such distances will be . . . well, impossible. The ships and their occupants will be gone forever, and we do this with only the hope that the births will occur properly in the ships, the ships will land, and the occupants will survive to perpetuate the human race. This hope that they *may* exist, that we *did our best,* is all we will ever have, and we will never have anything more than this."

"This project sounds like a monumental waste of time and resources," Jing said.

I held her gaze.

"To *most* people," she continued. "To me, this is how a great many species perpetuate themselves already. They birth their children and simply move on, never seeing them again. Maybe it is a weakness in us humans that we require our offspring, our friends, and our brothers to be by our side, within our reach. Perhaps this is why mankind never traveled outside its realm."

I agreed, of course.

"The Chinese government, however, is suspicious of you, Jason Argenon. At first they thought you were sending armies into space." She smiled. "*Are* you sending armies into space, Jason?"

I laughed.

"I didn't believe it, either." Jing's eyes became friendlier. "There are going to be stipulations for this kind of unusually large funding."

I sipped my tea. A siren came and went, down the street outside the walls. I heard gunfire.

Jing looked up at the top edge of the stone wall. "China's population is outgrowing its livable land," she said. "We have few alternatives, other than population control, and since the Western world deems this immoral, we find that we want to be a part of your journey, to extend our own race as well. China wants to be able to choose Chinese citizens to contribute specimens to the project—to seed the universe with *our* genes as well. And, of course, the Chinese government must be able to observe and assist."

I sighed. What was I expecting, a bailout with no strings attached? "That sounds difficult to manage," I said, "but under the circumstances . . . I'll find a way to work it out. Now, what is this 'something extraordinary' you alluded to earlier—this great experiment?"

"Yes, it is time," Jing said. She wet her lips. "Yimosu and I need a program installed into the ship's systems."

I stiffened. "Go on."

"It's an experiment for the children. It is Dr. Yimosu's life's work, and it will be in your hands. Upon certain circumstances coming to light, this program must be carefully implemented by the computers, initiated automatically—and the children will be the subjects."

I was measured in my response, trying not to offend. "You know we will never see any results from any experiments, right?" I said. "Also, any experiments we send up need to help the occupants survive, not saddle them with even greater challenges. We can't waste their time determining whether ants can do cartwheels in space, or anything like that." I leaned back in my chair.

Yimosu said, "It is only a few lines of programming and a few days of their time. I have spent much of my life working toward this." He asked me, "Remember my paper on dark matter, which Professor Ulrich called 'ingen-idiocy'?"

I smiled. "Yeah, sure, though I don't recall what it was about. Most of your stuff was like a dog whistle to most people—above our brain grade." I tried to recollect. "I do remember something—oh, yeah, but it all turned crazy when you implied something . . . what was it? Something physiological, something evolving in our brains. It really freaked people out."

"Yeah, I know," Yimosu said. He exhaled and gave me that squint again. "It's more developed now . . . more refined."

Touching Yimosu's arm, Jing said, "Maybe I should explain." She leaned closer to me. "Your ships are going to produce a condition, a condition that man has never known—a condition of *distance*. And it is this distance that will result in a great discovery . . . or become nothing at all.

"What you are doing with these ships, Jason, is fishing in an open sea. But when you catch your fish . . ." She crossed her arms and ran her hand nervously up and down her upper arms. "When you catch your fish, the whole sea may come with it." She looked deeply into my eyes, and I felt as though she knew death.

The monastery was silent. The chirpy yellow bird was still; even the breeze had stopped. I began to feel worried about Jing. What had she gotten into? I felt worried for the world—if the sea was coming down on all of us, it was a problem beyond our little project. But this sounded nonsensical. I pondered it further, trying to get my arms around it.

Yimosu said, "We all need this more than you know, Jason." His face turned to granite. "Now, I need to ask you something."

I was tentative in replying. "Go ahead."

"What are the *names* of the children?"

I had never looked at the list of donors, much less the list of names of the future babies. "I don't know."

"What are the children's names?" he asked again, more forcefully. The splinter of light in his eye manifested his anger in clouds and dark ribbons within the flowing fluid.

"I . . . I'm not sure," I said, meaning it. I was mesmerized.

Yimosu looked at Jing with a fierceness I had never seen in him.

"He doesn't know," Jing said, defending me.

Closing his eyes, Yimosu walked away.

"Jason," Jing said softly, "we are about to become something greater than who we are." She looked deep into my eyes, and at that moment I realized that *her* left eye embodied the same splinter of glinting, phase-shifting light as Yimosu's, except that hers was mother-of-pearl in hue, flowing with translucent light blue and yellow like the inside of an abalone shell.

From down the hall, Yimosu said, "The girl in your ship will be important to this world. Important to Earth. You should know her name." He shut the door behind him.

I regretted never once having taken the few moments to find out the children's names—not even on the ship that would carry my contribution, my specimen. I never looked at the label on the sample dish, the dish that would have my daughter in it. To be honest, I couldn't bring myself to look. It would have added to my difficulty . . . to know their names, then send them alone into space.

"There is little time," Jing whispered to me, holding my arm and leading me out. "Despite the complacency of this naive earth, everyone is in peril. You must go—go and launch these ships. They must launch soon." She turned away, her bare feet touching the ground the way a child's fingers would pat down newly planted seeds.

As I walked down the monastery steps, I felt as if it were my fate to have invented these things. There was some comfort in Jing's and

Yimosu's words to reaffirm my work's importance, to let me know that something greater was in play. Though I didn't entirely believe it, I had a thread of intrigue, a thread of acceptance—a *comforting* thread. I just didn't know how much time I really had, with the ongoing pressures, even with new money. For one thing, the Russians were starting to stir, and rumors were circulating that our military would be ramping up again, which, at his point, would shelve space flight entirely.

Outside the monastery, the green car hadn't moved. The passenger was dressed in a black business suit; the driver was a soldier.

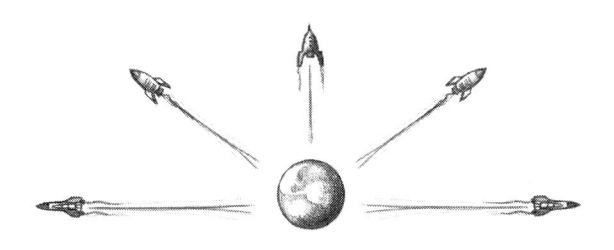

CHAPTER SIX

The two men watched me from the car. Through the windshield, I saw the face of the man in the black suit. He had a peaceful expression and almost American features. He nodded at me with a smile, as if he knew me, as if we were friends. The car began to roll forward, and I turned away and walked toward the waiting cab. As I entered it, I asked the driver to wait, and we sat there and watched the green car move slowly past us. I looked up. The man inside, in the black suit, the one with the peaceful face, spoke over his shoulder to the soldier. I saw this in an instance of perfectly aligned light, the perfectly synchronized speed of the vehicle, and the coincidental angle of the vehicle's rearview mirror to my line of sight. I watched him speak. Yes, my previous work in the military had involved certain specialized training. Sometimes I'm wrong with my interpretations when I do this, but this time I thought, no, I would swear to what he had said. The man in the black suit in the green car said to the soldier, "Someday I am going to kill Jason Argenon." To this day, I still recall it vividly.

My mind turned in on itself in analysis and rumination, visualizing the instant over and over: the movements of his mouth, the formations of his words. And the only plausible result was a death threat.

I rode to the airport, flew across the ocean, pulled up to our house where the artificial flowers by the mailbox had been blown over by the dry Texas wind. I hugged my wife, but with that moment outside the monastery foremost in my mind. The phone rang. It was Yimosu.

Before even a hello, I said, "Did you see the car in front of the monastery, the green one?'"

"Yes," Yimosu said.

"Then the Chinese government is after me."

"Yes, Jason, they are."

My heart sank.

"They still want you to do this, mind you. While you were in flight, they actually contacted your government and helped place the order to build more hulls—you'll get your forty-four ships. Jason, look," he said, "I know this sounds strange, but they will not harm you as you work, as you do what you need to do."

I was pacing through the kitchen. "But why would they want to kill me?" I looked over at Maggie and realized I should have stretched the phone cord to the dining room, or at least whispered. "What's wrong, Jason? What happened," she said, hurrying to my side. Her face grew helpless, cracking my heart. "Answer me."

I covered the phone's mouthpiece. "Relax, there's no real threat," I said.

I reached for her shoulder and squeezed. Her hands covered her face. She listened to the voice on the phone. Mrs. Crumwell appeared with her trusty Swiffer and began dusting the knickknacks on the shelf, her backed turned, her judgmental little eyes reflecting in the picture frame glass.

Yimosu said, "It's all a part of it, Jason."

My mind froze. I don't recall much of the rest of the conversation, but I do recall asking, loudly and angrily, "Are you a part of it?"

Maggie cried.

There was silence. Then he said, "May 29, 2091. He is an elite assassin. This is in motion. It cannot be stopped."

"That's sixty-five years away."

The phone went dead.

I considered Yimosu no longer a friend, as hard as that was.

Only days later, I received a letter at my house:

> Mr. Jason Argenon:
> I felt the need to write to you to explain myself, to let you know that this is not what it seems. Yes, the Chinese government is following you, but that is only part of this. My part is an extension of Yimosu's experiment. It is critical that you understand this. It is equally important that I not elaborate further. This is all I can tell you.
>
> I hope you are well.
> Chen Li Wu.

I folded up the letter and put it in a book. The man in the black suit—I was right. *The elite assassin reveals himself. He hopes I am well. Fantastic.* Yimosu must have spoken to him.

I walked to my closet and lifted a case from beneath a stack of folded blankets.

I'll work with Yimosu, Jing. Setting the case on the bed, I caught my reflection in the mirror on the wall. "Yimosu wouldn't do anything to harm me." I watched my reflection speak the words, to make sure I wasn't lying. I would launch my ships. I turned back toward the gun case and unlatched it. "When the time came, I would confront this guy. They gave me a date—a date to die. That was the edge I needed. I knew I had made my choice: to pursue my project, but also to live my life in peril. Would it haunt me, follow me? Probably . . . no, definitely. I would have Chen Li Wu in my thoughts every single day from that day forward, but this was the cost I would pay for creating my vision. This was the cost of bringing my work to fruition.

I pulled the gun out: my nickel .45 Colt Government. I used a rag to wipe it down. No one had ever died from this gun, although I had wounded some. But I had killed only one man—with a knife. With my hand, I felt the two parallel scars above my left eye, from an enemy hidden under a mattress in an urban stone house during night ops in Afghanistan. The enemy slid out and got me in the gut first. In the dark room with a sandy floor, I grabbed him and held him down. I felt his knife punch into my skull—he was trying to stab me in the eye then. The knife entered again, and my only choice was to pull my knife from its sheath and use it on him. After that, I noticed that my blue eyes were somehow duller. A dullness that only death can give you—death you see or, even worse, death you inflict. I was still only nineteen.

Hospitalized from the wound, I was just coming to when I heard the news about Tex from some soldiers entering the ward. He was piloting a troop chopper that crashed in the desert—sand gets everywhere, especially in the rotor gear boxes. He and six other men were buried for eighteen hours in the sand. While his companions decayed around him, he found a way to breathe through all that sand and stench of decomp.

I was to be on that night op with those men. If not for these wounds, I would have been in that crash, too. So I was saved by the man I killed.

After the Army, I brought Tex with me to the Wombs project. "Under your close supervision," they specified. When I went to give him the news that I could bring him on, I found him shirtless in the Safeway parking lot, in a shopping cart in the middle of summer, wearing gloves he had made from pigeon feathers held on by rubber bands. Sometimes the flashback veteran in him takes over. But he was getting better. Really. Sometimes I feel as if I were in that chopper crash, too.

I checked the sight on the Colt, threaded my belt through the concealed holster, and flipped my shirttail out. "Chen Li Wu," I said. I would continue to work on my ships, and Maggie and I continued trying to conceive a child. Although I checked out okay, the clinic said Maggie's worries and stress made things difficult. All these things were tough on her. We couldn't have a child of our own—not right now, not under these conditions. And because of this, I never once could bring myself to look at the names of the children on the specimen jars in the ships.

ACT II

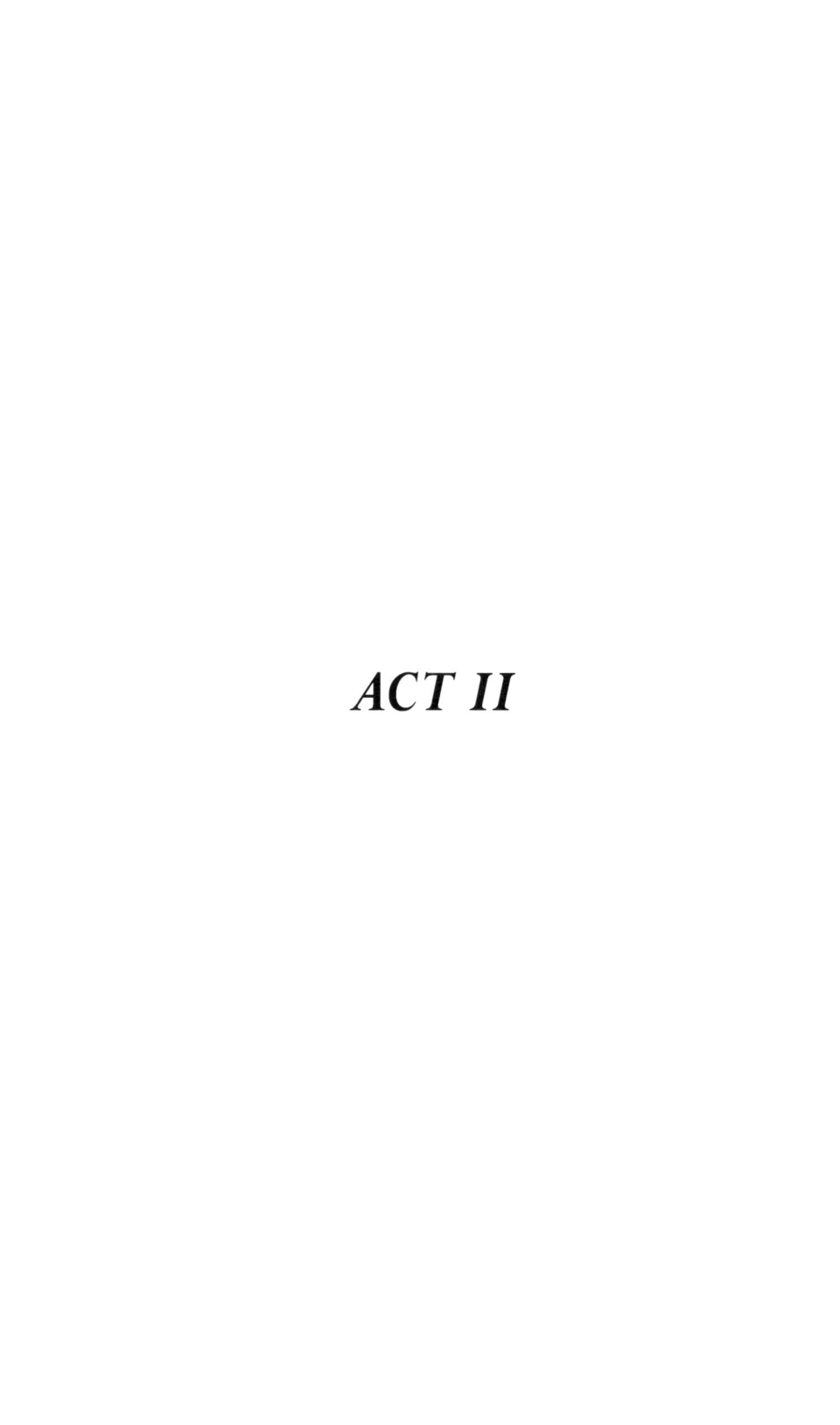

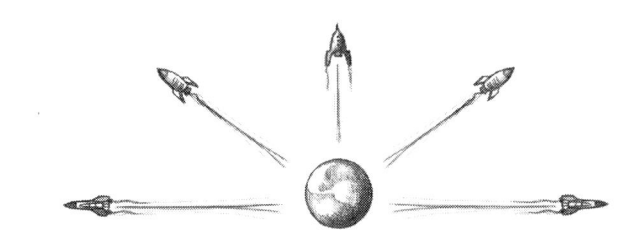

CHAPTER SEVEN

Sixty-four years later, with a severely wounded Tex piloting, I was navigating a cranky Chinese crane helicopter we hijacked a few hours earlier. The huge airship's controls clacked and rattled, the cabin turned cold and reeked of leaky gear oil, burning rubber, and hot wire insulation, and now the engine had begun to smoke. We were leaving the the patchy farm and woodlands of upstate New York for the gold and rust-colored parkland of Ontario. The hills would be our hiding place, these trees our immediate cover. Oscillating below us by a chain-and-strap tether was one of my ships, the ark *Amadeus*. One of my ships had returned home. I didn't know how or why—it was hard to fathom. But it was here below us. We had it.

Above a thick stand of alder, we slowed as Tex calmed the angle of the rotors, and the aircraft angled backward, settling into a steady hover.

"Looks okay," I said.

Tex was looking bad; his eyes looked strangely fake, like the marbles a taxidermist uses. He punched the big yellow release button, and the tether freed, snapping into the air as the chopper jolted upward. The pines engulfed the spacecraft, reminding me of how a child can disappear in high corn. I hoped I wouldn't see it roll down the hill—that would be awful, and I would have to say something to Tex about it. But he turned the chopper, and as we flew toward the nearby clearing, I could see that the ark *Amadeus* had landed soundly, making a dent in the ground for itself to rest in.

As we looked for a place to set down, the landing zone below us revealed blunt outcrops of rock, treacherous thickets of huckleberry, and decaying deadfall trees crossing deep gullies. But it was too late—we had released the cargo and we needed to land nearby.

"That's almost a death trap, old buddy." I said, looking down.

"Yup," he croaked, coughing with the effort.

The chopper emitted more smoke.

A bullet had plowed a groove across the top of my forearm. It hurt like hell, but it was a scrape compared to the large-caliber hole somewhere in Tex's belly. The cockpit was too cramped, the controls too confining, for me to check his wounds. I offered him a stack of cotton bandages, and He pulled red wet gauze from under his shirt and grinned, dropped it to the floor, and stuffed the new white dressing under his soaked shirt. His breath was loud in the headphones. His face was pale, and his heavy body swayed with the turbulence.

He centered the craft above the landing zone.

"Three tight rotors, Tex. Three wide, not five, like I thought," I said. "We're gonna hit a vortex from those trees." A vortex meant a ferociously spinning wind, which would twist us wildly. Blades would hit branches and chop into tree trunks and fly apart, going through whatever chanced to be in their way, and we would die in a very messy, metal-laden manner.

I reached over and put my hand on his arm.

"This is no joke—it's a bad idea," I said.

"Partner, it's an LZ," he said. That means there's a gnat's-ass chance or better of survivin'." He coughed and wheezed between rapid, rattling breaths.

I braced myself just as the big rubber wheels hit the stacked boulders and bounced us back into the air. We began to tip over, and the ground and branches and rocks approached my side window. But in a complex display of flight control bordering on insanity, Tex, in one sick motion, forced the cyclic to port, jammed the starboard pedal down, pulled the collective full up, leaned back and closed his eye—and the chopper righted.

Now, twenty-five feet above the ground and steady, I caught my breath and we had another go at landing. With the precision of an arcade junky pulling troll dolls from a crane game, he set one fat tire down at a time, tail wheel first, then each side. I felt us moving, starting to roll down the slope. I peeled off my com headset, opened the door, and jumped out, instantly reminded that my ankle bone had been cracked back at the heliport by the explosion those soldiers set off. I found a large broken branch and crammed it under the rear tire. The rubber dug into the wood, and as the huge bird began to crush it, I struggled to slide a large rock in front of the log. The chopper moved the makeshift tire stop a little farther, then stopped.

I took a deep breath as the downwash throbbed in my every wound. Peeking over my shoulder for a look at the precious cargo again, I said to the *Amadeus*, "There you are. I can't believe it." I gazed at the gold-and-glass spacecraft, looking bright and crisp in these foggy, wet woods.

I turned back toward the cockpit but noticed the engine was still revving at full throttle. As I limped toward the door, the next few moments ticked by as if I were stepping into a bear trap and aware of it too late to stop my foot. The helicopter's rotors, in a slow, pounding rhythm, divided the sun into slices, slowing all time as their suction yanked at my shirt in violent pulses.

When I stepped onto the metal stair and reached for the handle to pull myself into the chopper, my bullet wound shrieked and the sprained ankle made me gasp, but all the pain left my mind the moment I raised my head and saw Tex, slumped over the controls.

Frantic, I climbed across the stick to remove his headset and free him from his seat belt. His clothes were soaked, and one of his boots was full of the darkest, reddest blood I had ever seen. Gasping, I tore open his shirt to find a gaping hole in his stomach. I felt his neck for a pulse. I reached for the radio, but instead of calling for help, I pounded the radio with the side of my fist, gouging skin open on the knobs.

"There's no one to call," I said. "We should've flown to civilization, to somewhere. We should've gotten you some help." I sat back in the seat and stared through the dirty windshield.

"Maybe we should have surrendered." I closed his eyes for him and looked at him for a little while. "No—you would have wanted me here, to do this. You would have wanted me to find out if launching these ships did any good at all."

From a cabinet behind the headrest, I pulled down another first-aid kit, this time for my own wounds. I found a large, curved needle, a phial of Betadine, and suture thread. "I'll find out what happened in the *Amadeus,*" I said. "I won't make your death for nothing, old buddy." Weakened from the pain, from Tex, from the sight of my own blood, I looked under my sleeve and peeled away the drenched wads of cotton.

I flipped the switches off, and the engine wound down. It wasn't the world of pain I saw coming that made me hesitant to darn the hole in my arm. It wasn't that I didn't know how or didn't have the guts to grit it out. It was that I was slated to die soon anyway. For today was only three days from the date Yimosu told me I was to die by the hand of Chen Li Wu. A long and excruciating hour later, I had the skin stitched together over the bullet's path. With the pain, the sadness had pulled tighter inside me with the needle's every gouge and tug. At last, I bound more cotton onto my wounds.

The halted rotor blades shuddered in the wind. I holstered the .45, slid a sheathed hunting knife down the small of my back, clipped a canteen to my belt, and grabbed a rifle.

Heavy as Tex was, I dragged him out and grabbed the entrenching tool stowed beside the fire extinguisher. Then I found a clear spot with no big roots, overlooking the valley, and started digging.

I stabbed the rifle muzzle into the dirt for a marker, and with my ankle swelling tight in my boot, I sat there listening to the strap buckle tap against the rifle stock in the solemn breeze.

"I'd read you something from the Bible," I said, "but I left it in your pocket—thought you might like to have it. The only prayer I know is Henrietta Hospital's dinner table grace, but I don't think that would fly." I took a swig from the canteen and wiped my mouth.

"None of this would have been possible without you," I said. "I would never have been able to pull this off, get this close to one of my ships again . . . one of *our* ships."

The cold wind dried my eyes. "If Maggie were here, I know what she would say. She would say you were good at heart, lovable. She would say you were like one of those big bears that pry off the car door to eat your cooler at Elephant Butte Lake. That you were a friend who would carry a buddy on his back barefoot through a field of barbed wire and broken glass. That's what she'd say. That's what you did today. I will also never forget your help when Maggie and Connor passed away so long ago." Then I unsheathed the knife and cut a button off my shirt and tossed it onto his grave.

Looking out through the alders to the valley, I saw, maybe a mile away, the vacant yellow and white booths at the U.S. border, saplings and skunk cabbages piercing up through the crumbling asphalt, cars lying abandoned on flat tires and shot all to hell. Four deer moved lazily across the road. The wind was coming up from the southwest, and even up here the air had a stench and a staleness. And these woods were quiet—no magpies or bees or grasshoppers, nothing.

I walked back down to the chopper and stepped onto a sponson support to investigate what the smoke was all about: a loose lubrication line. I found a rubber hose patch and some clamps, slid them over the metal tubes, and tightened them down. That would do it; she was flyable again. On to more useful things. I found bandages, empty food cans, two packs of cigarettes, six pouches of coffee—thank the gods—and a half-empty liter bottle of water. Then I found, tucked in the overhead compartment, on top of a stack of papers, a letter. It was addressed to me.

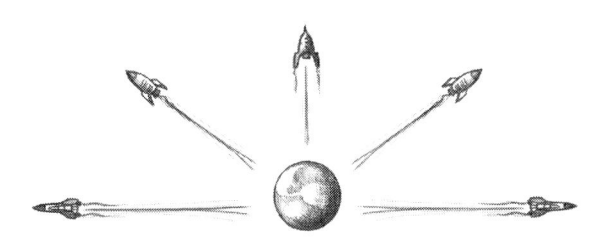

CHAPTER EIGHT

I sat on the chopper step and examined the envelope. The stamp was uncanceled—an old Chen stamp dedicated to some mathematician and not commonly used as postage. The lettering in the address slanted oddly to the left, the "S's" overlarge and the "U's" and "V's" indistinguishable squiggles subsumed in the long cursive rows. This, my home address in Texas, was penned by the same hand as two letters before it. The first, I had received just after my trip to China; the second, some years later This was now turning all too real: a third letter from my assassin-to-be, somehow here for me to find, and so close to the date when my death was to occur. It unnerved me that this assassin, Chen Li Wu, not only knew where I was but knew where I was going to be, before I did. He was always a step ahead of me. I checked the clip in my pistol.

Four bullets. "One's all you'll need, Chen," I said, chambering a round. I couldn't bring myself to read the letter—not today.

After covering the chopper's windshield and other reflective parts with fir boughs, I limped over to the spacecraft, which had settled into the dirt. Everything hurt, and I hadn't eaten or slept, but nothing would keep me from the truth awaiting me inside that spacecraft. It would be a simple, black-or-white assessment: had my life been for good or for bad? Had my mission and obsession succeeded, or would it turn out to be what many feared: a reeking failure at the world's expense?

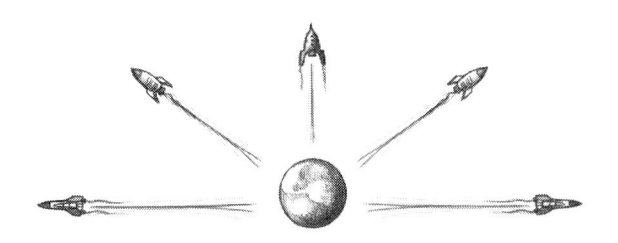

CHAPTER NINE

Running my hand over the hull, I felt the pocks in what was once the *Amadeus*'s glossy, perfect finish. One of the rear fins, curved like a chef's knife, had dug hard into the ground. I examined the back of the craft: the engine port, the retros. All was intact and, apparently, operable. A spot beneath the door frame caught my attention. Someone had repaired it with some type of weld. I found a pry bar in the chopper, and pushing it into the door frame, I bore down with all my weight. The bar began to bend, but at the very end of its strength, the door weld cracked and I landed firmly on the ground.

"Shepard?" I waited for a computer sound—an acknowledgment of some sort that he was working okay. "Shepard, open the hatch," I said. To my astonishment, I heard a click.

The cool, fresh oxygen greeted me as I looked into the ship with wonder, and the smell of the hybrid ivy we used in the hull walls for oxygen regeneration reminded me of the days when we were fortifying the ships. I took a deep breath and stepped over the threshold. My past was confronting me. The inside of the cabin of the ark *Amadeus,* something I hadn't seen in forty-eight years. It was awful. There was rust and sand and, most wretchedly, graffiti. The main cabin robotics were falling apart, most of the medicine cartridges were missing, and the EAs were bent and appeared inoperable.

I touched a monitor. "How did this ship even get here?"

Curiously, the center monitor seemed to have less wear on it than the other two, which looked as if they had been under sea water. *There are no spare parts in space,* I reminded myself. I saw a small collection of things, all of them black, stuck under clear tape. Little tufts, disintegrated over time—human hair, perhaps, though I wasn't sure.

Then something else caught my eye. In the corner, wrapped in plastic, was a bundle of books, tied together with a homemade twine of tightly clinging, still growing vegetation. The main cabin camera was hanging loose in the corner. Its wires were broken.

The video records, I thought, feeling a twinge of worry over how long the cameras had been out of commission. I only hoped they had captured something of use.

Outside, I laid down some floorboards onto two crates from the chopper for a rough table, cobbled more crates and a seat pad into a chair of sorts, then cannibalized enough wire from some ship components to bring the monitor outside. After setting it on the makeshift table, I went back into the ship and carefully lifted out the books. Brushing away the freshly fallen leaves and twigs from the table's surface, I set the volumes down.

This ship was never supposed to come back to earth, I mused. None of them were. I was just supposed to launch them and forget—I was supposed to follow the plan. A psychologist was assigned to me, to teach me, to help me. But I never could forget. And now it was here, and I was glad I hadn't forgotten.

"What secrets do you have for me?" I asked the ship. I asked the books. Over the years, my mind had often traveled to where these ships might have gone, how they fared, what they found, who occupied them, and how long they had lived.

I recalled, at odd moments during my life, hearing a whisper from the distance . . . the need of something, somewhere, as if someone were speaking to me. I always shrugged these feelings off, putting them down to lack of sleep, too much booze, or mental misfires brought on by stress or the painful torment of the great loss I had endured.

If I were to say, as I once said about Tex, that there were three people inside me when we were working on these ships, I would have said an engineer, an inventor, and a husband resided here inside me. But now I would have to say there were three altogether different people in here: an obsessed crime scene investigator, an apocalypse castaway, and, foremost, a familyless, regret-filled, washed-up, dilapidating old man held together by vitamin syrup, bandages, and, now, some Chinese suture thread. And yet, I hold out hope that there may be someone else in here, someone I haven't met just yet. I am hopeful.

I looked at my face, reflected in the monitor. I couldn't see anything unusual in my eye—nothing like what I had seen in Dr. Yimosu's, or in Jing's at the monastery so many years ago. Yimosu and Jing believed that something more existed out there, in space or beyond—something world changing. And that it was going to happen within these ships. I let them believe it. I don't think I ever bought into it. It was too unscientific—too out there.

"Shepard," I said.

As the monitor lit up, I heard "Yes."

"Show me the third records in the archives—the archives of this ship, *Amadeus*," I said proudly. "I want to see the heart of this, what happened in here." I expected to see nothing inside, because my skepticism that this mission would work at all had grown in the many years since the launch. My reflection gave way to a video flicker, and in front of me was a wide-angle view of the inside of this very ship's cabin.

I was sickened. The ship looked more like a filthy third-world apartment than the inside of one of my ships. Things were strewn about, the kale and chard growing along the ceiling were withering, and there in the center of the screen, gripping tightly to a chess piece and then letting it float away, was an extraordinary thing. Floating weightless was a thin figure of a teenager. He looked old and worn.

"Dear God," I said. "Oh, dear God."

The boy was dressed in a blue flight suit and, to my dismay, covered in red rashes. His hands and feet were wrinkled and dry. He looked like a very old young man. My heart sank at the sight of his unkempt hair, acne-pocked face, and spots of God-knew-what on his clothing. His curly hair, large nose, and big eyes filled with apprehension, filled with skepticism, filled with blame. How inhuman this must have been for him.

"Doc, what the hell are you doing now, you moron?" he said as Doc's arm tried to water a wilting tomato plant in the ceiling boxes.

"Gardening, Forsythe."

Forsythe swatted at Doc's arm and continued watching the center monitor of three, which displayed a small white dot near its center. The ship was heading for a white dot.

"Shepard," I said as I watched, "you found one! You found a planet." I looked closer at the image the young man was watching. "He's watching it come in!" With childlike excitement, I felt the delicate touch of accomplishment brush by me like a whisper, my expectations so close to reality . . . almost touching.

"Shepard, How old is Forsythe? He must be, what, twelve, thirteen? He'll be landing soon, then, if we can actually see the planet on his screens, right?"

Shepard didn't answer.

"Forsythe," I said.

His arms and legs were thin, gaunt. He had taped rows of paint chips, skin flakes, and wads of hair to the wall. It was now hitting me. This was my product, my efforts, my initiative. This real young man, who lived and breathed and scrunched his eyes up at his screen, was my doing—this was *all* my doing—and it all looked horribly, criminally wrong. I was now hoping he would hurry up and land. Hoping this weakening, nearsighted boy squinting at the screen would make it to the planet.

He had a permanent expression, tight and meticulous, one that Noah Webster might have worn when sternly correcting a schoolboy's word usage. This was the expression Forsythe wore especially when addressing the computers.

"Two more years of desolate travel—is that what's in store for me, idiots?" he said to Doc's camera.

Forsythe pushed off the floor and floated, grasping the metal bars around him to pull himself across the craft. "Four more years of reruns." He didn't smile. "Don't you Einsteins have anything new to teach me?"

"Forsythe," Doc replied, "you have excelled in all programs. Repeating them is good practice. There is an experiment in the queue, which will become accessible under certain circumstances, but that is the only variation on the lessons remaining."

"I beat you at chess within three months of trying," he said. "You don't think I am ready for your experiments?"

"It isn't your aptitude we await; it is a condition within the ship, which may or may not arise," Doc said.

"You and your 'may or may nots,'" Forsythe sighed.

"Yes," Shepard chimed in. "Only two more years left to land."

"Ah, yes, *only* two more," Forsythe said, pointing at the camera, eyebrows raised, his wrinkled finger quite large, the nail chewed, yellow with dirt in its cracks. "Only," he repeated, turning his eyes away.

Forsythe lazily stretched the EAs from the corner, attached them to his wrists and ankles, and moved around. The monitor showed that power was flowing, adding to the ship's stores. I watched him for seventy-one minutes. Seventy-one minutes out of the few remaining days I had left to live, spent watching someone exercising. But then the microphone caught a sound. It was a ticking, and it was out of place.

Forsythe floated to the nursery window, the EAs moving in concert with him as he looked through the glass. Scowling, his sunken brown eyes conquered his hollow face, the violet pouches beneath them ripening and his jaw tensing.

"Doc, what's wrong with your arm?" Forsythe asked. "This stage should have been completed by now."

"I am not detecting anything out of the ordinary," Doc replied.

Forsythe rubbed his face with his large hands, and some spit leaked from his mouth as he peered through his fingers into the locked nursery. "Your arm is stuck, you imbecile. You can't detect that?"

"No, Forsythe, everything is in working order."

Forsythe took a firm hold of Doc's camera and forced it to aim through the glass at the malfunctioning robotic arm. The lid was off the embryo dish, and the heat was escaping. The defective arm repeatedly tapped against the edge of the cradle, opening the lid wider, letting out more heat. The embryo jostled as if it were itself jelly. It did not look healthy.

A tiny residue of a heartbeat blip scrolled repeatedly on the nursery monitor.

"See, Doc? You have to let me in there to fix this," Forsythe said. He tugged on the door. "This would be the third child you have failed to bring to birthing—the *third one*! Your mission is failing. There needs to be *two* astronauts!" he yelled. "Two of us!"

Doc replied, "The protocol is not to allow entry into the nursery, only to let a new child out. We are not allowed to change the protocol at this point."

"The child will die. There will *be* no child to let out! She needs my help. You have to let me in to help her."

The malfunctioning arm's repetitive motion against the metal table exposed some live electrical wires, which were now sparking and smoking. The cabin lights began to blink on and off. Forsythe looked up and stared with undisguised hatred at the blinking lightbulb.

"Doc, you are going to let my companion die." He took in a deep breath and gripped a handle on the wall, squeezing it until his pale hand whitened even more. "And me—you have me in a horror film. I'm trapped inside the camera. . . . I am the shutter." The lights winked on and off, and on.

"How is it possible that I am at the mercy of the whimsical decisions made [off] by light itself?" Forsythe said in the dark.

"This entity—light—although a misfit in the world of trust, is only a pawn, poorly commanded by evil, murderous computers," he said. "You are evil and murderous, Doc." [On.] Forsythe's lips had a grim downward curl. [Off.]

He let go of the bar and rotated languidly in the cabin. The light from the galaxies outside tinged his face a lighter gray. Shadows showed on rows of thick wrinkles, and hairs bristled from his nostrils, as he gave a shudder, no doubt thinking of another birth uncelebrated.

A full flame established itself from the shorted wires in the nursery and flickered sinister shadows on the wall. Forsythe still floated slowly, spinning at an oblique angle, speaking outward to the walls.

"Your brain is now in decay, Shepard," he said. "You, too, Doc. You are deleting things—things like hope and my desire to live. Fire is deadly. You taught me that. Doc, you will die. Shepard, you will, too. As for me . . . I feel as if I were already dead." His speech grew tired. "After all this death, anyone would want to die—of that much I am sure. Anyone on that silly, mythical place you tell me of—that *Earth*. How possible is that Earth, anyway? How credible is your story that the place ever even existed?" Forsythe looked down at the floor in a long silence. "You made it up."

Doc's speakers were cutting out, replying with crackles and blips. And then, beneath it all, a constant sound, a sound Forsythe had heard all his life—the faint, almost undetectable sound of Doc's hard drive—ceased. Forsythe moved his eyes as if looking around for the source of the abrupt silence.

He clenched his jaw. "No control over anything. You gave me no control. We are going to die in a speeding, meteoritic fireball." He looked up at the surveillance camera. Forsythe was staring directly at me.

Judging by the distance between the flame and the oxygen petcock, Forsythe had perhaps a minute before the ship exploded.

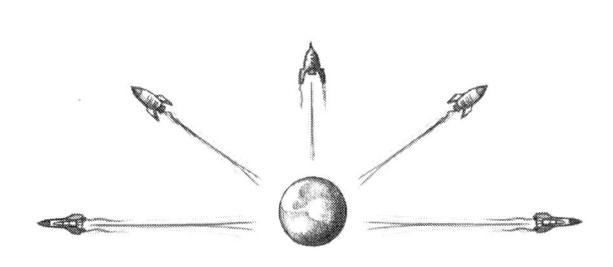

CHAPTER TEN

He was looking into the camera lens, looking directly at me. Although years and light-years separated us, he was looking into my eyes. The blue light of the monitors and the amber light of the flames lit his features as he spoke at me.

"Why would you do this to me?" he said. "Why could you not *wait* to birth me? Wait until the ship was on solid ground? You are an unfeeling bastard, you know. I see you in my dreams," he said ominously, slowly shaking his head. "A face of death—that's what you are to me."

He punched the aluminum bulkhead, denting it. "Lousy ship . . . lousy inhuman crew . . ."

"Forsythe, you need to put that flame out," I futilely said. "You need to save the girl!" I shouted at the screen.

He stood up. "My chess pieces will help me," he said. "They are my men."

"I shouldn't do it—shouldn't hurt them." He looked at them with regret as, with shaking hands, he removed the EAs from his limbs and pushed himself toward the chess table.

Ashamed, I supposed, he peered low and close across the chessboard and announced, "You are my friends. You are all my friends. I hate to separate you." His eyes became cold and disconnected. Almost tenderly he lifted the black bishop by its pointy head.

With eyes closed and breath held, he began to grind the bishop's head back and forth against the bottom of the chair, sharpening it. The sound was wretched, and with it came an equally wretched smoke-filled cough. He moved the piece faster and faster. The more he rubbed, sharpening it, the more he cried into his other hand.

In the nursery, the flame neared the oxygen.

He cut himself along the biceps—to test the blade, I assumed—and his arm bled in little ameboid dollops that floated around him and clung to his forehead and cheek.

I pounded my fist on the table. "C'mon! That's a *life* in there—it could even be my daughter!" In sober realization, I thought, it *could have been* my daughter.

Forsythe slid the bishop's pointy metallic head under the head of the hinge bolt and pried it up, then another one, and with a yank, the hatch released from its frame and floated away. Forsythe grabbed the overhead bar to swing into the nursery. Coughing and gasping, he looked at the fire as if it were a monster, foreign to this mechanical world. Fire. Forsythe seemed to study its motive, its intelligence, as he gingerly maneuvered to put his finger over the oxygen hazard. I watched the oxygen pressure sting him, watched the flame beginning to burn his arm.

"Don't let go," I said.

"You are a nameless and shapeless creature of pain," he said to the fire as I watched the hairs curl up and his skin smoke. He understood not to move his hand away—he was strong.

He unbuttoned the lower part of his flight suit and began sloppily peeing on the flame, in a stream that broke apart into weightless beads. But the fire still burned. Grabbing a towel, he peed into that and put it over the wire, and the wire hissed. The flame was out. Releasing the oxygen again, he beheld his wounded hand for a moment, then uncoupled the faulty arm and stuck it to the wall with a Velcro strap.

"Ah, Doc, you were supposed to be so smart," he said in the now powerless ship. He brushed away some piss beads and picked up the dish that held the deceased embryo of his partner.

"That's three—three deaths. Doc, you and Shepard really do suck at this." Floating out of the nursery and into the control chair, he held the embryo and put it in a clean towel.

His shadow moved in the gray. He rose up and connected the EAs back to his limbs. Standing on the command seat, he hummed Mozart's Requiem Lacrimosa, a very somber composition, and with his bare hands, he buried the dish in the garden box and said in the hardened darkness, "You lived for a moment. Perhaps that is long enough." I heard his sleeves rustling when he wiped his eyes. "Perhaps a short life is better than to struggle. To struggle, to venture from one place to another, to build things and to break things, to accumulate things and, worst of all, God damn it, to *lose* things. We all begin and end where you are now." A hint of a smile formed on him. "Maybe you led a full life—only you did it a little faster than most people."

He floated down and did a pretend walk with a funereal pace. The power meters rose again, and the light turned on as the circuit reset.

Shepard interrupted him softly. "Forsythe, now that the fire is out and electricity is restored, I wanted to inform you that we remain on schedule for atmospheric entry, barring any negative condition readings."

"Excuse me," said Forsythe, "did you say 'barring any negative condition readings'?" He closed his eyes and uttered a soft, plaintive laugh. "Of course, of course you would say *that* as I am trying to cope with all your other mistakes. 'Barring any negative readings.'" He mocked Doc's voice almost perfectly. The voice of a calm doctor who can inform you of the wonder of life or, just as easily, of impending death.

Catching a glimpse through the window as the planet swiftly neared, his naked eye moved under his blood-flecked brow. He pushed off the ground and floated back up to the ceiling to look down into the plant box. His face flushed cold. "I wish you were here to see this, my love . . ." He pushed a final clod of dirt over the female embryo and hummed the rest of the sad song.

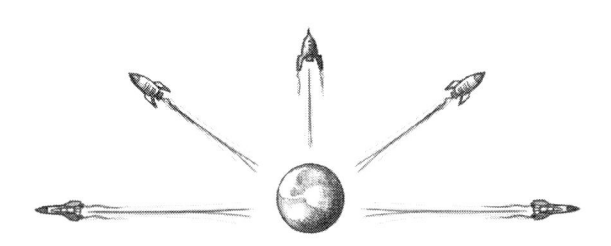

CHAPTER ELEVEN

On the final day of approach, Forsythe folded the aluminum covers over the wilting plants, resecured the nursery hatch, and placed all the chess pieces in their compartment. Then he took all of eight seconds to reread the thirty lines of the landing checklist. The ship navigated through the planet's rings, composed of rock, ice, and clouds of dust. His chair squeaked horrendously as Shepard's corrections jerked him in all directions.

"Cosmic whatnot," Forsythe said, gazing out the window. "No black—what a sight!" The gray and white planet was filling the entire window, and for a second, his eyebrows knitted in worry, and his lip quivered as if he were about to cry.

"It must be wonderful down there. Maybe this *is* my time," he said, gazing at the smooth features of the surface.

"I wonder how you're going to treat me, little lady planet." Pulling a hair from his head, he lifted the piece of tape from the wall where more hairs and other items he was collecting were held, and carefully pressed the hair in place.

"Three minutes to entry; twenty minutes to landing," Shepard announced.

Forsythe pulled the buckles tight. As he studied the monitors, everything looked like a go . . . except for one red line of narrow text, which he couldn't read from his seated position. So he ignored it. The sphere before him was enormous.

A quick blip issued from Shepard. Forsythe felt a slight tug on his suit, and his weight transferred.

"Are you steering?" Forsythe said. "Why are you steering? This angle was preset." The pressure of the seat moved against him, growing harder. "What are you doing!" he yelled.

"Abort," Shepard answered. An alarm shrilled.

"Abort what!" Forsythe struggled to release his buckles, but the G-force was too strong. He checked the window again.

"The planet is in the wrong place. What is going on?" Forsythe said, pounding his palms on the chair. He heard servos moving within the walls, retracting the fins and retro rockets; they were deep into a long turn. Free from his harness now, he slammed into the ceiling, banging his head. "This is no game, gentlemen! Abort *what?*" Feeling blood in his hair, he grasped for a bar.

"Abort the landing," Shepard replied.

"What's wrong?"

"At this close range, we were able to detect a harsh atmospheric element not found on Earth."

"Then how do you know what it is?"

"We can see the damage it is doing."

"What damage? I don't see any damage. I can *handle* damage."

Shepard showed him a close-up video of the surface, and Forsythe's eyes widened. "That's everywhere?"

"It's acid. Neither the ship nor you would survive the acidic content of this planet's atmosphere."

The planet below them had a landscape that looked as if someone had laid a thin gray blanket over it. Everything was worn and dull, as if the surface were melting, inch by inch.

"I can deal with acid." Forsythe's eyes were rolling into his head from the g-forces as the ship shuddered through the turn away from the planet's gravity.

"You could not survive there," Shepard said. "You could not set foot on the planet, not even for a minute."

"What about the space suit?" Forsythe said, pulling himself back into his chair. "I could live in the space suit."

"Not even the space suit would survive," Doc replied, "The ship and all its parts would corrode in a matter of hours."

Forsythe put his hand on the engine control biolock and moving his hand around on the glass. "Shepard, now, I'm serious about this. Give me control of the ship!"

Some screens displayed new controls that he had never seen before, but the two controls he needed were blacked out. "Nose retro, fire; center retro, fire," he said, "Give me those. Give me control of my ship! I want to turn around."

No computer responded, and the planet grew smaller.

"Give me control . . . of *something*!"

He felt disoriented, and a dullness came over his eyes.

Accelerating away, he sat back in the command chair and touched the screen. "Let me see who made this mess. I am fed up. Shepard, who made me?" Forsythe was looking straight into the camera. I shivered.

This was my fear coming true. All the pride I had, all the sense of accomplishment, was washing away as I saw this young man's hopes diminish to nothing. I recoiled at the memory of just how fervent I had been, how eager to send these ships out. My mind swam circles, and I felt the same defeat that I now saw in Forsythe's expression.

My inventions were a dream realized, but to what end? How selfish was I? I had created the deep-space version of the *Titanic*.

A photo of me appeared on the screen in front of Forsythe, and he slowly raised his middle finger at it.

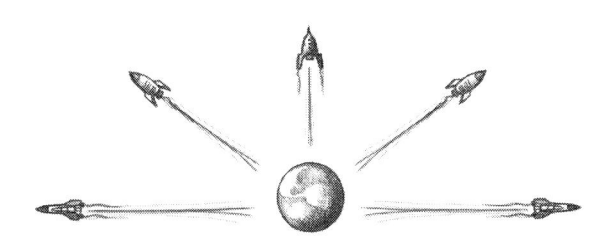

CHAPTER TWELVE

The next morning, the sun was breaking through spiraling evergreens to cast an orange glow on the camp. Light snow touched the canvas cover over my bed of wool army blankets and dried leaves. I was in pain, inside and out—irritating, numbing cold pain. Every sound throbbed in my head; the least movement shot lightning bolts through my ankle. The shrapnel pellets in my back reminded me to lift myself up off my side. I saw my breath on this crisp day, got up, and limped over to the chopper to throw some fresh pine branches over it. I tried to release my anguish by taking in a deep breath, but my mind's eye saw Forsythe's anguish and his disgust of me.

I watched a coyote scout me through some low branches, and with this eye contact, I was hopeful the new day would reveal something better than yesterday.

"Elite assassin," I said, "come and get me." I felt as though this thing—my life, my mission—were over, but I also realized, as I limped over to the bench, that I was at least a little bit lucky to be here and able at least to know something about the ships, even though none of it was good.

"Shepard, I'm afraid to watch what happened to Forsythe," I said. Already guilt was crushing me, and to watch Forsythe suffer more was beyond bearing. "Go deeper into the records; in fact, switch to another drive," I told Shepard. The screen changed views. I was expecting to see Forsythe's dead body floating around, his wrists slashed with the sharpened chessman, perhaps, because there was no destination for him now, no reason for him to go on. I thought. The image flipped, and I pushed on the screen with my fingers to tilt it back. It was the view of a ship's cabin again, although it looked new and clean.

"Something's different," I said, examining the cabin more closely. The image was distorted. I tugged on the wires I had stretched out from the *Amadeus,* and the feed became clear. Squinting to read the plate above the hatch on the screen, I gaped. "*Rhapsody . . . !* How is the *Rhapsody*'s hard drive in this ship?"

Shepard didn't answer.

The view now was from the camera on the *Rhapsody*'s fin. It showed both the outrigger centrifuge capsules fully extended and spinning about sixty feet out on each side of the ship.

Suddenly, I realized that both centrifuge units were occupied. How was this possible?

I wondered what date this was, but the time stamp on the screen displayed only blank dashes, as though it had lost power at some point. In small type at the bottom, it read, "Data loss."

"I understand why you didn't answer me, Shep," I said. "Data loss causes you problems." I picked up the canteen and took a small sip, savoring the cool water.

My view then switched to the internal camera of one of the centrifuge capsules. It was a fish-eye view of a girl. Her gaze gently drifted to one side, as if she were trying to see something so far away it was inside her, so close she couldn't touch it, so new it had not reached her yet.

Her pearly skin contrasted so vividly against the black quilt of space that the stars behind her seemed to dim. Her hair was well kept, long and black and straight, glistening and reflecting star trails.

As she became engrossed in the video before her, her eyes warmed ever so slightly and she formed a subtle, almost nonexistent smile. But I could see it; it was there, this minuet thing, in a single instant formed and finished and injected into my memory, as if I were inoculated by the sight of her smile. It felt vaguely familiar. Everything was spinning in all directions. The galaxies surrounded her, but now, beside this girl, galaxies seemed insignificant to me.

"Who is this?" I said. "She is so very fragile." She really was. Adorned with faded freckles, she looked shy and frail and infinitely vulnerable. Through her blue flight suit, I could see her ribs pushing against the fabric—muscle atrophy was taking its toll.

Her head moved gently back and forth as she read her lessons, periodically pushing on the screen. Her arms moved in uninterrupted, softly mechanical motions

"What have I done?" I asked the computers.

From the ship beside me, a familiar voice answered, "You launched your ships."

"Doc?" I said. "Doc, she is so *delicate*."

"She lived. Did you really expect her to build a whole society?"

"That was the plan," I said. Was it that far-fetched?

"Maybe—you programmed us to make the environments nurturing."

"Yes, I did."

"You programmed us to make them feel good and accomplished, no matter what the circumstances, no matter how small the achievement. Would it really matter how long that lasted, how much they achieved?"

"Well . . ."

In the small girl's eyes I was staring into, I saw a conundrum, the pale ghost of an unsolved equation on a chalkboard. But I felt as though—no, *I knew*—that the solution was somewhere deep in those eyes and that the answer would somehow manifest itself. As I said, there was someone else inside me whom I had not yet met. And right now I hoped this girl might help me find that person. I censored the impossible request at once.

She probably didn't live very long. I shivered at this thought. I never wanted to know the names on the jars . . . the specimens. I never wanted to look back. "But, Maggie," I said to the air and to the living wood in the forest surrounding me, "I am looking back now." I was hoping Maggie could hear me wherever she was now, but it was ridiculous, of course.

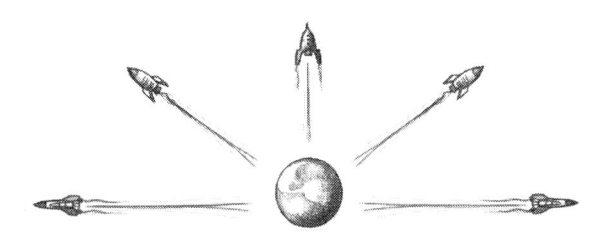

CHAPTER THIRTEEN

The camera switched to the inside of the ship, and this teenage girl and boy climbed out of the centrifuges and floated gracefully across the cabin, he to the top bunk to sit on the mattress, and she to the wide command chair. She picked up a blue strip of fabric that lay on the seat. Looking at it, brushed her hand over it as if it were a doll, and set it back down on the seat beside her. I noticed that this two-by-six-inch length of cloth had been cut from her bedsheet, and she looked at this mere rag as if it were a dear friend. She glanced through pictures on the monitor, tapping the screen to move to the next, while speaking to the boy in a softly trembling voice. And as she uttered the first words I heard, her personality came through. She was a caring, distant creature who enjoyed, watched, learned, and felt. She had great hopes; I could see them.

"In the lesson today," she said, "a teacher made a home video. It was of some day-care kids. The children were walking across a street. Did you remember watching this one?"

He looked over at her. "Yes, Angela, I saw it, almost precisely one year ago. It made no sense; it had no plot." He seemed calm and stable, checking the gauges often, floating past the window, surveying and pulling a loose edge of his blanket down tight to make the bed with military corners. His look was stoic, as if these tasks were automatic. That is what I saw at first.

She floated over to him and touched his arm. "The toddlers held the rope, Nathan. That was the plot. The teacher hurried them across the street. One totally fell down. It was so horrible, so-o-o-o predictable." Her eyes darted back and forth. "They look so clumsy down there."

"They *are* clumsy on Earth, Nathan said. "It's all that gravity garbage."

She stared at the floor, remembering the video Maggie shot to send up with the ship. It was one of the few noncommercial movies allowed in the media library, and I was pleased this girl was enjoying it, but Maggie always knew these kids would like something like that: a home movie of children.

Angela floated over to attach the EAs to her wrists and ankles.

"Doc, engage the EAs, please," she said. The arms applied downward force on her. She began to walk from one wall to the opposite wall of the ship, taking eight small steps and then curling into a ball. The charge indicator gauges would peak during the downward curling motion, and she would rest there looking up at the indicator's numbers, and when they started to decline, she would stand up again and take eight steps again and go back and forth from wall to wall. "The children never let go of the rope—none of them, not even when they fell. They never dropped the loop assigned to them; they held it so tight, their fingers turned white." Angela continued pacing the room and then resting in a ball. Now she was breathing hard from all the motion.

"But here's the plot, Nathan: there was a girl who used this chance, when the other fell—she used this opportunity to stretch the rope farther. I saw her do it. While the boy was down, the girl stretched the rope to where she was almost out of the walkway, almost with the cars. She was even pulling some of the other children with her. The cars beeped their horns, and the teacher tugged on the rope to start the chain moving again, but this girl, she wanted to let go of the rope *so-o-o* bad. She looked at the sky and then at the flower beds. She looked at the camera. She knew there was something more than hard pavement and hot sun and the flowers in the center of the road. I saw it in her face. It was like she knew she would never know anything more—unless she let go of the rope." Angela stopped walking and released the EAs, and they sprang back up to the ceiling. She leaned her head near the window to look out at the stars.

"Did she let go?" Nathan asked.

"No. But *I* would have."

"I know. You're going to be a big pain, aren't you?" He moved across the room to a command chair and loosely secured the seat belt. "I'm going to be saving your butt all over the place. You can barely lift your own food to your mouth, and you're going to be letting go of the rope."

Angela looked at him. "I would have let go."

"Don't go talking about letting go of anything," he said. "Once we land and get out of this emptiness, you'll want to stay put, believe me."

Angela moved her arm in a gentle arc to test the wall's temperature with the back of her hand. "I don't think space is empty at all," she said. She brought several strands of her long hair up to the window and compared its deep black sheen to the darkness.

An unusual low rumble interrupted the ordinarily solid hum of the Xenon engine. They both looked up at the gauges and then toward each other. "We girls are restless," Angela said, raising her eyebrows and smiling. Nathan's eyes looked worried.

I was enjoying the young astronauts' banter when words came onto my screen overtaking the *Rhapsody* video. "Diary Entry," it read. I pushed on the screen, choosing the link.

As we fly, I feel closeness, like a friendship with space. I think space is watching me through the glass of the ship, and it can hear me trying to speak. No words, though. Not words. I think it is because I am the only girl to have been born in space. The only one I know of.

I don't want to share these feelings of friendship with Nathan or with Doc or Shepard, because I fear this might be something that could be taken away from me and become forever lost, this warmth. This is my fear: to be alone on a planet, without space—me with just a boy. Boys are unruly, inconsiderate, and demanding. This is what I know about boys. Not all males are this way, I hope. A father seems solid, predictable, reliable, irreplaceable, I think. A missing father is unfilled space. This empty space cannot be filled with anything other than a father, I think. This is the emptiest space there can be, I think. Unfortunately, right now, I live in this emptiest space.

The children's ship approached a planet. It was close, very close.

"Recon satellite ejecting," Shepard announced. From the side of the ship, a steel ball shot out. Antennas unfolded from it, and it flew into space just above the atmosphere. The ship received the images from it.

Shepard reported, "Unknown anomaly detected."

"Oh, no," I murmured, sitting forward in my seat. I thought of Forsythe and how his journey was to end by flying into forever space after Shepard rejected the landing on the acid planet. That was another unknown anomaly. I threw a stick at the *Amadeus* in the woods.

Shepard reported, "The anomaly detected on the approaching planet is producing some form of echo. The soundings are strong. The anomaly's cause is unknown. We will continue to use caution in our approach to the destination planet. Planet name: Echo Kingdom, for this anomaly."

"Nice name," Angela said. She tightened her grip on the arms of her chair.

The satellite photograph displayed the surface of the planet.

"A tan desert with a tan sky," Nathan said. "No visible water." He let out a sigh.

"Anomaly still detected," Shepard said.

"'What is an anoma-laly?" Angela asked.

"It will not harm us," Nathan said to her. "Will it, Shepard?"

"That is unknown," Shepard answered.

The ship's engine ports had been diverting in full reverse for fifteen years, and as the craft entered the atmosphere, the solid-fuel thrusters engaged, sending a great rumbling through Angela and Nathan. They both gasped as their bodies shook violently in their seats; then the vibration dissipated.

"We are in atmosphere," Shepard announced.

The ship steered slightly upward, the skid plate deployed, and the parachute shot out, filling and billowing behind them in their quick descent, maintaining a steep angle. They touched ground and skidded into a rock pile, which raised the vessel onto its nose and spun it before letting it slam down onto the rear fins, with the doorway positioned at an inconvenient four feet above the surface. The dust of their touchdown stayed aloft for hours.

Nathan unbuckled himself and reached across Angela to release her. "Oh, shit," he said. "I never thought it would be like this."

"Oh, shit," Angela said. "It's not like the centrifuge—not at all. Gravity, it's everywhere. Ugh . . ."

She tried to stand, but her legs wobbled and buckled, and she fell.

"I think my legs are broken," she said. One arm held a grab bar as she dangled. "This can't be right."

Doc rushed to comment, "You will get accustomed to gravity." Doc's arm reached for Angela's hand. "We have more vitamin shots at this stage, and outdoor exercises to make you stronger."

Angela looked at his camera, tightening her lips and silently shaking her head.

Nathan asked, "How does this gravity compare to Earth's?"

"It is actually less—ninety-two percent of earth's gravity," Shepard said.

Nathan stood, wobbled, and walked over to his space suit. "Are we okay to exit?"

"Yes, the readings are satisfactory," Doc replied. "Oxygen excellent."

"Well done, Shepard."

He struggled with the bulky suit, falling a few times, but finally got it on, complete with oversize gloves. He stood above Angela.

"Are you accompanying me?"

Angela nodded. "Yes, I'm going with you."

Crawling over to the closet, she pulled her suit down from its hook. She wriggled around for the longest time. Nathan didn't tap his foot or say a word, and he even helped her put her helmet on. He walked over to the wall and unclamped the glass tube from it.

"What are you doing?" Angela asked.

"Retrieving my scroll."

"Yeah, like you'll need that," she said. "How are you going to defend us with that if there are, like . . . alien creatures out there? You going to scare them off with your pedigree?" She sat on the floor shaking her head.

"Shepard, are there aliens on this planet?" Nathan asked.

"None that we can detect."

Nathan sneered at her.

"If we do find an alien, maybe you can read your little scroll to him," she said. "He'll be the only one impressed by it." She pulled up her front zipper and grunted, pushing down the Velcro flaps on her sleeves.

"Here we go," Nathan said, reaching out a hand to help her up. She rose to her feet while Shepard opened the door,

"Say something famous," she said.

Nathan started to climb down. Hanging by his elbows from the door's edge, he let go and fell. He struggled but managed to stand, dusted himself off, and said, "Oh, al-i-ens, I have some excellent reading material for you."

"Great" she said, climbing out the doorway in the same clumsy manner. "One small step backwards for alienkind." She gave a loud "*Umph!*" as she landed on the hard-packed sand.

"I think I broke my femur," she said, brushing off the dust, which returned instantly to cling to her suit.

"You kids be careful out there," Doc said, moving his camera arm to the doorway to watch them in their oversize suits. The main sun was high above and hot. A light wind blew some tumbleweeds in the distance. They walked a few yards and stopped, panting.

"How's that scroll doing?" she asked.

"Shut up," he said. "We should go back."

"I'm with you," she said.

They climb back into the ship, accomplished by piling up some rocks, took an hour. The door shut, and the screens inside displayed their vitals.

"Are the space suits required?" Nathan asked.

Shepard replied, "Only the inner lining, to protect your skin from the sun."

Nathan set the scroll back on its shelf as Angela struggled to get into the command chair, where she watched comparison pictures of earth scroll by on the screen. Turning to Doc's camera arm, she asked, "Doc, is Nathan going to be king just because of that silly scroll?"

"Yes, Angela," Doc said. One of his gold arms reached for her hand. "And you, my lady, will be queen." She smiled and placed her fingers in his metal palm and said, "Queen."

"Wait a minute, Doc," Nathan said. "My relative cannot be my queen."

"She is not your relative," Shepard pointed out.

Nathan gazed over at Angela. "What are you talking about?"

"Since you have different donor parents, you are not related."

"We're *not?*" Angela asked. "If I'm not his sister, what am I, a robot?"

"No, not a robot," said Doc. "You both are human and simply have different parents, which makes you unrelated."

"Unrelated—so we may have offspring?" Nathan queried.

"Offspring? You mean *kids?*" Angela made a sour face and aimed it at Nathan. *"Eew-w."*

While Nathan squirmed a bit on the screen, I dug a cracker into a can of pink composite meat—the Chinese version of military-ration Spam. I reached for the metal cup, which had acquired a dry pine needle and a fluff of moss. Tex had done this programming—he liked fussing about Christian morality and things like that. That was a good decision to put him in charge of these things.

"Someday. Right, Doc?" Nathan said. "That's the design: for us to someday populate this planet, right?"

Angela was looking at the photos of deserts, and one appeared of a girl holding her father's hand at the Grand Canyon. They were standing in awe of the purple and rust–colored canyon sunset. "Dads and daughters seem pretty close," Angela said. "I would like to know who my parents are. Who are our parents, anyway? I think I would like to ask that now."

I could hear in her voice that she had been waiting to ask this question for a long time. Maybe she had been scared of the answer to what was through that nursery door, what secrets were hiding in the mechanical nursery. This would have scared me, too.

Through the nursery window, the machines glistened in this new sunlight. Metal contraptions, shrewdly devised only to function, never to offer true warmth or display softness or compassion. The centrifuge disks were strangely animated among dirty blue fluids, jiggly orange gels, and ugly red and black and gray wiring harnesses. The answer to her question "Where did I come from?" would scare me, too, if I were her, born in there.

"We don't really have parents," Nathan said. "Zero parents."

Angela stared blankly at him as I held my breath. I, too, wondered who their parents were. I never kept track. Forty-four ships to launch, with forty-four guidance systems, recycling systems, and outrigger centrifuge malfunctions to troubleshoot, and with poem plaques and scrolls to boot—it was quite enough to keep track of.

"Even if we did have parents, they don't care about us, whoever they are," Nathan said.

"Shit," I said. Feeling the welcome morning sun on me, I tilted the screen sideways to see better. Nathan stood up, picked up a pawn from the chessboard, and pushed it forward. She looked at his move and sat lower in her chair. He continued talking. "All they want is for us to be their test subjects—go start a new society somewhere, go live, have babies, and a big old 'Who cares?' to us." He went to the console and, leaning over her shoulder, tapped through the photos on the monitor.

"That's not true," Angela said. "I don't think what you're saying is true. I think our parents do love us and do care what happens to us. They just don't have any way of connecting to us—it's just too far."

"Good girl," I murmured. I moved closer to the screen, to their images, "Good girl for understanding the mission."

"I think they will find a way to find us . . . someday," she said. "I think the whole point of this is for us to start things up for them and then they will find us. They need to know we're okay. It's basic human nature."

Nathan laughed. "That is most likely impossible. You don't understand how far away we really are, do you? Sixteen years traveling from Earth before we were even *born*. The speed we gained over time was tremendous; the ship spent the last Fifteen years just *decelerating*. There's no chance they will ever find us. We can't receive any kind of signal—or send one. Right, Shepard?"

"Nathan is correct," Shepard replied. "Transporting a receiver or transmitter powerful enough would have been weight restrictive."

"Well, I don't care," Angela said. "I will do anything to communicate with my parents—anything."

Feeling my jaw tense in frustration, I felt sorry that her parents would never know she even existed. And in Earth's current circumstances, it would be just about impossible for them ever to know of her. There were just too many other worries here on Earth. Right now the world wouldn't even care. Watching these children, I saw them as forgotten. Yet I felt humbled and honored to see this much of them. At least I could see them.

She glanced at the chessboard's reflection in the monitor. "Queen's rook to bishop seven," she said. Nathan reached over and moved her piece. "Sorry, Nathan, check."

Suddenly, Angela was riveted to the monitor. She rubbed her eyes. "I don't believe it!" she breathed. "I got into the *archives?*"

"It let you in just like that?" Nathan asked, squeezing in beside her and anxiously sliding his finger on the screen, moving through the records. He found a folder with the word "Nathan" and a shield on it. I could see they both recognized the emblem from the etching in the thin glass case of Nathan's scroll. "There it is," he said.

I was dumbstruck. Starghard must have done this—added parental pictures.

Touching the screen, Nathan saw a photo of a man.

Angela said, "Then that's your father." Before them was a man in uniform—British and, by the ribbons and stars, an officer.

"See? I told you," Nathan said. "That's him." His eyes went far away—almost to Earth, in fact.

Angela stared at the man's strong jaw and wide shoulders, his graying red hair and pale-blue eyes. To me, she was comparing him to

Nathan: the curve of Nathan's mouth, the traces of age-old freckles on his sculpted cheeks. This man on the screen was the herald of what Nathan would become.

"My father," Nathan said softly.

He clicked to the next page, and a photograph of an aristocratic brown-haired woman appeared. She had a stuffy, stern expression, sorrowful with worried eyes. "My mother," he said. She's wonderful—very pretty.

"Yes, she is, but don't start talking all British and stuff—now it's my turn," Angela said, suddenly quick and happy.

Nathan looked at his mother a little longer. Then he typed, "Angela."

"No record found."

"Why?" she said. "Do it again."

He did. "Look," he said. "It says in this tiny type . . . here, at the bottom: 'The records of the founders were deleted for security reasons.'"

Confused, I paused the video. My hands were shivering. I had to think. Her father was a founder. Shepard must be talking about that guy, Colonel Bertrum. He had an Asian wife—yes, that's it; it must be him! Why they called him a founder, though, I had no idea. He didn't sweat a day over this. And anyway, that guy resembled a rhino. Angela probably favored her mother.

She tried typing and running through the folders one by one, but none had her name on it.

Angela stood up from the chair, went over to the bed, and pulled the thin blanket over her head. With a sympathetic shrug, Nathan climbed into the top bunk.

"Lights off, please, Shep," Nathan said.

An engraved plaque was fixed to the bulkhead beside Angela's bunk, recognizing the writer Annette Hensley from Maggie Argenon's fifth-grade gifted class, 2027. Angela recited this poem from memory each night, but tonight it sounded the saddest it ever had.

Sunflowers try to reach the sky, but they are never tall enough.
They remind us of how small we are.
Maybe our sight to see great distances,
So we will try to reach that far,
Try to touch everything,
Try to grow that tall.

She heard Nathan whisper, "Good night, Father."

Angela breathed out softly, exhaling hope, then inhaling wanting.

She heard Nathan say, "I feel bad that the computers messed up on your parents, Queen Angela."

She stared at the little plaque. "Off with their heads."

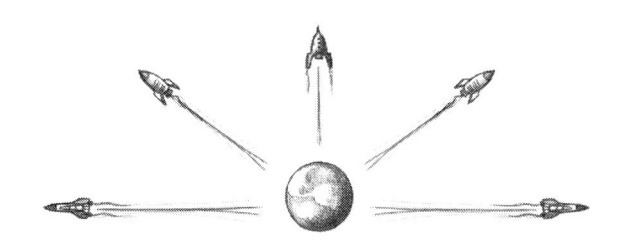

CHAPTER FOURTEEN

Two weeks later, Angela sat cross-legged on the ground by the ship, weaving together dried roots and tumbleweeds brought back from her last walk among the rock hills. Her lips were cracking from the dry air, but she scarcely noticed, absorbed as she was in the texture of the bark and the fine shavings falling on her bare feet. She looked up at the sky to catch a large purple planet passing directly overhead. It moved fast for a planet. Low and just above the hill was a pear-colored planet, solid in color, no clouds, no craters—just pear. Another planet, much farther off, glowed gray like a dull star, like our moon. Three moons circled it so fast, she could see their motion.

She heard Nathan's footsteps. "I've always wanted to discover something never seen before," he said, dropping a fist-size rock onto the ground.

"That's nothing new," Angela said.

"My point exactly."

"The body aches are new," she pointed out.

Doc responded, "You and Nathan are still adjusting to this environment. We landed only twenty-two days ago." Running diagnostics on Angela again, he said, "We're going to increase the carb dose frequency to every eighteen days."

Extending a few feet from the ship, Doc's medical arm lined up with Angela's shoulder, and the anesthesia puffed. The needle pricked her skin, and she leaned her head back, eyes half closed, as if nestling into a big brown leather chair with big, round, well-worn arms. Her neck, legs, and back felt uplifted, supported somehow, but this feeling passed. She looked at the horizon, then at the sand.

"I'm not sure I want my life extended," she said. "Is this all that there is going to be, Doc? Shots and rocks and wasteland? I don't think people on Earth live like this—not by choice, anyway. The lessons showed wonderful houses and brilliant lights, blue oceans of earth."

Picking up the rock he had brought with him, Nathan grunted, walked over to a random spot, and dropped it again.

"We'll start here," he said. "This is the beginning of our house."

"Whoopee," she said.

Nathan pressed on, moving another, bigger rock, and then another. These became the foundation, and soon they were using water from the ship's stores to create mud bricks. After laying two courses of stone and brick, they stepped away and admired the beginnings.

Suddenly, Angela turned her head toward a rocky outcrop near the first dunes. "I thought I heard something," she said.

Nathan dusted off his hands. "What kind of a something?"

"There was a clicking . . . like hooves."

"I'll go and see." He ran up to the hill and disappeared.

The brightest planet moved away, and the star-filled sky made her feel as if she were alone in a glass globe.

Nathan came back. "I didn't see anything, but if there is something, I'll hunt it," he said. They both gazed at the edge of the swirled orange planet sinking over the horizon with its moons.

"Shepard says there's a planet with rings," she said. "We can't see it yet, but when we do, it's going to be huge and pass very close. He says we'll need to find a place to hide from it."

She sat back down, closer to the light of the *Rhapsody*. Doc's camera arm watched as she began to press a sprig of tumbleweed into a flat piece of paper. I recognized what she was working on. It was a diary. I looked beside me on my makeshift table and pulled a book from the stack. It was the most primitive-looking one—her first. I opened it. She was there on the video, making this first page of this book before me. Its pages were made from flattened, dried roots bound at one edge by smaller, flexible roots. For ink, she must have found the reservoir of black armature lubricant behind the walls, in the workings of the ship. How ingenious. A thinly carved twig was her pen.

I watched as she began to write on the very page I held before me. The dry wind cracked off bits of bark as she wrote, and a piece lodged in the ink. Brown bark in black ink. She never restrained her long black hair from sweeping across the wet words. Indeed, everything seemed to be part and parcel of her work: the roots, the bark, the ink, the words, the movement of it all collected together like a reverse explosion— pieces falling into place to make her diary, all the elements combining to make her book. I could see her hair making the streaks in these very words I was reading in Angela's diary:

> *I never wanted to write about being in the womb. I wouldn't want anyone reading this to have reasons to do or not do this again. I wouldn't be here if this mission were scrapped. I would have been scrapped, too.*

> *I am glad to be here, but once I found out what kind of baby I was, I have never felt human. I am another thing. Though Doc and Shepard try to convince me I'm the same as those I see in films and videos, I am not. There are no pictures of children going to school with mechanical contrivances attached to their arms and legs, sucking their energy as they move. When I was an infant, one was stuck to my head. I remember that one the most. I guess they thought I wouldn't remember it, but I do. Later, when I was four or five, I used to look at it through the window of the nursery. It felt like it was a part of me left behind, still attached to the servos and devices, as if I were part of the ship, jettisoned. Yes, it would help power the ship. Yes, everything everywhere is so important, but what about me? What about me growing up thinking a metal rod was one of my limbs? An appendage—that's the word, appendage. One day it simply detached, like my arm fell off.*
>
> *I feel detached from the human race sometimes. Today I was looking in the nursery for any supplies we could use, and there on the floor, beside the refuse container, was my dish. The dish I was born from. Lying there, degraded. It isn't so much that the dish was unimportant; it's that the ship's name on the label was not even correct. It said "Amadeus." Was I supposed to be born on another ship? Would that one have landed in paradise, and the Amadeus people, would they now be in this desert?*

I could scarcely believe what I had read. Understanding swept through me like a tide. Angela was originally to have been on the *Amadeus*, and had she been, she would have been dead because of that faulty arm. She would have been one of the three failed births Forsythe had witnessed.

I watched her lonely eyes read back what she had written. Her features then struck me. She had this subtle smile buried amid her contemplation—a familiar, faint curve of expression. I had seen it on only one other person, one other face . . . *Jing.* I thought, *That smile belonged to Jing.*

I recalled then that Jing was one of the last late egg donors and that, for some reason, she had requested that her eggs be transferred from the *Amadeus* to the *Rhapsody* . . . but *why?* I watched Angela read the last words she had written on the page. I watched her lips move, and moved my lips with hers.

I could think of only one reason why Jing would transfer her eggs to the *Rhapsody:* because my samples were on the *Rhapsody.* I recalled how Tex liked to work on the *Rhapsody* over any other ship. It was all making sense. He fussed over the *Rhapsody;* he was watching over it.

I wrestled with these notions. I thought, the signs were there; oh, the signs were definitely there. The galaxies had filtered through millions of people, and this lonely girl, writing on her pages, just might be . . . I didn't know if I wanted to believe it. She used the oil so inventively . . . *If she truly is my daughter,* I thought, *this would change everything.* If she was mine, I was unworthy of her. A man would never do this to someone so frail and innocent—leave her out there unattended, with no way to communicate. A man would never do this to his own daughter.

I was still unsure; there was not enough proof.

A spider had crawled into my coffee. I ate it and reached for the second book, from the toppled pile of diaries on the makeshift table in my camp. *A daughter,* I thought. One who could make things like this. I held the book by its binding. It weighed as much as a book should weigh. It had life in it. I tried to steady my nerves, to rationalize this whole mess. I determined to put my attention forward. I should spend my days finding out the truth. This could be my *daughter* out there. I opened the book and studied it. A tear almost dropped to the page, but I fought it.

"This was a good thing, to know of you," I said. "I so admire your work."

I looked at the stack of books differently now. Each diary varied in size and in the patterns impressed into its cover. Most contained the same light green paper, painstakingly pressed from a tree or some kind of plant pulp. The edges of the pages looked as if they were cut to size with flint or obsidian, and remnants of this rock fell from between the pages, flakes of grit sifting onto the table. I pushed my fingertip down onto the grains to pick them up. There was a time, I realized, when this would have been so important to the world. This particle of rock would have been a great discovery. I looked around to show them to someone, these granules of rock from another planet, but the desolate woods revealed no person to see them. I tasted them and they tasted like dirt.

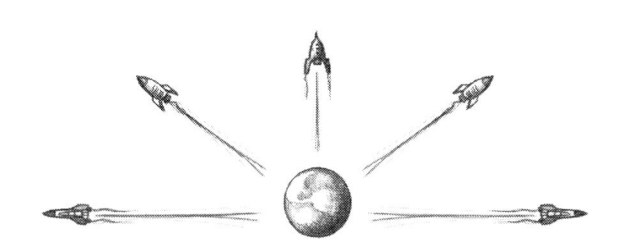

CHAPTER FIFTEEN

The next day, Angela was scratching her skin, made itchy by the dusty desert air. She looked at the ship as if pondering whether they should go back inside it to live. She and Nathan now occupied what he annoyingly called "not your traditional English mansion," for he had often said he would have a mansion by this age. The door was a warped, tight weave of hurriedly wrapped tumbleweeds; the floor was sand. He sat in the center of the room, on a larger rock. Angela sat in the corner, writing in the sand with a long, thin stick.

Nathan is getting more set in his ways. He wants so bad to be the king of something, and the only thing here to rule is me. I brought the tea late today and he got angry. My eyes always go to that rolled paper in the glass tube. I can't help it. Who else is here to admire it and bow to it? Only me. What a torturous device this scroll has become. Yes, it is his lineage, and his father is noble and intelligent. Well, I bet my father is strong and hardworking—two qualities that trump noble and intelligent in this place. But we are here and have so few things—especially me. I long to touch real paper, and this is my dilemma. Should I bow to it? Today I will, but tomorrow, well, we'll see what tomorrow holds.

"Angela, it's time for tea."

She sat quietly.

"Angela?"

She slammed her pen down and said, "Nathan, we're not supposed to be the Echo Kingdom version of *The Flintstones*." She went outside, picked up her tray, and brought him his tea. "Traditional tea and a wafer for you, master?"

He took the aluminum cup. "Thank you, Angela." He sat up straight and surveyed his home. Angela went back outside in the dust, but she looked at him through the holes in the walls. He tried to conceal his self-consciousness while she spoke to him from outside.

"Are you ready for the hunt tonight?" she asked.

"Yes, I am," she heard.

"Good. We have only one tomato and three squash left."

"The rabbits should be breeding soon, so I wouldn't worry," he said a little defensively as two scrawny rabbits made pathetic, wobbling hops in their tumbleweed cage.

She picked up her stick and began to draw a calligraphy character in the sand. Nathan came from the hut.

"That language is deceased," he said, coughing.

"Anything can live that you and I keep alive," she said. "Let's keep the beautiful things alive—the wonderful lettering—and ditch the lack of equality. That's the only thing that is dead."

"Tradition—let's keep that alive," Nathan said. "People traditionally honor their husbands, their fathers and mothers."

"Tradition is easy for you to say and try to emulate, but if my society had the tradition of men being women's slaves, that wouldn't be fine with you, now, would it?"

"On Earth, you will find that men are greater because of our strength and our ability to defend the female." He picked up the bow he had made from a piece of metal door trim and strung with braided roots. It was a good bow.

"Remember, I will defend you forever. Your respect for me and for the old ways will make my defending you worth the effort."

"Worth the effort—*huh!*" She stormed into the shack but then came back out to lift the door up and swing it shut. Part of the hinge broke off.

"I will go out tonight and hunt," he said to the hut in a loud voice. "You will be a good wife and remain here and prepare something, *do* something. This will make us equal." He headed for the rock hill and looked longingly up at the seven stars, as if they were his only friends.

The sun was rising behind the plain pear planet, and the wind was still. Nathan's muscles had grown fit, and he moved quickly and quietly over the large rocks, which were sharp like coral and pocked with holes. The surfaces felt like sandpaper, and the granules that crumbled loose clung to his skin and got under his fingernails like fine-ground glass.

Leaping over a deep trough, he heard an odd, faint tapping sound. He squatted and listened. Angela was right—there was something out here.

Another tapping noise traveled across the craggy rock pile. And as he peered through a stone fissure, he heard it again, this time closer still.

He slipped the bow from over his shoulder and set a brittle arrow. He heard a harsh exhalation.

"A dragon," he whispered, "with or without fire . . . come to me."

From behind him, he felt breath on his calf and turned and launched the arrow. It flew and broke against the wall.

"You're playing with me," he said. With shaky hands, he nocked a second arrow and drew it back. Again he felt breath on his back. Whirling, he pointed the weapon nervously up and down and sideways. In frustration, he yelled, "Fi-i-ight!"

The ground trembled, and he heard the tapping of hard feet again. The rocks began cracking underfoot. He moved away and watched the cracks growing and making the sounds like the impacts of hooves.

Feeling with his palm, he traced the air to a crack in the ground. Air was forcing its way through these cracks in periodic gusts.

"Nothing," he said, lowering his bow. He looked at the seven stars as they began to fade and hide in the daylight. "You, my useless companions, have failed me," he muttered. On the way back to the hut, he picked up the launched arrow with the broken tip.

Coming across the dune, he found Angela waiting. She searched in his eyes and then wrapped a blanket around him. "Let's get you inside," she said, her breath clouding from the cold. She hung his bow on the wall. "Your empty hands are those of a warrior—a warrior who's still learning."

"Yes," he said. "Now I think I know everything I need to know. It should be a good hunt tomorrow." He sat in the center of the room, and she sat on the ground beside him and looked up at the scroll. He looked down, and dust blew on him.

Two days passed, during which he did not hunt.

Finally, Angela spoke. "Nathan," she said, "I know that you want us to survive on the land. But we need to lock ourselves in the ship so Doc can control the environment. The plants need to grow. They need to be nurtured. We could have edible things in a few weeks."

Nathan threw his cup against the wall. "It's too late. We won't survive even one more week. I will not close myself in that ship ever again. I will go and I will get you food."

He swung the bow over his shoulder, then picked up her drawing stick and moved it across the sand. She looked down. It was a dragon. She gasped and bowed her head as he walked to the rocks.

He sat hidden on the other side of the rock hill for hours, waiting for what he knew was nothing.

Suddenly, his muscles tensed and his stomach turned as a wretched scream came from the camp. It was Angela. He felt the ground rumble and heard another cold scream, this one cut short.

Running down the rocks and up to the top of the dune, he stood at its crest, but he could not locate her, so he ran to where the hut had stood. It was now a pile of rubble.

"Angela!" he yelled, pulling rocks and crumbled bricks away from the collapsed structure. Nothing moved.

He spun and saw something that made his legs weaken.

It had come from nowhere and grown like the plague. He stepped back and stared at a leering black hole in the ground—a seemingly bottomless crack in the surface of the planet.

"Angela!" he yelled. The hole seemed to swallow his voice.

He turned back toward the hut. There was a trail of faltering footprints . . . and blood. Red spatters came from the house and ended at the crevice. The house had caved in on her. She staggered, fell in. She was gone—the ship, too.

He looked into the dark hole. "Whoa!" he said. *What are we living on?* he wondered. *This place is a giant trap! Echo Kingdom is only a shell of a planet.*

He paced the rim. This could not be happening. Yet it was.

"Angela, where are you!" he shouted down into the cavern. He lay flat on the ground and peered in, trying to make his eyes adjust. He took a pebble and dropped it in, and hearing nothing, he dropped a larger rock. Again, no sound of anything hitting bottom.

He yelled her name again and again. Night fell, and he kept yelling until he was hoarse and no sound came. Hanging his head over the edge, he listened, periodically dropping another rock or pebble, but he heard nothing. He rolled onto his side and looked at his home, the pile of rubble, the dirt.

"Angela, where are you?" he said faintly. "My love, you are so wrong—we are nowhere near equals." His dusty cheek showed the single trail of an errant tear.

"You are so much braver than I . . . so much truer." Nathan looked at the smeared drawing of a dragon in the sand, the crumbled mud bricks, and the scroll's glass tube, now smashed. He stared at it blankly.

"Why would anyone believe a scroll could do anything for us out here?" he said to no one. He threw a fistful of sand at it and rolled onto his back.

"We traveled so far, for *this,*" he told the wind. "I hope the others have better fortune."

He lay there for a while, then stood and hung his bow over his shoulder, his arms hanging low and motionless "I cannot do this alone," he said to the crevice. "This conclusion is easy for me to reach: I am no one without you. Without you, Angela, I myself cease to exist. What would be the use of it—to struggle just to die?"

Stepping to the edge, he closed his eyes before the yawning black maw. And with his back straight and arms raised high above his head, he pushed off with his toes.

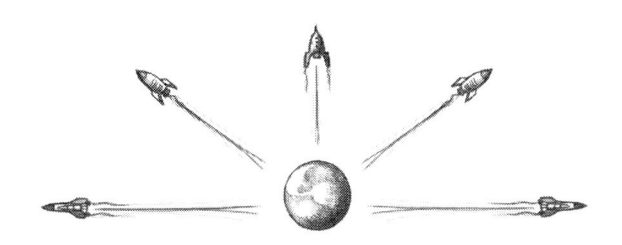

CHAPTER SIXTEEN

I was mortified watching Nathan jump over the edge of the cliff after Angela and the ship. Just like that, they both were gone. I was numb. My own demise would be soon enough, but these *children* were dead—my daughter was gone. I thought about Forsythe, still in space, the only one left.

"Shepard," I said, "let's go back to the *Amadeus* drive—I want to see how Forsythe is doing." The screen blinked and brought up the *Amadeus* cabin.

The ship had veered away from the acid planet, and Shepard could not detect an alternative—not one reachable within Forsythe's lifetime. There he was, a shirtless, hopeless, haggard kid, traveling into the forever darkness. His frame reminded me of a rickety card table with thin, spindly legs and wobbly joints. I could see the smallest skeletal detail right through that thin parchment skin. His large eyebrows made him look like a professor of botany or fungi or germs. Fast-forwarding the video, I saw him, between bouts of cursing and whimpering, kicking and punching things. Then he would sit motionless for hours on end, barely even blinking. By my calculations, he was twenty-four.

He plucked a green bean from one of the plants and laughed maniacally at it. He set it down on the window ledge and kept looking over at the bean and then away, laughing in spurts. He would compose himself, look at the bean, and laugh again.

"This is how I am going to live out my life?" he said, chuckling then calming down. Floating over to the chessboard, he picked up the edge-sharpened bishop and began scraping words into the wall. The sound was like a wrench tightening a rusty bolt.

"Why would the world believe this could be done?" he wrote. "What madman concocted such a farce?" He looked toward the nursery, as if pondering the failed births, then up at the planters, now composted by the dead embryos. "Why is this our destiny?" He looked at the writing and floated backward, away from it.

He said, "I have very little regard for you anymore, Doc and Shepard. You people make me sick." He threw the bishop against the wall, where it bounced and spun in slow motion.

Many months passed, and the ship maintained what appeared to be a random course. With the slightest light from a star, Shepard would frantically change directions to inspect the light, investigate it, test it. He felt responsible for this. Forsythe couldn't tolerate being in the same room as Shepard, so he moved the computer case into the nursery.

One day, Forsythe sat floating in the center of the room. His hair was long and his pants shredded, and the floor around him had an even greater collection of filthy debris. Doc observed him and knew that this destinationless flight was wearing the patient thin. The code from Yimosu's program kicked in.

"Forsythe," Doc said, "I know you are upset with us for miscalculating the viability of the planet you were to land on."

Forsythe remained motionless on the floor.

"We understand that," Doc said, "but we have something that might help you."

Forsythe moved his eyes—only his eyes, and only opening them halfway.

"There is an experiment on board we would like you to perform," Doc said.

"Go away," Forsythe mumbled

"This may help you."

"I said beat it." He gave the air a sluggish swat.

"If you do this, we can give you a steroid injection. It might make you feel better."

Forsythe bit down on his finger. He lowered his head, and his hair fell forward again. "I like shots," he said. He smacked his lips, sounding like a cat lapping milk.

"When do I get it?"

"After."

"Of coarse you would say that. What is this experiment?" He licked his lips. "A Rorschach test? Or maybe it's a survey: how I like my journey so far. I'd give it a bad recommendation—needs improvement."

"No, it's nothing like that," Doc said.

The screen showed a monk. It was Yimosu.

"Yeah, this guy's a real winner," Forsythe said. "You think I'd look good bald, Doc? With epicanthic folds, maybe?"

"We need you to begin," Doc said.

On the screen, Yimosu said, "I need you to think of something, which may be quite painful. I understand that you have no companions and that you feel all is lost."

"You're psychic," Forsythe said, pulling himself into the chair.

Yimosu said, "Please repeat the following words until I tell you to stop: 'The pain I am trying to reach is this: I am alone. If I were to walk at any pace in any direction for the rest of my life, I would never reach or see anyone. I am hundreds of millions of miles away from any living soul. The future holds no people for me; I can contact no one. I will live alone. I will die alone. The pain I am trying to reach is this."

Forsythe listened again and then began to say the words. For three days, he repeated Yimosu's statement, dozing off and, the moment he awoke, continuing it, like a Hindu pilgrim repeating a mantra.

Seventy-four hours later, Doc turned off the experiment, and Forsythe stopped repeating the words.

Silence again took over the *Amadeus* as it kept traveling for two more years. Forsythe was little more than a living skeleton. His face drooped from lack of fat and muscle content, but he had a calm about him, maybe even some sort of disturbed smile. On this day, he was lying low above the floor, with his chessmen in a circle around him. In this circle, from out of the silence, he heard a tick. It occurred just once, a frail, minute sound, a nonevent that, on earth, probably could not be detected except with very sensitive equipment. But Forsythe's equipment had grown very sensitive, and he heard it.

"What was that?" he asked. He tried to focus on the screen. "Was that electricity? Shepard, are you powering up the filters?"

Checking for activity lights on the screen, Forsythe floated over to the chair, and the center screen turned on.

"Shep . . . *Shep*," he whispered. "What do you have?" He spoke as if he were approaching a child who was holding the car keys over a drain. "Shepard, my dear old friend, what do you see? What can you see? Can you show me? What could you possibly see?" Saliva was accumulating in the pouches of Forsythe's withered cheeks.

Shepard's screen warmed up. "There is a planet," Shepard said.

A blur appeared. Shepard adjusted the focus, and a magnification lens locked into place to reveal a sun with a planet passing in front of it.

Forsythe bit his fingernail.

"I need to remind you, this may be a wobble."

"I know, I know, a wobble: an event that occurs when the sun is too close to the planet and would make the planet too hot to occupy. The planet's gravity itself forces the sun to move slightly; hence a wobble." Forsythe watched the planet swing around the sun, and as it did, the image of the sun moved slightly to the left.

"That's a wobble, all right, Shep," he said. "I know I'm desperate, but I don't want to land somewhere where the planet is a fireball. *Is* that a wobble, Shep? Is that planet too close to its sun? Might the planet still be habitable? If maybe the planet passes by its sun only once every few years, maybe I would do that." He rubbed his chin through his patchy beard. "We could land there so I could touch ground just once—let's say, a minimum of one year. If I could live on a planet for one year before dying, I would do that. Yes, one year and I would like that." Then he muttered, "Maybe less . . . yes, maybe less." He blinked rapidly, swallowed, and caressed the screen with his fingertips. "Maybe less."

Doc moved an arm toward Forsythe.

"Don't touch me, Doc. I told you not to touch the hair." Doc's arm retracted.

Forsythe said, "How about if we could time it so that we would land just after the wobble, so the planet would be cool enough for me to live on until either it freezes me into a beautiful ice sculpture or the sun melts me into wet ashes."

"We are unsure of the terrain at this time," Shepard said. "If the wobble has produced extraordinarily harsh conditions, we will determine this by our current study of emitted chemical signatures and—"

"I could use the suit—take walks outside and live in the ship." Forsythe began to rock back and forth. "I could go in and out, in *and* out. Okay, I am willing to chance all those things if you can give me a window, so I can make a decision on how short a time I would be willing to live. A year, but maybe less . . ." He wrung his hands and leaned nervously to one side in his chair. In this position, he was at an angle that enabled him to see, through the nursery window, something he had never noticed before, something previously hidden by tubes and water storage containers.

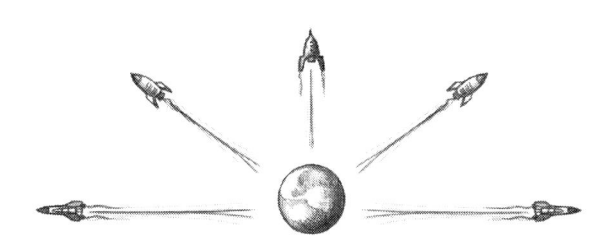

CHAPTER SEVENTEEN

Forsythe was looking through the nursery window, turning his body completely sideways.

"What's in there? he said. "What is that?" He floated to the window.

"Secondary specimens—animals," Doc said.

"Those are little animal friends?" Forsythe said, his eyes wide and childlike.

"Yes, we have twenty-four varieties of animals."

"What kind?"

"Earth animals."

"I don't want any sharks in here." He shivered at the idea.

"Don't be silly," Doc said. "We have no sharks."

"Good. No sharks." Forsythe pointed his finger into the air as if making a important decree.

"Shepard and I could allow you to have a dog."

He peered into the nursery. "Does it bite?"

"Some do."

"Why would I want that?"

"For companionship. You can teach it not to bite." Doc put up a photo of a rather ordinary-looking brown dog.

"A dog. Do people eat dogs?" He cocked his head.

Doc hesitated on this one. "Not ordinarily."

Forsythe remained with his face squashed against the glass, He didn't move any muscles or grit his teeth, or even blink very many times. A few hours later, he said, "I'll have a dog . . . please?"

"Yes, one dog, then," Doc said. Forsythe anticipated that machines would start to move, and he smiled when the smaller nursery arms became animated.

"Oh . . . ," Forsythe said. He reached over to the top bunk and held up the arm that he had repaired after the earlier malfunction. "Do you need this?"

Doc looked at it with his camera arm and said, "Oh, yes."

Forsythe frowned. "This isn't going to go very well, is it?"

Forsythe often looked at the picture of a Chihuahua on the monitor. The embryo grew and was passed from a small centrifuge to a larger one, then into the blue fluid of the womb sphere above. Two months later, from the thickened gel came a wet blob. It was alive. Forsythe watched the puppy being handled by the robots.

"When can I have him?"

"We need to wean *her* first," Doc said. "She needs to be strong enough to be in the main cabin with you." The puppy remained in a quilted bed, with small robotic arms holding her gently in place and attending to her.

Finally one day, Shepard opened the nursery door, and Doc handed the wiggly puppy through.

Forsythe got down on his knees and let the puppy go. She floated around him, legs struggling to grip something, anything, and peed everywhere.

Laughing and crying, Forsythe said, "What have I done?"

That afternoon, Doc said, "We're supposed to name her."

"No, no, you're not naming anything. You named that shit-hole acid planet back there 'Triumph City.' What a piece of crap that was." Forsythe stood up and paced the room. "No, *I'll* name her. How about 'Robot'?"

All Doc's arms retracted.

"I guess not." Forsythe sat back and took in a deep breath through his teeth.

He said names he had heard from films and lessons: "Wilson . . . McGregor . . . Mr. Belvedere . . . McClintock . . . McDonald . . . Mendelbaum. Whoah!" he said. "Wait, I like that one. A long name. I like saying names, especially long names."

"Mendelbaum." Forsythe sat up and lifted a chess piece from the circle and threw it. "Mendelbaum, fetch."

The chess piece clinked and bounced to the floor and floated into the air. Everyone was quiet. Forsythe had a companion.

He stared into the puppy's droopy eyes, then reached a finger out to touch the dog's eye.

The video advanced to six years later. Forsythe was much taller and struggled to fasten the EAs, which were bent from overuse and his unusual size. He frequently attached them to his calves instead of his ankles, and to his forearms instead of his wrists—I supposed because of the rashes produced by the friction. Some of the pivots were loose, and the meter still showed a positive charge when he moved around. He was running in place the best he could, when Shepard spoke.

"Forsythe, the planet on target is, in all probability, habitable. The wobble was a mistake—a glitch in the lenses; however, there is a slight chance—"

"Shut up!" Forsythe interrupted. "Shut up and do it." He stopped running and panted.

"Do it?" Shepard asked.

"I don't care about your 'however's.' Initiate the sequence to land. I don't care how long I live on it. I just want to live for a little while, and I don't care if this planet is a giant ball of snot with oceans of giant sharks and purple, rabid flying monkeys slinging feces at me—I am not going to let my dog die in here."

He sat down. One of Doc's arms approached him; it had scissors. Forsythe flinched. The arm retracted, then moved in again. Another arm held some of Forsythe's hair, and the scissors snipped the strands away. Forsythe watched the locks fall away, then took a deep breath and closed his eyes.

The ship traveled another year and was moments from skimming the atmosphere. Forsythe was only halfway strapped into his seat this time, watching intently for the red line of code that aborted the last landing. A scraping sound began. The sound grew into what could only be described as a pile of brass band instruments being dumped into the sea. Welcoming the sound, he took a deep breath and raised his arms to conduct the musicianless undersea ensemble.

"I hear no retros," he said. "What is going on?"

"The vessel is old; ice may be clogging them," Shepard said.

"Go into entry, dude—that will warm the ice up," Forsythe said, raising his arms again in hope. An uninvited tuba sound hit a flat note; then silence. He felt a familiar tugging.

"Oh, no. We are *not* turning away!" Forsythe stood up, and the straps fell away.

"We bounced off. Two of the retros did not angle us in," Shepard said.

"You know, fellas, this does not surprise me one *bit*!" Floating in the air, he squirmed and twisted like a fish on a hook. "What is your problem!" he said. Green lights turned red in succession.

"Forsythe, we will need another three months to circle and make another attempt."

"Forget it!" Let me into the diagnostics.

The diagnostic screen appeared on the far right monitor, and he started entering a code. A few moments later, he said, "Let me into the rear compartment."

The compartment's door latch clicked, and he climbed through. "I have been thinking about this for years: how to control this ship without dying of old age in the process." He pried the paneling away with his fingers and peeled off some inner wall stays. The main guidance rocketry mechanisms were now exposed. There were levers and switches—leftover test controls.

"If you butt-heads did your job, I would have landed years ago."

He pushed in a breaker, switched on a primer unit, and spun two wing nuts off a governing bar, which flew against the wall. Now he forced the fuel valves fully open, and the retros fired outside. "I am tired of executing a turn at one degree per year!" He pulled down the test levers, and the ship began to turn, the G forces slamming him against the wall. The loose bar headed at him, and he caught it just before it could smash his face. The ship then pulled Forsythe from the compartment and threw him against the ceiling of the main cabin as it banked into this deepening turn. He was beside the planter, and he lifted the lid and shoved the bar inside. The forces against him doubled again.

"Holy shit!" he crowed, crab-walking gleefully down the wall. He picked up Mendelbaum along the way to get back into the command chair.

"Never felt G's like that, have you, Shep?"

"No." Shepard said.

The planet approached, and a momentary rumble quickly gave way to loud wind. The ship cruised and leveled. Forsythe looked out the window. The recon satellite shot out from the side of his craft and fell away. "What the hell was that?" he moaned. "Was that my satellite?"

No answer came from the computers.

Then Shepard said, "Forsythe."

"Is this about my satellite falling to the ground? Because I just saw it—it fell to the ground. What good is a satellite going to do on the ground?"

"This is not about the satellite. This is a more pressing issue," Shepard said.

"Well, let's hear it—what could it *possibly* be now?"

"Forsythe, there is no land in sight."

"No land? What do you call that below us, then?"

"Water," Shepard replied. "A mixture of water and sand, with a very strong current."

Forsythe stared at the uniformly beige ocean on the screen.

"A current . . . doesn't that mean land would be somewhere?"

"Not always. It could be winds or moons driving lunar tides."

Forsythe calmly petted his dog. "Mendi doesn't know how to swim."

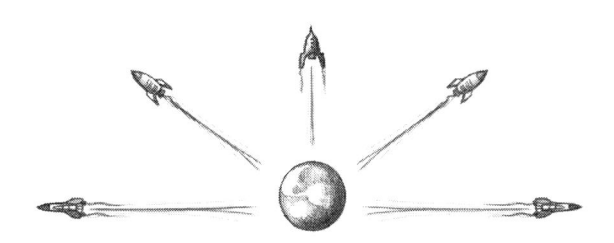

CHAPTER EIGHTEEN

The ship splashed into the turbid water, throwing Forsythe forward in his seat. Shepard shut the rocketry down, and the parachute followed the craft down.

A glassy-eyed Forsythe stared at the bubbles outside the window. "Water," he said. "I can't swim, either." He bit his lip. The ship hit and tossed sideways and up and down , throwing Forsythe around in his first-ever experience with gravity, before settling at the bottom.

"Well, it's a change of scenery, isn't it, you fuckers!"

"We are all going to die sometime," I said. I inhaled the cold, crisp woodland air. "Some of us more humorously than others. Shepard!" I yelled across the camp. "I can't take one more minute of Forsythe!"

The video turned off.

"I was thinking about the kids, Nathan and Angela. Shepard, show me anything you can find with a time stamp after Nathan jumped off the cliff," I said. "What about the overhead view from *Rhapsody*'s recon satellite?"

The video came up. I rubbed my eyes. The distant view showed the crevice and the crippled house in the Echo desert. No ship, no people. A lone cloud passed by.

"Hey, what about the ship's hull camera?"

Shepard switched the view to a tilted angle; within it was the ship's fin—and darkness.

"Rewind," I said. Carefully, I looked through the footage. I caught a glimpse of motion—distant and faint, but definitely an object falling. It was Nathan jumping over the cliff's edge. I was watching Nathan die.

Nathan's body arced in a graceful swan dive into the cavern. The air cooled rapidly, and he awaited the impact of the ground. Something touched him; then lots of things touched him. Wet and slimy substances wrapped around his body, tightening as he fell farther to become systematically engulfed by a web of vines. The pain from the lashing strands whipped and stung him. Through his sticky, blood-covered eyes, he could see the dull, unfocused blur of the opening above. Vines—hundreds of them, some as thick as tree trunks—dangled from the ceiling of this cavern and held him suspended like a spider's prey.

Drawing breath was difficult as the strands of thick goo tightened with his weight, constricting his chest. He rocked his body into motion, wincing each time, but noticed some relief when he applied pressure backward with his elbow. It was his bow—the metal edge of it was cutting through the vines. He was grateful for the air, but his ribs cried out as he breathed, and his fingers and palms burned and stung from the plant juices. Slowly moving his arm, he cut away more vine and grabbed a thick stem. Loose vine meat shed away, and his hands found a solid core. He took a deep breath.

"Angela," he whimpered.

The plant life muffled him. He tried to follow the damaged portions of the ropes from the top down to see her path, but his eyes would not adjust to such detail.

"Angela," he said. He began working his way toward the wall by grasping the slimy ropes, slipping down as most gave way, each time finding the solid portion deep inside each vine. This barely but satisfactorily held his weight, but with each sideways advancement, he slid down a few feet. Soon he was exhausted, and also terrified at the prodigious depth of this cavern—who knew what creatures lurked below?

He heard a sound: "Nay . . ."—quick and stifled.

He wanted to try to speak her name one more time. He coughed and wheezed but could get out only "Ange . . ."

"Here," he heard. "Over here."

She was right beside him, camouflaged in the vines. Her eyes blinked three times; then she fell limp. Nathan wrapped his leg around a vine and cut her away with his bow, and she was free and in his arms. Breathing deeply, she opened her eyes.

"My love . . . ," she said with eyes glistening, wrapping her arms around him tighter. The pressure of her against him was something he never wanted to live without. He would follow her down again if she fell. Getting the hang of navigating the vines, he moved more easily, holding her faithfully as even more of his strength surfaced.

From below, a reflection caught his eye. "There's something down there—I can hear it." Cautiously, he slid them down farther, but the vines came to an end, like a ragged curtain of thick, gooey tentacles. Nathan and Angela hung there, their eyes adjusting.

"Water," she said. "That's water I hear."

Nathan dangled his feet and, touching solid ground, let go of the vine. His knees buckled. He and Angela fell onto the pebbly bank of a clear brook. He crawled over to it and pooled water in his hands. She followed him, and he offered the water to her, and she steadied his hands with her fingertips.

"Water carved these caverns," he said.

"Look," she said. "There, beside that boulder in the wall."

"It's the ship!" Doc's familiar light peeked at them through the porthole.

He helped her up, and as they walked beneath the vines, she ran her hand along their bottoms, moving them like curtains. The space felt cozy and secure; the acoustics made their voices sound perfect, isolated, and private.

Some sunlight broke through, and the light revealed marvelous colors within the cavern.

"This is wonderful," she said. She touched a plant that swayed gently in a soft, misty breeze.

"Astonishing," he said. Flowers resembling tropical fish swayed, their luminescent petals animated in circular and spiraled motions, reaching toward the light. Some plants moved like seahorses in a current, some like crabs. Some seemed to have eyes. She waved her hand in front of one, and it did not flinch, though it blinked once in a while. She plucked a gold and blue petal from a red stem. It was like touching the cheek of an infant. She put the petal on her tongue, and it melted away, leaving a trace of perfume . . . the perfume of a movie star.

"This is the *real* Echo Kingdom," Nathan said, holding his side. He looked proudly into her forgiving eyes. "This is our real home."

"Your mansion," she said.

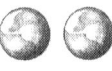

Nathan had marks and dried blood as if he had been whipped. For days, Doc kept him asleep under the influence of morphine and sedatives. Angela gathered fresh food, planted the ship's plants in the tender soil along the edge of the wall, and made a table and chairs out of flat stones, all the while keeping an eye on him as he rested. Nathan struggled to open his eyes.

"My love, are you okay?" she asked, approaching. "How do you feel?"

"Still weak," he said, trying to sit up as his joints popped. "Wow, something smells good."

She had a pot of stew on the coals—mussels she had found in the creek. He was mesmerized by Angela as she sat illuminated in Doc's blue light, her delicate, flowing hair held in place by carved sticks. She poured his supper into a bowl and handed it to him. "You, my love, are about to eat aliens," she said with an evil grin.

He smiled and took the spoon, then noticed something on the ground beside her. Recognizing it, he flushed. Setting the bowl down, he took her hands and looked at them. Fresh rope burns. His mind raced. How could this be? What had she done? Slowly raising his eyes to meet hers, he gazed at her in wonder. Through tears, he looked at the one thing he had once cherished above all others

"The scroll," he said.

The *Amadeus* rocked at the bottom of the sea. In the cabin, Forsythe lay curled in a ball. He steadied himself every half minute or so by outstretching his arm, touching his fingertips to the floor. Even in the monitor, in the cabin's dimming light, I thought he looked like hell, even for Forsythe. Dried blood encrusted his hands. Something had happened to his fingers . . . gashes.

After hours of silence, he held his stomach and rose, reached out, and took Doc's camera arm. He peered into the lens with one bloodshot eye.

"What the fuck am I supposed to do now?" he muttered.

Mendelbaum was frazzled. She scurried, tripping and tumbling, consumed with the motion of the waves.

"Doc . . . Mendi and I have had a full life," he said. "I look like crap, the power's not regenerating—not without me exercising myself to death—and I'm tired of this."

He put the camera to his mouth and spoke into it as if it were a microphone.

"Doc, teach me how to swim."

He wobbled, barely keeping his balance in the jostling ship, and wrestled with attaching the EAs to his body. Though they were loose and improperly located, Doc began to operate them anyway, in a manner that made Forsythe's arms and legs move in the crudest approximation of swimming—stand-up swimming, one might say. Although stand-up swimming seemed ineffective, he looked proud to be doing it. It reminded me of some sick horror puppet show in which the puppeteer toys with all his victims in sad and demented ways and, in the end, everyone dies. Forsythe was learning stand-up swimming—something I, unfortunately, somehow had a hand in inventing.

A few days later, in the morning, he decided it was time. He knew the basics. He thought he and Mendelbaum would float to the top, breathe in some fresh air, have a look around, and then drown. It would all be over.

With an inflatable pillow, Forsythe made a small bubble for Mendelbaum and put her inside it.

"This should do it, little girl," he said. He donned his own space suit, tied a line to her bubble, and held the loose end. But just before putting on his helmet, he plucked several hairs from his head and, with his thick-fingered gloves, awkwardly lifted the tape on the wall and added these hairs to his collection, there on the very end, nearest the skin flakes, a thumbnail paring, and what had to be . . . a booger.

"Water temperature eighty-four degrees Fahrenheit," Shepard said. "Current six miles per hour."

"Unlock the hatch," Forsythe commanded, latching his helmet clamp to seal around his neck and picking up a grab bar. The door slowly cracked open, and water poured in.

"Ah-h-h-h," he said as if settling into a warm bath. Mendi struggled in her ball, squirming and stumbling, try to keep her balance. Within seconds, the water lifted both of them. He released his grip, and they flowed through the door. He felt uneasy, then fearful. Swiftly ascending in the murky water, he screamed.

He saw pieces of parts of things, things moving, and things appeared to be grabbing at him, circling him, following him.

"Oh, shit—sharks! I never thought of that, Mendi," he said, shooting upward.

The turbulence tugged on his legs. He swam to get away, and the current twisted his body, and then, unexpectedly, they both popped up through the water's surface. The sun beamed on them, and he swam a few strokes.

"Mendi, that's it," he said, paddling and breathing hard.

He stopped swimming. He stopped struggling. He stopped.

But instead of sinking to the bottom as he had predicted, instead of gurgling out his life then and there, when he stopped swimming, he floated on his back, holding the string of the dog ball. He took in the undersides of tan clouds and opened his faceplate. The sun warmed his forehead, and he closed his eyes and breathed in the cool air. He cracked open the zipper of Mendi's ball, and they made their way south.

"This should elongate the inevitable, don't you think?" he said to her.

With his arms and legs extended, his body swirled, and he took a drink once in a while from the sea by tilting his head to one side and catching the salty water in his mouth.

"I just don't want to be eaten . . ."

Mendi looked around.

". . . by sea people," he remarked as they drifted.

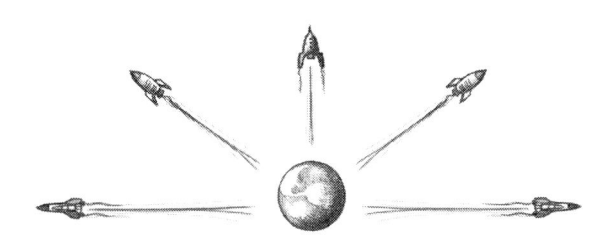

CHAPTER NINETEEN

Forsythe had passed almost a full day in the ocean in his space suit, face to the sky, when he woke to a pleasant splashing sound in a star-filled night. Although he was still floating, he was being nudged by something, as if someone were poking him with a plank. He reached down and felt beneath him. Not a foot below him was solid rock.

"Whoa," he said, standing up. "I can't believe it." He looked around for Mendelbaum, tugged on the line, and pulled her close.

"Mendi, we made it," he said, though there was no dry land to be seen. "It does feel good, though, to be on solid ground, doesn't it?" He let Mendi out of her ball, and she ran around in the chest-high water.

"Water feels a little like Doc's womb, doesn't it?" he said. Under the sun, he sat in the water, bathed in it, laughed in it, splashed in it. The current strengthened, and Forsythe soon realized that if he were to misstep, he would be swept away.

"This wasn't in the lessons," he said to the mysterious ocean. "This wasn't one of the landing scenarios." The current across the shelf was moving faster now. It was running away.

Grabbing Mendy, he put her back in her ball.

He looked to the horizon and noticed that some of the area ahead was now exposed. The current moved even faster, and within minutes the water had drained away entirely, leaving a smooth, glossy plateau of slippery black rock.

"It looks polished and new," he said in openmouthed awe. "Just for me. I am like some form of wizard—a real one. I wanted the water to go away, and it did!"

The stone floor steamed. Beside Forsythe was the edge of the plateau. He looked over it, at the water eight feet down. Waves smashed against the cliff side, against crystal-faceted spires, roots, and jagged rocks that protruded outward and captured flotsam. Timing his actions to avoid the waves, he reached down and snatched a seaweed clump from the rocks and ate it as he walked, humming a piece from Mozart's happier period. His voice rose in volume as he hummed. His pace quickened, and his song became vibrant, allegro appassionato.

"The shore!" he cried. Just ahead of him stretched a sandy beach. "I never would have imagined you boys would get me here!" He jumped on the land, knelt down on it, and gripped sand in his hands. It felt glorious, sifting through his fingers. He turned back toward the ocean.

"Doc and Shepard, I commend you," Forsythe said. And he stood and raised his arm in a firm wrong-handed salute. His eyes twitched when sand landed in them. Night was quietly approaching, and in the eerie absence of walls, it felt dangerous.

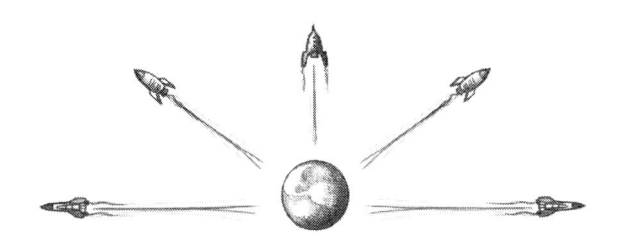

CHAPTER TWENTY

In their new cavern home, they sat on rock chairs beside the playful creek. The fire snapped sparks into the air, and the mussels blew bubbles mimicking the sound of crickets. "You're almost back to normal—healthwise, anyway," Angela said.

Black scabs had formed on Nathan's wrists and ankles and around his waist. "I feel kind of crusty, though," he said.

Seeing the moon through the gap above, Angela sang, "'Livin' after midnight, rockin' to the dawn . . .'"

Nathan smiled. "We'll need to build a ladder to get back up there."

"Why would we want to go back up there?" she asked him.

"I don't know yet. If this cavern was cut from water, the water might come again. We'd need an exit. We can do it with the vines—shear off the gunk and make a rope ladder." He threw a tight bundle of grass on the fire.

She stepped over and scraped a slimy rock with a spoon.

"Did you see this?" she asked, pointing at the scar she had made in the stone.

"That might be metal," Nathan said. "That'll come in handy." He brushed sand from his hands and legs. "This place is a utopia compared to the desert upstairs."

A sound from the ship startled them.

"Oh, man, I forgot to shut the recycler off," he said. He stepped into the ship and flipped a switch.

"Yeah, no more piss-water, *puh-lease*." She made a sour face and scraped more shavings from the rock. "Maybe we can melt this." She rubbed them between her fingers, and Nathan came out of the ship.

He heard another sound. Raising his hand for her to stop, he said, "There's something out there."

Angela's eyes widened. The vines were moving. Then she heard something she had never thought she would hear on this planet.

A throat cleared. Loudly, sharply cutting through everything she knew about this planet.

"How would that sound be here?" Nathan asked, looking at her.

Again a throat cleared, this time hawking up phlegm.

Angela gasped, hand over her mouth, and said, "What is it?"

"I do not know."

"It was like a voice almost."

"I know."

Just around the corner of the ship, they heard footfalls on the pebbles. The feet stopped. "Hello?" Nathan said.

"Hello," a voice answered.

Doc announced, "That is a human voice." He contorted his camera arm to see, to locate the origin.

Nathan looked for something to pick up. Running into the ship, he grabbed a chess piece from the table and stood just inside the doorway. Angela was on the far side of the fire.

"Kids," the raspy voice said.

Angela saw the figure. She stepped back, her face growing flushed and her knees shaking, as a tall shadow eclipsed her. "What are you?" she said, stepping farther back, almost touching the cavern wall "Are you a person?"

Nathan waited for the answer. Angela's teeth chattered twice. The light from above failed to reveal any detail of the intruder.

Nathan moved slowly toward the floodlight switch.

"Go ahead, turn it on. I have nothing to hide." The shadow moved closer to Angela.

Nathan hit the switch, and the light shone on a scraggly man with a crooked gait. He was dressed in a blue flight suit with rips and tears throughout and plenty of dirt on the butt and back. His skin she noticed most of all. It had wrinkles all over it—an endless number of wrinkles, it seemed. She was amazed at the distance his tangy, foul breath traveled to sting her nose.

"*Are* you a person?" Nathan asked.

"Yeah, are you one?" Angela repeated.

"I was," he said. "I was." The words sounded sad.

"So *now* what are you?" she asked.

"I am a shell of a man, much like this planet." The man exhaled loudly and stepped toward the fire. The sparks released from the palpitating flames, and he seemed enchanted by them. He put his hands out over the flame tips and closed his mouth, as if keeping to himself how good the warmth felt.

He turned his head halfway toward Nathan. "I have one of those," he said. The man pulled the sharpened bishop from his pocket, crossed his arms, and spun it between his fingers the way a prestidigitator might manipulate a quarter. Nathan looked surprised to see an object so familiar. "Don't worry. I am one of you, you might say. Right, Doc?"

Angela could not stop staring at the man and at what an ugly process he made of forming words. He angled his jaw downward, and it popped audibly. He often stuck his tongue out and licked his lips—too often.

Who are you? How do you know about Doc?" Nathan asked him.

"My name is Forsythe. This is Mendelbaum." The scrawny dog with buggy eyes and a matchstick tail stood by Forsythe's leg and then spurted into action, running and sniffing around him like one of those little fish that clean their host.

"Forsythe," Doc said. "This name *is* in the Wombs name bank. On the first ship."

That's right Doc," he said. "I keep telling you, I am one of you guys."

Angela looked at him and slowly shook her head back and forth. Forsythe smiled a fake smile directly at her, and she knelt down and picked up a dried grass stem.

"The name Mendelbaum is not recognized," Doc said.

"You computers don't control everything, Doc. I named her," Forsythe said proudly, uncrossing his arms to reveal the Wombs insignia on his uniform, above his heart. "Ark Amadeus" was stitched below it.

"Now, from the looks of things, I must have been the first person born in space. I don't know what your numbers are, you guys, but I am guessing four or five—seven at the most."

"Two," Nathan answered. "Our ship, the ark *Rhapsody,* was the second ship. What are you doing here? They weren't supposed to send two vessels to the same planet. It's all about spreading us out."

"Yeah, we don't need anyone else here," Angela said. Her teeth chattered three times. Forsythe put the chess piece in his pocket and picked up some dried vines.

"You look glued together," Nathan said, "My guess is morphine."

"Throw in some bitterness, and, kid, you just nailed my ingredients." Forsythe changed his tone to friendly. "You, uh . . . got any of that?" He licked his lips again.

Nathan stared at him. "Morphine—are you injured?"

Forsythe frowned. "Guess not."

"What's with this thing?" Nathan said, looking down at the dog. Mendelbaum sat, bulbous eyes worrying.

"The human births didn't work out. This was the next-best thing."

"Oh, my God," Angela said. She stood and walked over to stand by Nathan. "What happened to the other astronaut? What happened to her?"

"Yeah," Nathan said. "There are supposed to be two of you."

"It's not like that," Forsythe said. "It was a mechanical failure—an unforeseen problem."

Nathan cocked his head back and said, "We didn't experience any . . . unforeseen problems. No failures at all."

Angela didn't say anything about the computer files being blocked.

Forsythe knelt closer to the fire. "Really? Hm-m-m," he said. "'Shit happens,' they say. You ever hear that one? That's a good one. Anyway, I'm here now and I have been through a lot of shit-happenings." He sat down and crossed his legs. "But everything is all right now. I'm kind of hungry. Do you have—"

"Of course," Nathan said. "Angela, can you put something on the coals?"

"A campfire—how ingenious," Forsythe said. "There is no fuel whatsoever topside. Those tumbleweeds burn in two-point-one seconds flat." Forsythe picked up a stick and fiddled with the embers; some flew out and landed on him. He didn't even flinch. From her pocket, Angela pulled out her blue fabric and held it tight, then stepped over and stirred the broth in the pot.

"So . . . you have the same type of ship as us?" Nathan asked.

"Yes, there were supposed to be many ships. Something was happening on Earth. The world needed a future it could count on, I believe—that was their excuse for this whole mess." His eyebrows rose. "They wanted to believe in us." He stuck his tongue out and licked one side of his chin all the way to the other. "Believe in the rocket men," he said. "Rocket men . . ." He sang, "Early in the morning and the morphine's gone, 'cause I'm a rocket man! Come on, join in."

"You have the words wrong," Angela said.

He stared at her. "Anyway, I think Earth was headed for trouble. That's another reason why I think we're out here, doing this. My journey was rough, you guys, I have to tell you. It was horrible. Hey, you guys have any morphine left?"

"You asked us that already," they both answered together.

"Yeah, I did," He looked around. "Hey, nice ship. Mine's all beat to crap and sitting at the bottom of the sea somewhere."

"The sea?" Angela said. She poured the soup into a bowl and handed it to him, never letting go of her blue rag.

"Yeah, there's a sea. Landed in it. Water sucks. Don't go near there; you guys'll drown. Sha-a-a-a-arks."

Angela stopped, and with the fire at its brightest, she examined Forsythe's wrinkles further. "Why are you so much older than us?"

Forsythe chewed and slurped and looked around.

"How old are you?" she asked.

He snapped at her, "People with no wrinkles don't know crap! You haven't suffered yet. Life's hell, kids."

Nathan stepped forward. "How did you find us?"

"I saw your fire"

"Why did you come here?"

"I stopped by to see if anything was better for you guys than it was for me. You guys made a nice place for yourselves." He nodded and looked at the stone bowl. "This is a nice place."

The camp was quiet except for Doc's arm servo's adjusting and Forsythe's slurping.

"Um, I'm kind of tired," Angela said.

Nathan added, "Yeah, I've been out hunting."

Forsythe spat out his last gulp of soup. "Hunting? *Hunting,* you say?" He laughed. "What the hell can you hunt here, some wild and lascivious rocks? Herds of pebbles? Schools of wind? There is nothing here, my child. There is nothing but us miserable humans, here to wither and decay. We might leave some bones behind, but even those dry to dust.

And the metal ship will someday disintegrate like no one was ever here at all." Forsythe stood.

Angela took a half step toward the large man. "I need to ask you a question," she said.

Forsythe turned toward her and said, soft and sweetly, almost pleasantly, "Yes, what is it, my dear?"

"I need to know if you know who my father is."

Forsythe wore a serious look followed by a broad smile and a single diagonal nod/shake. Angela stood on her toes. "I know who my father is," Forsythe said. "And if you are in fact Angela—is that right . . . Angel A?—then, why, yes, I do know who your father is."

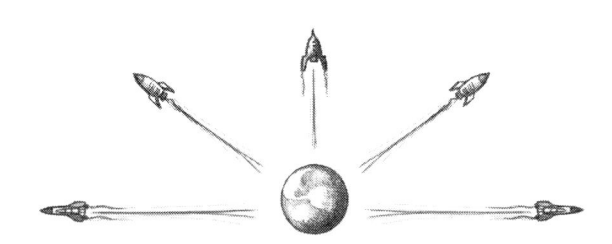

CHAPTER TWENTY-ONE

Forsythe set down the bowl and spoke to her as if telling a story. "Your father was one of the founders of the Wombs Project. He was a captain in the army or something. He was pretty young. This information should be in your ship."

"No," Nathan said. "No records found."

"Young," I said, staring at the monitor, hoping that this record Doc had captured was true, was real. "A captain?" I exhaled. This was my daughter. She had to be. Forsythe was talking about *me*. I sat back in my chair and looked through the woods. I was looking for someone to tell, someone to celebrate with, someone to hear that I was joyful. I *was* joyful, for a moment, in these woods.

"I am a father again," I said. I felt a cold, shattering euphoria. "She is so . . ." I felt the warm, dull pain of shame in my face and in my head. ". . . distant."

Angela spoke again. "How do you know all this—about my father?"

"My ship," Forsythe said, making a circle with his sore shoulder. "Yeah, the U.S. military was being sensitive about their people; there were discussions in articles in the ship's library about keeping that information out of future ships. My ship had a lot of information about the project in it. That's how I know about you, Angel A. Wanna trade ships?" he asked. He gave her a broad, stained-toothed grin.

"No," Nathan said, stepping forward.

Forsythe looked at him. "There is nothing in there about you anyway, Nathan." He nodded at him once.

Forsythe inflated his chest. "I secured that drive. I put it in the overhead planter, in a plastic bag to keep it from getting wet." He let out a hurt chuckle. "But it doesn't matter; that ship is lost now."

He tried to look deep into Angela's eyes, and she looked away. He said, "Among other things, one of the lessons in my computers indicated that my ship, the *Amadeus,* was to be the only ship that contained information about war—war in history. They were going to edit out war. Can you *believe* it?"

"War," Nathan said. "Like *Star Wars?*"

"No, like *real* war," Forsythe said. He looked darkly at Angela.

She took another step closer to him. "What is real war?" she asked.

"They did delete it," he said quietly. His eyes went cold, and he tugged on his chin. "Forget I said anything. I don't want to mess you guys' minds up. Let's just say they were trying to delete Earth's wrongdoings, so those things wouldn't happen here—or anywhere. Earth's mistakes. Things like war, money . . . print money, pass it around, print some more—how could this ever last? Things like crime, criminals, torture, rioting, general mayhem . . ."

Nathan and Angela looked at each other. "Well," Nathan said. "I think that maybe it's time that you go."

Forsythe's mouth tightened. He stood up. He towered a foot taller than Nathan.

Nathan walked over to him. "I think this is what we're supposed to do," Nathan said. He extended his hand.

Forsythe slowly and awkwardly grabbed it with his sweaty palm and overlong fingers. They shook hands. A blank look swiped across Forsythe's face, and he promptly pulled his hand away and looked at his palm. In a whisper, he said, "Wait."

"Wait what?" Nathan said, and moved a step backward.

"Wait. Try again."

"O-o-okay." Nathan looked at Angela and then stepped forward.

Forsythe reached out and shook Nathan's hand again. This big, daunting man squished his eyes tight. Tears began to fall from his cheeks.

Angela and Nathan looked at each other. "What happened?" Nathan said. "Did I hurt you?" More tears fell from Forsythe, and he began to chuckle and soon began to laugh, and Angela and Nathan laughed, too. Nathan shook his head, smiling. "Are you insane?" Nathan asked.

Forsythe laughed louder and started shaking his head. "Probably," he answered. Everyone was now laughing and crying, and then Forsythe said through the tears and the sniffling and the entire ruckus echoing throughout the cavern, "No one has ever touched me before." Everyone dried their eyes.

"Well, I gotta be going," Forsythe said. He sniffled. "Thanks for the soup, Angela," he said finally, vacantly. "Thanks for the soup." He peered at Nathan and moved back into the darkness.

Angela's Diary:

> Forsythe looks like a worn-out shoe. I hope I am not going to look like that when I get older, or smell like that. I swear, if I do, I'll kill myself. If I turn out being the girl version of him, I am ending it. I tried to see something good in his eyes, to look

past his slovenly appearance, but everything I saw was blank and cold and inappropriate for a new world. I never want to be like him. I will end it if I do.

A week or so later, on a dull gray day, Angela and Nathan trekked through the desert. The wrinkled dunes swallowed their footprints as she ran in quick spurts, eight long steps and then a rest—and by "rest," I mean curl into a ball while catching her breath. Eight steps, then rest. Nathan watched her. He didn't laugh. He loved her, and he kept a slow pace to accommodate her crude traveling procedure. It was, after all, by design that he was to have feelings for her, and at that moment he realized for the first time that the design was working. Eight steps, then rest.

It was almost a full day of walking to the sea, near the end of the day. She ran a few steps farther than he and looked out over the last dune's crest.

"There it is, Nathan."

"Ocean water." He raised the corner of his mouth. "I think we just found something we can name after you that isn't a rock or a weed." He took a deep breath through his nose. "Can you smell that?"

She inhaled. The salty air was sweet, thick, and new to her. The ocean exploded onto the shore. As far as they could see, there was water, complete with swells and breakers, and tan, swirling sand throughout it all.

"Let's call it the Sea of Angela," he said.

"You are very good at naming things, Nathan." She ran up and hugged him and pecked him on the cheek.

Nathan grinned with a mischievous glint. "That was our first kiss," he said.

She shrugged a shoulder at him and walked toward the Sea of Angela.

"That is our first kiss," he said, louder this time, and he followed her.

"No," she said. The edges of her smile, unseen by him, wrinkled playfully. "When it's our *first* kiss, you'll know it."

The sun started to set, and Angela saw something shiny out in the ocean but dismissed it as the top of a wave cresting and catching the sunlight. The water in front of them began to turn quickly. "Look. It's rushing away," she said.

"Receding . . . Oh, boy, am I glad we are not out there. It looks treacherous."

Soon the water was gone, and in its place they beheld the expanse of flat, shiny rock. She walked up to the edge and bent down to touch it.

"It's slippery," she said.

"Yeah, let's not go out there. Wait a minute . . . what is that?" Nathan squinted, then pointed to the ledge where the sea met the plateau. Splashes erupted into the sky, and bright, reflecting metal gleamed. "Wow, that is crazy!" he said. "It's the top of Forsythe's ship. It's the ark *Amadeus*!"

"When will the water come back?" Angela asked. Tempted to walk out there, she already had one foot almost touching the stone.

"I don't know," he said. "This whole planet seems unpredictable."

"Yeah, it is, for sure." She pulled her foot back.

Then they saw what had to be Forsythe, running from the south side of the beach, barreling toward the ship. Reaching it, he scurried into it like a crab into a crevice.

"Oh, my God!" She laughed a little. "You think he lives in there?"

"Looks like he gets in and out of it with the tide. What a strange dude."

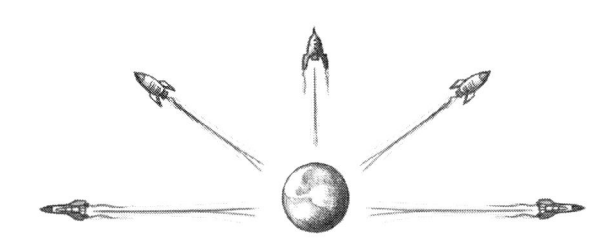

CHAPTER TWENTY-TWO

Back in the cavern, Angela sat cross-legged on the ground, admiring a sketch she had made with her fingertips and sooty gray dirt. Water droplets leaped from the ends of the vines onto the sand, and once in a while onto her.

A shadow approached.

"Ah, the architect's drawings," Nathan said.

"We could build this. We truly can," she said, touching the lines lightly, smearing one line into another.

"We cannot make this," Nathan said. "How do you suppose we make glass?"

"How does *anyone* make glass?" she said. "Progress."

"*Se-lec-tive* progress," he said. "And I select that making glass is way beyond the capabilities of two rather slow-moving computers and a fairly incompatible couple of humans."

"Incompatible?" Angela said.

He walked over to a bush growing out of the wall and snapped off a twig. "I'm just saying, we might have different views on what this place should be like. Most of what I know about society, about planet Earth, is that people were breaking their necks to make cities and huge, complex organizations, which all eventually fell apart. We don't know what condition Earth is in right now, but by all evidence, it does not look good. Forsythe himself said something was happening down there. He would know—he flew in the unedited version of our ship.

"I'm just saying, we have a chance to make it simpler. We have a chance to start out right. We can live our lives and enjoy a modest existence under the stars and not kill ourselves to build or fight or die under a rock." He walked over to a rock and smacked it with his twig. "Die under this rock just because we wanted it moved from here to over there."

"I know what you're saying, and it seems good for now," she said. "But when population demands—*and it will demand it*—we need to grow and become a civilized society. And I wouldn't mind a few creature comforts along the way . . . like ice cream."

Nathan shot back, "I am not spending my life making a window or a refrigerator." He walked to look up through the crevasse. "I do wish there were birds here. We could make a new bed, made of feathers."

"You mean to share?" she asked, blushing, bright pink on off-white.

"Hey, let's make a list of things we want." He said it warmly, more casually than ever before. He walked over to her and touched her shoulder.

"We'll need to run the idea by Doc to see if there is anything that might destroy our future or anything, like Forsythe said."

"Yeah, like not making me ice cream."

"I would make you ice cream if we had a cow."

They both looked up at the moonlight becoming blocked. Through the cracked ceiling they witnessed a massive purple planet passing by. She leaned toward him and touched his cheek. She kissed him on the lips. His lips melted into hers, and they shared a solid, wanting moment . . . testing . . . tasting. Doc's camera whirred up close, and from it came a blue vertical-line laser, which quickly scanned across the two of them, together.

"Doc, stop it," she said during a half kiss. The arm pulled back about a foot. Both hard drives etched, recording the event.

Nathan reached to hold her head tenderly, embracing her warmth. Her hair fell beneath his careful fingers, in a simpler essence that they had never-ever known till now. Gracefully, they flowed from the bench to inside the ship.

They lay down on the lower bunk, and she kissed his closed eyes and he caressed her shoulder beneath her shirt. His lips explored her neck. She paused. Softly she asked him, "Can we wait?"

He stopped kissing her and looked into her eyes, blazing.

"I want to wait," she said.

"For what?" he asked, then covered her lips with his fingertips as she tried to answer.

"Don't worry," he said, turning a little red. "Doc still has not backed off the LR yet."

"Oh, I see." Angela looked down and playfully covered her mouth and whispered to her blue fabric, which lay nearby, "Libido reducer." She giggled.

She turned and stared a little longer into Nathan's eyes. "You have some of Forsythe's wrinkles, you know," she said.

"Then just kill me," he said.

"Then we agree." She giggled again. "No wrinkles."

Nathan looked down the creek. There seemed to be enough room to walk beside it even as it widened, and a glow of natural light beckoned down beyond the bend.

Angela tenderly, softly cupped his chin, turning him to her. "Please don't go down there without me," she said. "I want to discover things with you."

He nodded, her hand slowly letting him go, with only a fingertip now touching his chin. She said, "Incompatible?" She blinked and looked away, then back into his eyes. "Maybe you can talk to Doc about something . . . you know." She breathed in the air of the moment. "Backing off the LR."

Watching the monitor, I felt a little ashamed to see this intimacy—a father would rather not get this close a perspective on such a thing. But its innocence was heartwarming, and soon I only felt honored to watch these kids growing toward each other. My fire had gone out, and I was too tired to light it again. It had been days since I really slept. A *daughter*, I thought. *One who is in love. Jesus.* I smiled inside over it, but only a little, because I knew that all this was going to be lost forever—all of what I had learned, all of what had happened. These kids might not even still be alive.

I had Chen Li Wu to deal with, and who knew what the outcome would be? He had always been one step ahead of me, and this last letter, still unopened, the one I found in the chopper—this was proof he had not let this thing go, this threat on my life. If I were to die in two days, the world would forget about these ships and about me, and no one would ever know what happened. The history of Echo, of Angela. No one would ever care. I closed my heavy eyes, just for a moment.

Yimosu wore a black robe now. The rain was loud in the courtyard, in the room built from logs and held together by wooden spikes and ancient clay. The monks stood before a single worn candle. "She is confident," Yimosu said. The flame flickered. "I think she will like the experiment."

"Most people enjoy science, I think," the tall, thin monk, Gossum, said.

"Yes, it is unusual to find a person who does not," the short, stout Monk, Plato, agreed.

"She will find her way." Yimosu turned, examined their eyes, and turned back to the candle.

Gossum said, "She seems quite curious about her place in the universe."

"I think we all are," said Yimosu. They all nodded.

The candle's random dance of amber flame reflected in Yimosu's eye and brought out the brilliance of his silvery entity.

"When will we know?" Plato asked innocently.

"It is always the young monk who asks when. When is nothing, my brother. When does not exist, nor does how or why. It will be a dramatic event, though—an occurrence—that changes her."

"Will she fall from a cliff or become injured or ill?" Plato asked.

"No, it will need to be something worse," Yimosu said. "An event much worse." He walked over to the window and looked out. His eye facet reflected off the window and brilliantly beamed onto Gossum and Plato. Yimosu said, "She will need to understand. She will need to thoroughly understand that she is completely, helplessly alone."

Gossum blew out the candle. Plato looked sad in the sparse light allowed through the cracks of the walls.

I came out of this dream and shook my head. Things like this were now so vivid to me. It must be the pain, the vitamins. The visions were more frequent, though. I reached for another diary and saw that I had them, Angela's books, out of order. I lifted one with a dark black binding. A charcoal substance smeared all over it rubbed off onto my hands. This book was more ornate, with a scalloped border and a drawing of some form in the center, which had been scribbled out with angry circles of the sort a child might make when throwing a tantrum. The engraving on the back cover felt rough and angry in its depth. The impact of the die it was struck from had definitely been affected by emotion. Black birds—crows, I believe. Angela had drawn crows.

I ran my fingers over the center emblem, trying to make out what was beneath the scribble. Then, when my fingertips dug into the cover, I realized what the impression was. It was a figure, a person with X's over the eyes. Stitched X's. I whispered, "A corpse."

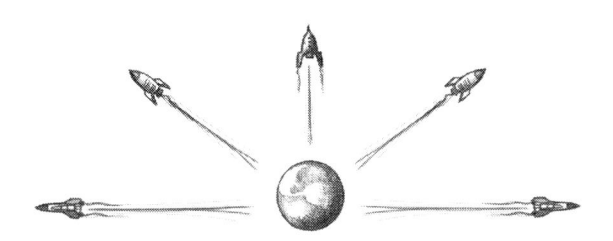

CHAPTER TWENTY-THREE

The cavern's pale-gray mist was like a wet rag wringing out drops of moonlight onto Angela and the creek. She sat up quickly from a dead sleep. "The *Amadeus*," she said. She looked at Nathan, then quietly wrote a note and set it on her pillow. After grabbing her pack, she climbed the rope ladder and set off toward the ocean: eight steps, then rest. At rest, she sank a few inches in the sand. Her hair tickled her neck, and sand sifted into her shoes. Sweat dried on her skin. She smiled at all this.

When she reached the water, it was already receding, and she visually scanned the beach and the ocean. Once the plateau had only a few inches of water remaining, she stepped out, slipped, caught herself. But she learned the trick of it, sliding and walking as the floor dried, and soon she was moving spryly toward the ship.

Cautiously, she peered over the rock's edge, then searched the beach and all across the plateau behind her. "I don't know where you are, but stay away from me," she said. She looked up at the pinnacle of the ship.

The much-battered *Amadeus* was wedged in, pointing out to sea, like a leftover dud bottle rocket.

Angela timed the waves. Waiting for the lull between sets, she climbed down and entered the ship and swung the door shut. Removing her pack, she steadied herself with one hand against the wall. The writing just below her hand struck her.

"'Why would the world believe this could be done?'" she read aloud, stepping back from the grafitto. "'What madman concocted such a charade?'"

She looked around again. Raising her eyebrows, she said, "A little nuts . . . or maybe a lot?"

The chess pieces were so worn, they were almost indistinguishable except by height and vague differences in shape. They were configured in order of royal and feudal hierarchy instead of by their true opening positions for traditional chess play.

After quickly rearranging them, she went toward the nursery.

"Doc . . . ? Are you there?" she asked. Shepard's computer was not in its normal location. It had been moved to the nursery. Wires had been spliced, some of the clips had come loose, and the main power cable was disconnected.

She opened the nursery hatch and squeezed herself in, bumping into rods and loose jars. A blanket was bundled in the corner, and some insulation was loose in the ceiling above her. Just behind the smallest centrifuge was a row of copper coils and a dangling cable. She connected the cable, and a spark popped and she smelled burning wires.

She pulled her hair back from her ear. Water slapped against the hull. A pale blue light flickered on a screen in the corner. To reach the monitor, she had to climb over more mechanical works. She pushed the button on the monitor, and the screen powered up. After looking around a bit, she climbed out of the nursery but left the hatch cracked open just a bit. Looking back in through the window, she could see on the screen blank white snow, which soon gave way to a video of

Forsythe. He was lying on the ground, cursing at the faulty arm in the nursery. She stepped back and touched the manual controls on the wall, fast-forwarding the video. Now it showed him scratching his angry words into the wall. Then he was urinating in the corner. Then he was scolding his dog and kicking her. Then he was making small cuts in his own forearm, in almost perfect rows.

"Oh, my God!" she breathed. "You *loon*!" Her eyes darted in confusion.

The window she was leaning on fogged a little. But she had turned away, looking for the thing she came for, so she didn't see this. There up above, in the planter, she spied the edge of a plastic bag, so she got up on the chair and pulled it down. It was the hard drive, right where Forsythe had said it would be. She wiped the dirt off and tucked it into her knapsack, found a root-meal cookie in there, and took a nibble. Leaning closer to the glass to watch the video, she tried to wipe the fog away with her sleeve, but the moisture was inside. She moved closer to the glass.

From behind the window frame, an eye appeared, mere inches from her face. The eye studied in microscopic movements the detail of her hair, the curves of her eyebrows, the suppleness of her cheek, her tongue tasting the sugar of her cookie.

The eye was close—so close to her own eye that if she were to blink and there were no glass, their eyelashes might have touched. The wrinkled skin around the watching eye grew fierce. Forsythe. He had been hiding in the floor of the nursery, crammed between the joists like a folded-up wooden doll. Her attention was on the monitor, and it displayed a horrifying image.

The footage was bringing to life Forsythe's ordeal beneath the sea. On the screen, he was punching himself in the face, smearing his clothes with his own blood, and then sucking the blood out of the threads. She shivered and brought her hands to her mouth.

Forsythe's eye studied her facial muscles; watched her fingers, her lips, her nostrils flaring in reaction to the video of him suffering—this recording of his disintegration. The video began to show him peeling back his own fingernails. Seeing this image, he started to whimper, and a tear ran down his time-carved face, through his gritted teeth and into his contorted mouth. He slid down the nursery wall and cowered in a ball, pulling out single hairs from his head. The video skipped and flickered and played again. "What the fuck am I supposed to do now?" rang through the cabin.

Forsythe—the real one, not the one on the monitor—then raised himself up, his face red and tightening. He stood in the window, his breath hitting the glass. Now she saw the breath, saw the saliva smears on the window. Then, out of the corner of her eye, she saw him and screamed.

He gripped the framework of the hatch to climb out, and the hairs he had pulled from his head drifted down. She stepped back and froze as he unfolded his gangly frame from the port. Standing at an awkward angle to the tilted floor, he looked at the chessboard.

"I don't play with them like that," he said. "I play with them another way."

She looked at the door.

"Those pieces were set up according to how this world should be," he said, walking over to the board. "The horses are below the pawns. I think I had that right, didn't I? In what world is a horse more important than a man?"

"That depends on the allegiance of the man, I think," Angela answered. "If he goes against his own kind, the horse is then better than him . . . so the horse."

"Maybe," Forsythe said. "Maybe." He raised his eyebrows and looked at the floor as a blind man would. "But in the end, the king is the oldest and wisest in the game." He looked at her with blind-man eyes. "All the rest of the pieces don't matter at all." And he swept the pieces to the ground with his arm.

"Let me show you how I play," he said, and lurched toward her.

She held up her hands. "Look."

He paused, hovering above her, breathing on her.

"I am here only for a few components—since your ship is dead, we can use some things to keep ours working."

"My ship is not dead, lass." He made an artificial smile. "She just needs a little less water on the brain." He walked toward the door. Angela's back was against the wall, and she looked up at him as if they were about to perform a slow, dark tango. "I had to pry the door open to get back in," Forsythe told her. He kicked the door open with his foot. "She was submerged way down there." He pointed out to sea. "It takes about two hours to fill up with the door closed."

She blanched. She looked across the sea and at the big, daunting waves. "I guess it is your ship," she said. "I don't really need anything from it."

He looked down at her and suddenly, awkwardly pushed down on her shoulders. Her knees buckled, and she fell sideways and slammed her head on the corner of the command counter.

She touched the blood with her hand and then, looking for something to hit him with, grabbed one of doc's arms—the closer one. It was his medical arm with the syringe. She found the release and engaged a new needle.

"What are you going to do with that—inoculate me?" Forsythe asked. "I've been stuck with that thing more times . . ."

She ran at him with the needle and hooked him in the wrist, where the needle caught bone. She levered it upward, tearing at veins and tendons and making him warble out a high-pitched scream. Releasing the needle, she stepped back and engaged a new one.

He looked at his bloody wrist and then at her with confusion, as if he were just bitten by a tiny poisonous butterfly. Faking a lunge to his torso, she instead attacked him at the knee, stabbing the needle in and forcing it sideways. It ripped and popped and broke off in him.

He laughed through a perturbed cough that ended in a low growl. "You little bitch," he said.

Chambering another needle, she ran toward him again. But this time, his long leg whipped out in a front kick to her jaw. The force of the blow lashed her head back, and she hit the floor like a bag of sand.

He wiped the blood from his arms and stared at her, lying there unconscious. Closing and latching the nursery door, he twisted the EAs through the handle, then grabbed some bandages from the first-aid kit and threw them at her.

"Here . . . have a nice day," he said, and exited from the ship and slammed the door shut. With waves bashing him in the back, he clung tightly to the rock wall and wrestled a large loose stone in front of the ship's door. Climbing up to the flat plain, he yelled over the waves, "You can have that old piece-of-crap ship, 'cause I am *freakin' taking yours*."

He ran away, moving like a badly designed robot, his muscles obviously working in poor cooperation with his mind.

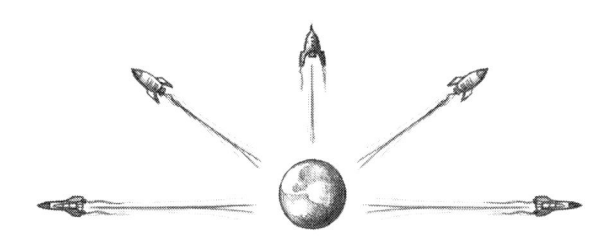

CHAPTER TWENTY-FOUR

Water was entering the ship at the gap where Forsythe had once pried it open, and Angela lay unconscious on the floor. Her arms were beginning to float. Pulses of water woke her, and she coughed and choked on them. Groggily she sat up to look at the bent door, and her stomach tightened as she looked back at what had happened . . . at him touching her. She moved her jaw around and winced, touched her forehead and checked her fingers for blood. There was some watery red. She looked at her thin arms, then managed to stand for a moment to try to open the door, but the rushing water pushed her away to floor. Pale and shivering, she saw that the nursery door was hopelessly obstructed with the twisted metal arms intertwined through the handle. She pulled herself up into the chair and watched a bandage float by and twirl in the deepening water.

"Maybe it's over," she said, looking up at the thin ceiling, the marked walls. "Maybe the world can turn without me. It always has, this place."

She picked up the silver bishop and began to sharpen it on the bottom of the chair.

"Angela," she etched into the wall. Then she wrote, "Why are we interfering where we don't belong."

She scratched in a period. "That silly mud house was destroying the landscape anyway," she said. "Nathan's better off without me." The water was nearing her knees now. "One less mouth to feed."

She looked at the ceiling and the plants. "Forsythe . . . Maybe we are alike. The difference is," she said with a look of realization, "even you know who your father is."

She waded over to push on the door, and the boulder blocking it moved only slightly. Looking in the nursery, she noticed that Shepard's computer was disconnected, so she reached into the battery cabinet, pushed down on the cable, and tightened the wing nut. A hard drive engaged. A monitor turned on and fizzled out. It smoked. Around her, other things were booting up. She put her palm to her forehead to keep the throbbing at bay. Drops of blood came from her nose and rolled down her chin, falling into the cold, sandy water.

"Doc?" she said. "It's Angela."

"Oh," she heard. There was a great pause. "What are you doing in this ship?" Doc said.

"Forsythe beat the crap out of me."

"Shepard and I knew he was unstable," Doc said. How did you get on this planet?"

"I was a Wombs baby. Two ships landed here."

"That's not supposed to happen."

"I know. A lot of things aren't supposed to happen, but they do." She wiped away more blood. She shivered. "I need your help."

"What is it?"

"I need you to boot this drive. I don't have much time. There's a rock blocking the door, and if I do anything before I die, it's find out who my father is—what his name is, at least. I know it's too much to ask to hear his voice. I was hoping you would have something in your archives." She started removing the cover from Doc's computer. "I need to exchange your drive with Shepard's." She waited for a moment, knowing that Doc would be ruined, essentially gone forever. Then she shut him down and worked.

She loosened Doc's drive and set it on the console. From the plastic wrapping, she removed Shepard's drive, held it by the wires, and plugged it in. The corner of it dipped in the water for a moment. As she worked, she made soft sounds, like a dove. She shoved the drive into the slot, and as the ground wire engaged, her unusual smile shone. Pushing the power button, she stared at the water line and realized that it was rising faster than the computer was booting. She stretched her body over the box to protect it as, throughout the ship, one thing powered down at a time, shorting in fizzles and hisses. The water had won. She lay perfectly still across the metal. "This is as close as I will ever be to him," she said, opening her eyes and imagining a face. Any face of any father would do, she thought, but she saw my face. She had written it here, in this diary, how she saw my face:

Nice eyes, blue, alive; trusting bold smile surrounded by a virtually invincible jaw and a caring innocence and strength only present in a loving father. I was sad to see two scars above his left eyebrow . . . a scar from war, I think, from a fight.

I felt her thoughts at that moment. I recall, years ago, the moment she was able to imagine me—my likeness, even the detail of the scars above my left eye. I remember this moment, this feeling. I knew when it happened, over thirty years ago. I felt her see me. I was asleep, and I felt the cold water. I felt her lack of air. I felt as if I were the one drowning.

"I can see you," a voice said. She was alone in this struggle, and distance had worn her down. She was trying to have strength beyond this world where she was trapped, where she desired only one thing, and that thing was to know of me. She was trying to let go of the rope in her mind—that rope the children were holding in the street. But the teacher was screaming her name to stop and warning her not to let go, not to go any farther.

Her eyes became heavy as water entered her lungs. I couldn't see her anymore.

"No!" I remember screaming out that night. She was lying on the floor.

"No!" I said. She opened her eyes underwater. She saw the weak ceiling where the water was now reaching. With newfound conviction, she took a firm hold of the ledge under the command counter and curled into a ball, gained spinning momentum, and kicked the ceiling in with such force, she practically flew into the crawl space.

She spat and coughed out water. "You're not going to win, Forsythe," she gasped. "You don't even know how to play the game." In the ceiling, she looked down at the rising threat and surveyed the space filled with plants and tubes. She touched the foliage. "You are not to blame," she said to them.

With her wet eyes, she followed the leafy stems and felt their skin and their furry roots and admired the knotty intersections beneath the soil. Something poked her hand. It was a metal rod from inside the workings of the ship, the governing bar Forsythe had removed and, under the g-forces, placed there in the planter. A rod to pry with. Taking hold of it with both hands, she dived into the water and stuck it into the doorjamb. Then she pushed with every ounce of her rage. The boulder outside started to rock, so she pushed again and felt its grating motion. Then it fell away into the waves. The door cracked open.

With the rush of escaping water, she floated out and bobbed on the surface, but she was instantly dragged under again by the current of the open sea. She fought the raging water until her head popped up again. Even farther from shore this time, she eyed the vast ocean. She focused on the ledge. *This is not Forsythe's evil ledge,* she thought. *It is part of the sea of Angela, and it is mine. I am going to conquer it.*

The rolling waves grew larger and manhandled and tormented her exhausted body, sweeping her away, lifting her up in the next scend, the crest folding over her and dropping her deeper in, pulling her yet farther out. Then, mischievously, the current reversed itself and pushed her toward the platform, slamming her against the rocky side, where hundreds of other things had collected, and those sharp things punished her frail body like steel rods gouging her ribs, and sharp blades into her skin.

She grasped at the slippery rocks until another swell took her back out. A swirling trough sucked her under, and she grasped at the water's surface, but it gave way, as it is water's nature to give way, as if water itself were helpless to do otherwise. Water did not seem to laugh, though, because it, like her, was also the victim of diluted strength. Another wave came, and this one felt more rigidly made; the shoulder of it had built up extraordinary might. It brought her forward to where the very tips of her fingers found one thin seaweed stem, a stem with the minute details of a painter's finest-point brush, which was anchored to the rock face where she saw her own helpless expression reflected. Another strand entered her blurred vision, and reaching for it, she let go of the first and grabbed this thicker one with both hands. The swirling sea must have decided then that enough was enough. And it reversed all its treachery, all its bad deeds were nullified, as this good sea, Angela's sea, gave her a modest but gracious swell, lifting her upright to land on her feet on the plateau.

Disbelieving, se staggered and looked back at the waves and sighed, then ran toward the shore in the rapidly rising water. When she reached the beach, she collapsed facedown in the warm sand, coughing out remnants of the Sea of Angela. But then she saw indentations in the sand dashing up the dune. She rose on all fours. *Footprints.* Forsythe was headed toward home.

"Nathan," she said.

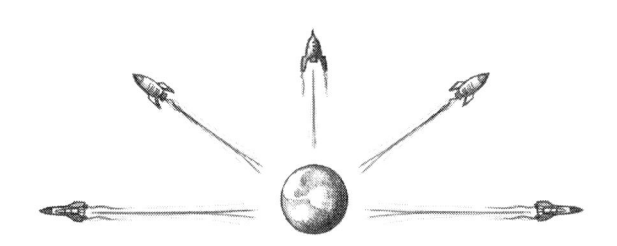

CHAPTER TWENTY-FIVE

Dusk was pulling Nathan's shadow quickly across the floor as a small, bright planet speeded across the sky. From his pocket, he pulled out Angela's note and read it again. He looked skyward through the crevice.

"Be back soon," he said, hoisting up another of the ship's solar panel segments by a pulley system he devised today. But the cumbersome load caught near the top.

"Bloody hell," he said, tying the rope off. He began climbing to free it. He noticed that many of the ladder's rungs were worn thin, and he needed to keep to the outsides of them if he wanted the ladder to hold through the many trips of this project. He was about twenty feet from the top, a good forty feet from the ground, when something passed beneath the light above him. The rope ladder shook. Something shiny was moving back, just below the intersection where the ladder grew from the ceiling. Nathan put his hand to his forehead to block the sun, trying to focus on whatever it was.

"Angela," he said.

He heard the deep rasp of a throat clearing.

"Who's there?" Nathan asked.

A drop of blood landed on his hand.

"Jesus Christ," he murmured. He fumbled for some words, any words. "Uh, you look hurt. If you're hurt, I can help you."

Something moved through the light again. The rope was moving faster, jerking side to side. "I think we found some morphine . . . but I will need to go down to the ship and get bandages."

The shiny object was sawing. It was cutting the vine, which started to give way. Nathan slipped and missed a rung. He grasped at another nearby vine. At first it swung away from him, but then it came back and landed firmly in his palm. He had prepared many of the vines by stripping away the loose meat, just in case an event should come along requiring an emergency hold.

He wrapped his legs around the new vine. The old ladder fell. "Doc, I need help," he said.

The remaining light from above was quickly swallowed. A large rock struck him, ripping him from the rope. The ground shook, and Doc's camera arm pulled back. Nathan's eyes were open and lifeless.

Forsythe walked backward, away from the crevice, and sat down on the rubble of the collapsed mud house. Leaning back, he took in a deep breath and wriggled into the crumbled dirt to get more comfortable. He looked at the sky.

"Ah-h-h." He smacked his lips. "Alone at last," he said, enjoying the stars coming out. Mendi was scavenging in the dunes. She was very thin. "What am I to do with all of this time?" he mused. "Build a huge society?" He laughed.

A meteor whistled down and made a sound like "poof" in the sand. He stared at its impact crater. Another meteor landed in the distance.

"That's crazy," he said. Nearby, a third made a fist-size hole in the ground, zipping right through the surface. He stood and started to run, zigzagging and covering his head. He made it to the rock hill and found a crevice to squeeze into. Many more rocks fell from the sky, and Forsythe yelled, "Screw you, Nathan!"

Angela walked the desert, hungry, thirsty, and worried. Meteorites fell in her sky, too. One hit heavily beside her. She ran eight steps and rested, and her face turned in frustration with each repetition of the pattern: eight steps, then rest. Several moons changed the light of the sun on the dunes, casting faint images of Forsythe's wrinkled face onto them. A smaller meteorite puffed into the sand close behind her. On the last stretch of flat ground, the broken mud house came into view in the starlight. As she approached the crevice, she found the flashlight in her pack and aimed it around the entrance. She saw many large footprints, pacing, scurrying. The wind, meanwhile, was trying to cover them up, fill them with sand.

"What happened here?" she asked. She looked behind her and thought she saw a black ghost heading up the rocky hill. Kneeling down beside the dark, cavernous sliver, she shined her light down into it.

She made the flashlight follow the vines down to the cavern floor and search the familiar ground beside the ship. The circle of light caught the limb of a person in an unrealistic pose. Her eyelids dropped, and she turned the flashlight off.

"Nathan," she said in the dark. The only sound was her breathing, the only moving thing the fog rising from the cavern and moving away from her.

Jerking back into motion, she climbed down, sliding desperately down a vine. She watched for his head to lift or for his hand, his foot, a finger—anything—to move. Reaching him, she fell to her knees and delicately lifted his head. "Nathan . . . Nathaniel." She could not see his injuries: his crushed skull, his broken limbs. She saw only a boy.

"Doc . . . do something!" Her voice shuddered. Nathan was drained of color.

Her fingers moved in rigid, robotic spasms. She rose to her feet.

"How could you do this??" she moaned, staggering about the cavern floor and wringing her hands. "How could you leave me . . . here, alone?" Her words perished in the air. She fell on the ground, her legs contorting in a strange and painful way. She washed her face in the pebbles and tried to collect her tears. She was trying to force the tears back into her eyes with her muddy palms.

"All right, Doc . . . Doc! We need everything to go back to the way it was," she said, looking sternly at the ship.

She stepped over and tugged on Nathan's limp arm and dragged him within Doc's reach. "Tell me you can save him." She stared into the camera; the monitor flickered. "Tell me this is only a bad dream," she said.

Doc's arms touched Nathan, pushing on his limbs. Angela sat back, pulled her blue rag from her pocket, and passed out. She dreamed of the day she first laid eyes on him. Doc had opened the nursery door, and there he was, waiting for her in this great big white room. Although the EAs held them apart, she felt the warmth of Nathan. From the distance of a few inches, she knew he was warm. His face was so bright, his eyes so alive. She awoke.

"Where did the light go?" Angela said. "Where?" She pleaded for an answer from the computers, the mechanical arms. "In his eyes—where did it go?" She pressed her hands into the pebbles, turning them up. "Where did our friendship . . . our love . . . where did everything go, Doc? Everything must be somewhere." She threw rocks into the creek. "The light and love must be someplace. I cannot believe all those things are wasted. I cannot believe that something as lifeless as a rock can outlast something as beautiful as this man." She stood and ran her fingers down Nathan's cheek and looked up at Doc. "He needs to get better, Doc. I cannot do this without him. You need to make him better."

Doc's arm's slowed. "You are so delicate," Doc said. "Humans are altogether too delicate."

She looked away.

"Death is certain," Doc said. "It is in every human's future, this certain death. Because you have death, you have something greater. You can live on through one another. He lives in you right now because you remember him. A rock cannot remember. You are connected in this way. Humans have so many lives connected together in this way."

Adrenaline rushed through her. She recalled the visions of me, the ones she saw when she was trapped and drowning in the *Amadeus*. She glanced over and saw the large rock that had hit Nathan.

"A meteor," she said.

"No," Shepard replied.

"This happened before the storm," Doc said.

She began swaying in a slow rhythm. She imagined a sad sound coming from the walls. "Being one of two is warming and enjoyable," she said. "There is so much hope and life. Being one of one is cold and useless. Time stares at you as it passes by, and sticks its tongue out at you as it shuts the door."

"Some people believe in reincarnation," Doc said. "Some people believe that his light, his love, go to someone else . . . someone new."

"Another person? There *is* no one else," she said.

Doc was silent for a moment and then said, "Not yet."

Angela glared at his camera and said, "Don't mess with me, Doc."

She buried Nathan and said sad words over his grave. The numbness reached the point where she wouldn't speak, couldn't hear the ordinarily pleasant plant sounds or the screeches of the rabbits fighting, and she did not stop them. She did not eat. When she looked in the mirror, she noticed that one of her eyes was gently and lazily floating away. Late that night, she sat on the bed and wrote in her diary.

> *Anguish is reading me. It is taking hold of the very most innocent part of me, the most vulnerable area. Anguish is speckling me with a burning powder and salting the exposed wounds. Anguish is folding up hope, pressing it paper thin, and noting on it, "This is ruined. Dispose of it and never open it again."*
>
> *My mourning mind runs in a ruminating circle, forming a treacherous riddle that climbs to great heights of peril and pushes me over the rim of a grass-edged hole. The landing is painful, and the concussion awakens my mind, and I realize that I am standing right where I started: at the top, ready to fall over and over again as I think about him. My loss is still real.*

As Angela was desperately reaching for something on Echo Kingdom or far from that planet, on Earth, the monks of Psi Monastery were chanting her words—the same words she was writing, at precisely the same time she was writing them. "My loss is still real," they said. "Here we are again, looking at ourselves with one eye floating away, pretending that we aren't even here."

Angela dreamed of a black feather and a small porcelain doll, most of whose eyelashes were worn or torn away. A long brown leather coat rests on the back of a man in the distance. A doll holds a book with many pages but no words. These are tests, wordless oral exams, and each one is more daunting and harder to pass than the last. *How does one conquer this?* she asked in her dream. A gun appeared to her. A black gun, an earth weapon of pain, of war—*real* war.

She shivered and came to the cold conclusion, the devastating truth, that she was alone. With this, she saw a new vision.

"What is that?" she asked the stars. "I see dim light. Someone is there." The movement of light caught her eye: the outline of a person. The vision was imperfect and sustained for only a moment. "I know who this is," she said as a broken and faded view of another world circulated in front of her.

"Who is it, Angela?" Doc asked.

She exhaled in horror. "It is Nathan's father."

London

England was cold and wet. The wigged man had taken ill and excused himself from Parliament today. He walked down the cobblestone road, talking in a forced whisper.

"My child . . . my son."

Cars drove past him; street lights illuminated him; the rain hit him. His scarf caught the front door's hinge, and he staggered to pulled it free. Removing his white wig to reveal his graying red hair, he climbed heavily up the stairs, put his hands on the wall, on the large mirror and the antique painting and frame. Entering the master bedroom, he did not remove his coat, and Angela of Echo saw this graying man wearing his coat and scarf inside. This event, Nathan's death, had the high ground on him, and this man's hand trembled when lifting his pen.

"Quickly," he said.

> *Evidence is difficult to gather when there is none, for it is within the mind. These feelings are foremost to me. Something has captured my thoughts, and today something is using them against me. Light seems at odds with, and is never able to make amends or pardon the darkness for, its unseen crimes.*
>
> *I am wielding an imaginary yet very sharp sword. It is often the madman who pretends to feel something extraordinary, yet I am not mad. I have knowledge of the extraordinary, but to discuss it here would not do it justice, for the words to*

explain it do not exist. Nor do I possess the energy to explain it, because all is now lost to me.

The only thing I still hold is a secret. I will tell my secret now. I have seen my son. I have lived with my son within me, and we both possessed a loneliness unspoken. He exuded a power and energy that thrived in both of us and traveled this far, and I was fed in this complicated and unfeeling world by these meager morsels of hope. But all this hope is gone; it has left me today. Light dilutes nothing, and Nathan's pain arrived to me as thick as if it were my own. Hope is fluid. Hope can run off.

Inside me was a splinter of light. This was the internal taste of fatherhood. I have become accustomed to the warmth of knowing of him. But today, where I once felt power, I feel death. Death on the other end. Everything has shut down and gone to black. I sense that he is trying to reach me even in death, but neither of us has the tools or facility. It is as if I had been dropped into an abandoned well. I hear horrendous and unearthly sounds down here, and sinking beside me is a book which can never be read from again, because its language is yet unknown.

It is impossible to argue with death, for it is deaf. Death is also unwilling even to pretend to offer words of sympathy through the loose ground on which it dwells. My son Nathan is dead, and I do not have the means to find him. It is because of this that I take my own life. Again death begets another death.

His wife, her worried eyes, found her husband lying in a pool of blood beside the bed. This letter was next to him, and a black handgun rested in his palm. An investigator read the last few lines aloud: "Death begets another death."

The policeman asked, "Where is your son?" and looked at her. Through her thick glasses, her frantic red eyes displayed only truth.

She said, "We don't have a son."

On the day of Nathan's father's death, some nineteen years ago, I received a letter at our new Georgetown residence. I walked up the stairs to my den and pulled a letter opener from my desk to open the second letter from Chen Li Wu.

> *Mr. Jason Argenon,*
> *I wanted to contact you again to see how you are faring. My life here in China is one of simplicity: no objects to call my own, basic living with a few necessities.*

Why the hell was an assassin telling me all about his lifestyle? Why did he think I gave a crap what the hell he did? But I pulled a bottle of scotch from my desk drawer and, pouring some into a dusty glass, read on.

> *I wanted you to know that the delegates and Yimosu signed the orders for your assassination, to take place in 2091. You will see that China is not behind you in science.*
> *I am also writing to warn you. Some within the government are trying to stop you. They are trying to keep you from launching any more ships. I am at odds with my superiors; hence this letter. Don't let them persuade you to stop. No matter what they do, you must continue to launch more ships . . .*

I stopped reading and set the letter down.

More ships. How did he know? I took another sip of whisky and looked at my reflection in the glass. "Nothing is a secret," I said aloud. Why did he suppose I would listen to him?

I stood, opened the window, and looked down onto the brick street. A woman walked her dog past the antique store, and college girls swished their feet through fallen leaves, laughing.

So I have been warned—again. He was still after me. I turned and eyed my pistol case, then went back to the letter.

Life here is chaotic, and those who cannot let go of material things are suffering the most. I admire you and your vision and hold your life as one of distinction and honor. We all will honor you for this thing.

Be safe in your physical life.

Chen Li Wu.

On planet Echo, Angela rubbed dark coal rock beneath her angry eyes. With gritted teeth, she stained her lips gray. Beside her, a rabbit scurried, and instead of reaching down to stroke his downy fur, to enjoy his company, she cut him open with her knife. Picking up his limp body, she skinned him, carved the meat, and ate it raw. Then she wrapped pieces of gray and white fur, still smeared with with rabbit blood, around the ties in her hair and wove metal threads through her cheek and straight through the cartilage of her right ear. The metal had to hurt, and her eyes grew dark. She looked like a prisoner. She was embracing the darkness of death. The creek water reflected her features: She had gone goth.

Angela watched the ripples interrupt her likeness. She swam in silence. Next to her, on a stone, was her drawing of her city. She lifted it and touched the paper, smearing its lines, its intersections, and set it on the water and watched it float away. It bobbled in the current and soon quietly sank. Angela swam in silence and then broke it with a fierce voice.

"What to do about Forsythe?" she said, licking her lips. "I need to find you."

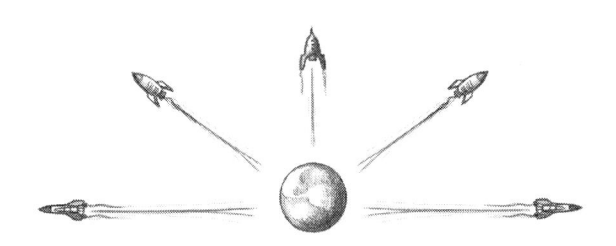

CHAPTER TWENTY–SIX

She assumed that Forsythe must be watching the exit above, so she followed the creek south to discover a way to the surface without climbing the vines. She headed downstream, and soon the light was brighter. She found some metal stones that lay in a large hollow, apparently brought here by water. She heard a waterfall, and soon the cavern opened into a wide sky. Below was a vast valley. This valley was filled with black trees, black bushes, and black soil. Some young green trees outlined the darkness in the far distance, but below her the black trees were prolific.

"So this is where the trees are," she said. She stepped to the edge, surveyed the climb, and worked her way down by scaling the roots. Reaching the bottom, she walked toward the forest, and an asphalt stench permeated the air. Between the pools of bitumen, she walked in the mud. A thin white electric charge passed between two branches of the black trees, making the hair rise on her arms. Passing another one, the metal chain in her cheek stung her skin.

"Bring it," she said.

She moved slowly through the forest. Stopping to scrape the thick mud from the soles of her boots, she grabbed a branch for balance, and at her touch, the entire tree disintegrated into ash. She slipped, and her body hit the ground at precisely the same moment that a bolt of electricity arced out from a branch to strike her in the arm. Four more bolts in succession shot across the woods and snapped at her body. Her ears clogged, and white and red bees swarmed and darted in her vision as she tried to get up. Three larger, louder, harder bolts punished her. When one struck her temple directly, her eyes closed and her breathing all but stopped.

Meanwhile, on Earth at precisely the same time, distorted thunder jolted my attention away from the computer screen. The television was blaring in the background, and I heard the words "Wombs Project." It had been twenty-four years since launch. I was forty-six; Mags and I had a bright baby boy, Conner, only five years ago. But we had a son and we were good parents, helping at school, going on family bike rides along the towpaths of the Potomac. I looked in the corner at the little TV. On the news was writer Drund Cashmen, arguing his point against D.C.'s nightly news anchor, Nancy Saranda, on the split screen.

"Billions of dollars have been thrown out into space, and for what—hope?" Drund was saying.

"Yes, for hope, Drund. And we still have it," Nancy replied. "We still have hope that the Wombs ships made it somewhere, that human life will continue no matter what happens down here. We all desperately need some hope right now."

I raised my glass to her. "Hear, hear!" I said to the television.

Drund replied, "I am sorry, but those Wombs ships will never make it anywhere. The science was a farce. Sending kids into space—my God! You can't even leave your child in a minivan in the Walmart parking lot! Also—this is serious, now, Nancy—the Chinese are accusing us of retrofitting some of the ships for nuclear warheads."

"So you're saying the Wombs missions were a ruse, a disguise for us to launch weapons into space?"

Outside the window, the lightning flashed closer.

"That's what I am saying, and now we have information that this Jason Argenon is at it again. He is dangerous to our country, and he's a gambler with a multibillion-dollar habit."

"You heard it here, folks," Nancy said, "Drund Cashmen of the *New York Chronicle* says it was all a fake and we're in the sights of some pretty powerful nations. We'll be right back."

"Screw you, Drund," I said drunkenly. I turned off the television and printed my notes on manufacturing a lighter-weight oxygen unit, but I was too angry from the newscast to go over them. I missed Duncan Right now his tail would be wagging against my leg, his eyes looking up at me as if I were a kindly disposed god. The B58 works only on people, though—no life-extending serum yet for dogs. Maggie would be home soon. I poured more scotch.

I felt odd, as if something tapped me on the shoulder—as if the room, the bookcases, the chair were waiting for me to do something. I stood up to shut the window, when a breeze brought me the scent of wet and freshly cut hedges. Distorted headlights appeared through the wet glass. A lightning strike lit the road, and I saw my white truck. Maggie had used it to take Conner to the grocery store. I smiled at the thought of her arrival and our all sharing the rocky road ice cream I asked her to get. Through the rain, I could see the wheels of our truck slow almost to a stop when the headlights of another vehicle came from behind her. "Maggie," I said. The car behind her was traveling very fast, and the silence of this moment was something I would never hear the likes of again. The speed of this incident played out in such slow and agonizing motion that I felt it was years of my life. The car hit our truck and forced it against a lamppost, bending it. Our truck spun and flipped horrifically—her hair was visible through the side window. The truck slid fifty feet on its roof.

Afterward, the only sound was my footsteps running down the stairs and into the street. The wretched rain soaked the pages in my fists, and I saw red under the crushed roof. The boy who cuts our hedges huddled in the shrubbery, shivering.

"Maggie?" My breath hung up inside me. One orange turn signal pulsed innocently. The rear passenger seat was flat, with no room . . . no room for anything.

I fell.

"My son . . ."

On the planet Echo at this same time, within the black forest, was Angela. I could sense her lying there semiconscious, and we became joined at that moment in distant thought. We both saw pools of something. Hers was tar; mine was blood. As I could see her, she could see me in this terrifying scene on earth, this unfathomable accident. She could see my pain.

"Machines and men are skilled in final and definitive violent things," I said to her in the rain. "All these things we have created, these systems—they are developed one on top of another to form a great, disorderly mechanism. And this disorder is a weight on us, which will finally collapse us. It will."

Angela moved slightly. She could taste the antifreeze steam lifting from the crashed truck. The image of me, my family, became sporadic, interrupted, and soon it left her. She felt something rough and callused touch her. She passed out again.

Wearily, Angela opened her eyes to find herself at the top of the cliffside, above the forest, with the crest of the waterfall splashing small droplets on her face. She looked back down to where she had fallen in the electric forest, and saw footprints. Hers headed in, and larger ones headed in, then out.

"Forsythe," she said. Her temples throbbed. "No." She looked around.

"Forsythe. No," she said. "You will never be safe. Never! Saving me is like pulling a dead body from the water—you have already drowned me. I am coming for you! I am still coming for you! You will never be redeemed."

She looked up and saw me in the distance, in her splinter. I was walking into the house. "Father," she said.

With the fire trucks approaching the accident, I was walking into an empty house. Nothing existed—no loving sounds of dinner dishes, no boy laughing by the fireplace or doing his homework at the table. I thought nothing of the visions of Angela. I wrote them off as insanity, which I was now on the brink of. Right now there was nothing that could convince me I had anything left. Right now this earth was boiling under me, over me, and I had just been scalded by the first drop.

They were blaming me for the approaching chaos, the inevitable turmoil. Some would name me as the point of origin, the epicenter, ground zero of the evil unfolding, the destruction that loomed over us all. They would blame my ships.

China was eager to accuse us of installing nuclear weapons into the Wombs ships, to say that my ships would come back and release the devices over their country and over the world. China was prepared to attack us for this.

Russia strengthened relations with China and was using manufactured evidence—false documents, doctored photographs, paid witnesses—to recruit nations and form a multinational coalition against the United States. And they were succeeding. Yes, there were other reasons for war against America, but my project took the brunt of the blame. I was the flashpoint. Me. Starting with the missing ships.

The trigger pulled back so effortlessly on my silver pistol. My blood must have been everywhere. The red lights of the fire trucks were already outside. The men must have heard my weapon discharge. I was ordinarily an excellent shot, and at point-blank range, how could I miss?

Weeks later, in my hospital bed, I stared in the mirror. The back section of my jaw, much of my left cheek, and six teeth were missing.

There was something holding me back. My aim was untrue—unheartfelt, that's what it was. Perhaps I was encountering unconscious glimpses of an element left in my life: the element that Yimosu and Jing had. I felt something there, within me—very far away and very faint.

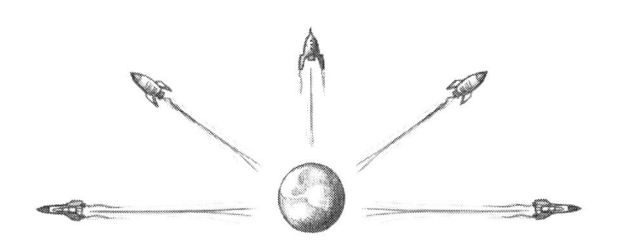

CHAPTER TWENTY-SEVEN

On planet Echo, by the creek, Angela drew a circle and sat down in the center of it. She acted out a series of motions, blocking the air and then leaning and twisting her body. She repeated this sequence for four days. By the fifth morning, her routine was smooth and ingrained into her muscle memory, and on this morning she pulled on her boots, patted her ship good-bye, and climbed the vine. In her pack, she carried a six-foot length of rope, a chisel, and a jar of water. She walked to where, Shepard had calculated, it would be very hazardous for a person to stand a few hours from now. Looking around, she found a large, flat stone, chiseled an eyelet in its center, and ran the rope through it. She then tied a thick knot at the end, and on this she poured all the water. Wrapping the other end of the rope around her waist and securing it with another knot, she then dragged the rock disk and rope to lay it over a two-foot hole in the planet's surface nearby. Now, tied to the rock, she sat down. In the desert, alone, she sat. Nearby, a meteor rocketed into the ground. She did not flinch.

She began to yell. "Forsythe!" She waited. "Forsythe!" she yelled again.

Exactly one minute would pass, and she would yell again, "Forsythe!" The clock in her mind was precise. "Forsythe! Forsythe!"

During the many hours of issuing this challenge, daylight was dim across the flat plain, and some stars sat as witnesses above her. Overhead, the large purple planet went charging by, and she remembered kissing Nathan beneath it. But as fast as it arrived, it was gone.

The wind picked up, and the temperature rose eight degrees in only a few minutes.

"Forsythe!" she yelled.

After six and one-half hours, she heard the wrinkling of stiff cloth, and she saw movement out of the corner of her eye. A form was uncovering itself from beneath the sand. It was him. Forsythe. Clods of hardened sand fell from him.

"I cannot stand this yammering anymore!" he said. He moved toward her with his slow and awkward stride, the obvious work of malcontent appendages. His every movement seemed painful, as if his body itself hated him. She almost took pity but shook her head clear of any vestiges.

"Nathan would have made a great husband," she said softly, rising to her feet, turning to face him directly, and then sitting back down. He scowled at her. She closed her eyes and bowed her head.

"What are you up to?" he said, dusting himself off, walking faster toward her. "Why are you all the way out here without your needles?" He held his wrist where she had stabbed him with the needle in the ship.

"Angela, are you okay?" he asked, angling his head.

"You know I'm not," she said. "I know you killed him."

He slowed. He pulled the sharpened bishop from his belt. She rehearsed her sequence once more in her mind as she heard a faint rumble from the north.

Forsythe saw the flat rock beside her, and the rope leading to her waist.

To watch this event unfold was to enter a Kabuki theater through an alley entrance and stand beside the workings of the side curtain. The stage had faulty planks, overstressed from previous performances, water tanks of magic acts, and chained crates of the freak shows. Now appearing was the hideous character Forsythe, with makeup caked on and dark lines thickly penned in so that his features of disgust were distinguishable even from the very back standing row.

If this were a play, the only sounds would have been the tiny sputtering taps of candle flames casting brown shadows on red velvet curtains, the rustling of starched garments that have endured a thousand mediocre performances, and the pounding of heavy bare feet on the wood.

But a play it was not, so instead they heard only annihilation, as a gray and white planet approached. The ominous sphere had such a near trajectory that its rings, comprising mostly rocks, large and small, were ravaging the surface of Echo. Forsythe and Angela were in this path of destruction.

But she remained still. Forsythe looked at the dust on the horizon, and one eye quivered. She calmly opened her eyes. From behind Forsythe came Mendelbaum, and Angela reached for him.

"What do you want with my dog?" Forsythe said. He took one long stride and stomped on Angela's outstretched arm. She gritted her teeth and yanked her arm away, and he stumbled. Spinning, he swiped at her with his makeshift blade, and she leaned forward as it passed across her back and grazed her shoulder. He thrust forward again and fell into the realm of her practice. In one continuous motion, she leaned sideways and used her inertia to flip the rock over as she slid down into the hole she had been sitting beside. As she fell, the rope tightened and pulled the rock over her, effectively shutting her into the planet. And there she dangled by the rope around her waist.

She listened. Seeing fingertips forcing their way under the edge of the stone cover, she leveraged her feet against the ceiling, tightening the rope and pressing the fingers against stone. The tips turned a deep pomegranate.

"God damn it!" she heard, and the fingers came out.

Forsythe examined the wet knot as a raccoon might look at a cupboard latch. The ground was now rumbling. He became mesmerized at the closeness and speed of the planet above and the growing cloud of pulverized materials heading toward him.

He looked at Mendi, then back at the planet. "That's the acid planet," he complained to his dog. "That little girl knew this was coming. She set me up."

The actor paced across the crooked wooden stage, his makeup mixing with his sweat, and to his surprise, neither horsemen nor archers miraculously appeared to assist him. For this theater was home only to a small troupe of loyal players, all of whom despised actors who displayed pretension and self-indulgence in their craft, so those loyal players sat backstage around a folding table, legs casually crossed, Frenchly pinching cigarettes, sipping tiny cups of coffee, shuffling cards, and leaving these two to fight it out on their own.

"What have you done, Angela!" she heard him yell. Through the rope hole, she could see his evil eye peering back at her. "I see you in there," he said.

The wall of rocks now screamed across the entire expanse of the landscape, some bouncing, some skipping, some sticking in, some punching through.

"Angela, let me in there." He knelt down, very close to the lid from which she hung. "Do you know Dr. Yimosu's experiment?" he asked. "I know who your father is, and I know how you can reach him."

For the first time in all this, Angela was frightened.

"Do you know I can speak with those on Earth?" she heard him say.

Through the hole, she looked closely at his eye, and the age lines around it now appeared wise to her, the eye itself truthful.

For a moment, she saw something else. Horizontally dividing the eye, she saw a splinter of light. Though it was dingy and dark like the tan, turbid waters he had emerged from, he had a splinter of light in his eye.

"What have I done!" she cried. She looked up again, and Forsythe was gone.

He was running away, trying to find shelter, looking for a crevice of his own. He found a small hole and chipped away at its edges and tried to lie in it. But he could fit only one leg in, and only up to his thigh. The first pellet from the spray hit him, making a hole clean through his hand. It burned him. More pebbles came; they penetrated his flesh like burrowing bees. He left the incompatible hole and tried to run. He looked up at the origin of the attack, and another pellet hit directly in his eye. The eye smoked and cooked in its socket.

He covered the wound with his burned hand. Multiple perforations occurred, with the pellets themselves cauterizing the wounds they made, sealing rocky debris inside him.

A boulder landed ahead of him, cracked the surface, and fell through. He headed toward the hole. "That little girl won't survive this, either," he said.

Two rocks collided above him, and a whistling shard of shrapnel zipped into his knee. From this puncture, he collapsed into the sand, and his eyes rolled upward in his head as if he had just gotten a dose of morphine.

Forsythe covered his head with his arms and heard another band of stones approaching. Larger rocks were coming. Mendelbaum's eyes were down, her ears back. Forsythe raised himself up on hands and knees and fell over on top of her. A round rock punched through his upper back. A thin plate, like the sharp end of a spade, gouged a trough in his calf, and a diagonally approaching meteorite scraped across his face like a claw. Numerous smaller rocks entered him, and he no longer moved when they did.

With the sound diminishing to a warm, rolling, rainless thunder, the downpour subsided, and the heat turned into a cool, moist breeze.

With twenty-eight holes in his body—his face had six wounds alone—his features were now distorted. His wrist was broken, and his foot nearly severed at the calf. He rolled onto his back, and Mendi scrabbled her way out from under him.

"I don't think . . . I'm going to make it, Mendi," he said.

Forsythe put his finger in a hole in his chest and felt his own breath coming from it. He wheezed with each inhalation of dusty air.

He turned his head toward the worried dog. He could see the sphere's path of destruction and watched it nonchalantly float away. Blood leaked from his eye.

"That was . . . quite a surprise she . . . had for us," Forsythe said. His words brought on a coughing fit, and red spatters came out of his mouth.

Angela pushed off from the vines beside her, swung back and forth, and hummed. She didn't want to come out, didn't want to see his dead body.

"His dead body," she said, trying out the words.

She thought of life with no one. No Nathan, no father, no mother, no Forsythe . . . no Nathan. Once in a while, she could still hear a rock or two hit the surface. But soon her world stopped making noise, except for the comforting sound of a tiny, trickling creek below. She contemplated the new holes across the ceiling and feared her stone plug might break through at any time. And so, patiently, she untangled herself, made a loop in a nearby vine, and stood in it to slide the lid over and climb out. Under the setting sun, she brushed her knees off and surveyed the ground. She found Forsythe's body and walked toward it.

His eye, and only his eye, moved. She recoiled.

"You disgusting wimp," she said.

She began to walk toward him again, but when she saw his wounds, her head throbbed, and she shook.

"Aw, God," she said, walking around him.

Forsythe raised his arm. In his hand was his weapon. But instead of reaching out to stab at her or writhing to grasp her leg or doing anything else she imagined he might do, he tightened his fist around the chess piece and began to carve at his own wrist, where a projectile had cut to the bone already.

Angela watched in horror.

"This is nothing, my dear," he said. Nothing compared to what has already happened to me—*cough*—desolation, near drowning, and now molten projectiles. Hah! Nothing." He continued sawing, slowly and steadily, speaking calmly to her as if he were writing a letter to a younger sister.

"My dear Angela, we are marionettes in the puppet show," he said, "but the puppet master has let go of the strings. We move about on our own now."

She stepped closer to him.

Forsythe became calm. "I want to see you happy," he said. "I know it sounds strange."

Instead of watching the gruesome activity he was engaged in, she looked into his remaining eye.

More blood came from his mouth, and she knelt down and wiped it away.

"Thank you," he said. He blinked his eye. His cheek muscle twitched. "I am happy to leave here . . . all this horrible mess. I am happy to give this to you."

When at last he finished cutting, he lifted his severed hand and set it aside in the sand. She pulled out her small piece of blue rag and placed it on Forsythe's arm, over the charred black stub where it was bleeding most.

"This is the key to enabling the rocketry on my ship, to the biolock on the flight deck. *Cough.* You can do what you want with the ship; it is yours now."

"What about my father?" she said. "You said you knew how to talk to people on Earth."

"Yes," he said. He moved his tongue and cheek as if sucking on a pit of knowledge, which turned out to be a piece of rock. She could hear him sucking on this rock, moving it about, clicking it against his teeth.

"I was traveling alone in space. Doc ran an experiment, Yimosu's experimental video. Alone—that is the condition which . . . *cough* . . . prompts this experiment and also makes it work. We must be alone and miserable, I think. I spoke to my father. I did not tell those computers that it had worked (they are so ignorant and controlling), but I spoke to him."

"How did you do it?" she asked.

"The instructions are in your ship, but as I found, they are even more so in your mind. There is a place unused in people." Forsythe spat the rock out. "Man seems to be evolving in a way no one knew or even suspected. We are the first signs of this evolution surfacing. The physical mechanism is already within us and fully developed. Distance and loneliness awakens it. *Cough*—I am awake now." Angela looked at him and reached for a passing tumbleweed, which she bunched up and put under his head.

"With my death today, you will find this condition may be stronger. You will finally be completely alone. You will also be more in need of it." He looked at her deeply. "Obsession seems to feed it. Obsession makes it stronger." He watched her move so succinctly, precisely, so unlike himself. "Obsession finally displays its useful purpose," he said.

She reached out and touched his cold cheek. One of his fingers stretched toward her shoulder. She did not pull away. She did not move.

"Forsythe." She said his name softly. When she did this, all the muscles in his face relaxed; then all of the muscles in his body went limp. His eye closed.

Ignoring all the horror surrounding his loose hand, she lifted it from the ground, wrapped it in her jacket, and walked toward the ship. As she reached the peak of the final dune beside the rock hill, she looked back. She could not see his body.

> *Today I noticed that Forsythe had something familiar about him. It was a look that I thought only Nathan and I had. I have never seen it in any picture of anyone on earth. It was a subtle and deeply rooted expression on his face. It's like the presence of an unanswered question in the air, I think, ever present; however, it seems like a useless device so far. I am certain it is a characteristic only afforded to a human born in space. Mendi followed me home. She has this look as well.*

Shepard's voice met her at the ship as she stepped onto the ground from a vine. "What happened out there?"

Angela didn't answer.

Doc tried to look into her eyes. "Are you okay?"

"Yes."

"Where is Forsythe?" Doc said. "We noticed him heading your way."

"He's dead. I'm glad. We talked. It's over. He gave me a gift," she said, pulling it out for him to see, "although it is quite nasty. I now have two ships."

Doc examined the hand. "You'll have to warm it up or the biolock won't work."

"Doc, I have seen him," she said.

"You have seen who—Forsythe?" Doc asked.

"No. My father. I've seen my father. Once in the *Amadeus* and once in the electric forest." She set the hand down and looked toward the sky, and Doc attended to her slashed arm. "The Yimosu experiment."

"But we have not initiated it yet."

"His wife . . . his child. My father is going through the same thing I am. He has lost his family," she said. "Like me."

Another meteorite cracked through the surface and sizzled in the pebbles by the creek.

"But the visions have not happened since. He needs me. I know it. I must find a way to see him again—my father."

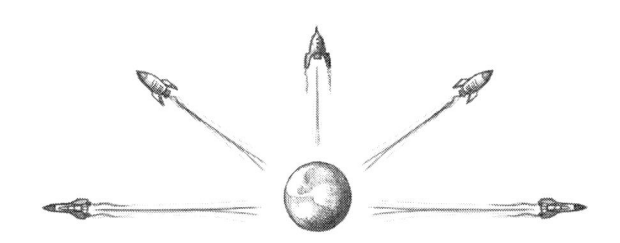

CHAPTER TWENTY-EIGHT

At dawn, she awoke to a crash and looked through the doorway. A meteorite had taken off a three-foot length of her picnic table. She got up and checked the cabin for damage, and through the nursery window she could see that everything was intact except a loose item now dangling by aged duct tape from the underside of the freezer.

"Doc, what is that?" she said, pulling her jacket on and opening the hatch. It was black, wrapped in plastic with gold lettering. While Doc's camera examined it, she cocked her head to make out the lettering.

She read aloud, "Texas Bill Hawthorn. It's a book—a Bible. Why is it here?" She reached in through the porthole and pulled it down.

This item was not on the load manifest," Doc said.

"At liftoff, fuel consumption was incorrect by approximately this weight," Shepard said. "It made things difficult to calculate. We had errors."

"A real book . . . one troublemaking book," she said. "Must be good." She carried it out to the table and sat, and while the edge of the table still smoked, she carefully unwrapped it and sat staring at it. By afternoon, she had read only the cover and had not turned one page. She was saving it. She put it away in a basket. This was a good morning: damaged table, new book—it balanced out.

Later that day, Angela was drawn by the new perforations in the ceiling, which projected light like spotlights onto the moving water and brightened the areas she had not yet explored. With adventurous eyes, she grabbed her pack and started upstream. Fairly quickly, the water became deep and the banks steep, and soon her only path was to scale the wall, using the protruding footholds of stone and grasping muddy roots. She pulled her flashlight out of her pack and stepped onto a toe-size rock, grabbing for the next root and knocking mud clods, *plunk,* into the water. The root began to pull loose. She could see, a foot beneath the water's surface, a rock. She leaped onto it and kept her balance. She stood on this pedestal in the creek and caught her breath.

Like cold tentacles touching her leg, a whisper came from the darkness.

"What are you looking for?" a dreary, phlegm-coated voice asked.

"Oh, shit!" she said, dropping the flashlight into the water.

"Oh, God, oh, dear God!" she said. "There are not supposed to be people here." Frantically, she searched for a way out. "How come people keep being here? Oh, God!"

"It's me," the voice said.

Slowly, she turned and tried to find the origin of this statement. The sunken flashlight projected the creek's spasmodic ripples onto him.

"Oh, no," she said. "Forsythe." She shuddered.

"Yup, it is me." Parts of him began to reveal themselves. She saw a hole in his hand.

Her voice quivered. "Oh, my God . . ."

He moved back a step.

"But you're dead," she said.

"I *was* dead. I am now, apparently, in an intermediate existence between life and death."

"Is there such an existence?"

"You tell me." He stepped into a beam of light. He had many holes. His torso had long, thick brown gashes. Much of his skin had melted and blistered. It was white and pussy where he had cut off his hand, and a yellowing bone end stuck out from her blue rag, now black, crusty, and unrecognizable.

"You *are* in this intermediate state," she said, and bit her lip.

"The hot rocks fused me together for a little while," he said. He moved back into the shadows. "I don't like you seeing me this way."

Angela stood stranded on the rock.

"I imagined you would come for the meteors," he said. "You're a smart girl."

"Meteors?" she said.

"They're in the walls, on these banks, and under the water. The springs here bring up the gas—don't breathe it in," he warned. "On Earth at one time, xenon gas was an anesthetic." The pebbles crunched under his feet as he moved about.

"Xenon—that's our ship's fuel," Angela said.

"Yes. And if you had enough of it, you could launch a ship again. The ship has the facility to compress it. Collect the gas and distill it. The meteors are the first key. " He walked forward, breathed in. "And the second key is . . ." He dived into the water.

She stayed perfectly still and looked for him to pass through the flashlight beam. She saw his shadow and waited. He never surfaced. She turned and jumped onto the wall, catching random rocks and roots and being ever so careful not to touch the water. "A ship launch," she said.

As she approached the ship, she heard a commotion, and looking inside, she found the robotic arms moving by themselves—all of them.

"What is going on?" she asked. Even the smallest arms were moving.

This was strangely familiar to her, and although she had never been to a carnival, she imagined the rickety clank of worn-out mechanical rides on a crisp fall day, the scent of electric rubber bumper cars, and the shivery touch, wild turns, and sudden stops of a cold metal roller coaster.

This nursery, where she was born, felt like that to her.

**"I asked you what is going on," she said again, looking into Doc's camera.

"We are beginning the new birthing. Shepard and I believe it is time for more children."

"What are you *talking* about? You two decided it is time for more *children*? What are you, nuts?"

"Mission protocol," Shepard replied.

"Yes, mission protocol," said Doc.

"I see. A convening of the committee of idiotic computers," she said, pulling off her dirty shirt and putting on a clean one. "There is a crazy man out there trying to kill me—did you consider that? He'll take your children and eat them, probably." She walked over to the nursery window. "You know, it's not a puppy or a rabbit."

"And it's not only one child," Doc said. "It's in the protocol that, upon stable conditions, we birth five children over the course of the next year." He moved his needle arm to the dish. "There you go, little one."

"What! Oh, no. Five kids—I saw that show. That is one messed-up family. I'll take my kids one at a time, when I'm ready." She sat down on the bunk, arms crossed.

"It's already done. The process has begun. Life has begun."

She rubbed her fingers in her eyes. "This is not happening."

She stepped forward and pressed her face onto the glass. Five cradles where warming; blue fluid was squirting into the glass columns; orange fluid filled the smallest basins.

"There are boys and girls in there," Doc said.

"It's the future," Shepard said "All from different parents, all to be nurtured and grown here. The directive was to wait until we established that your relationship with Nathan was healthy. With Nathan's death, we needed to modify the society-building process. We are prepared to make this world complete."

"This is your family, your neighbors, your friends," Doc said.

"My mailman, my plumber, my clown." She sat on the floor, against the wall. "*Nathan* was my family, my friend." She lightly kicked the door to a cabinet; it opened and shut. "I really need him for this."

"May I show you something, Angela?" Doc asked.

She sat hugging her knees on her bed, mostly disinterested. "Well, what is it?" she said finally, ambling over to the nursery window.

The dishes within the freezer shuffled, and one with a blue label appeared. The letters read, "Nathan C."

Doc spoke. "Nathan A never made it. Preliminary embryo tests failed before insemination. Nathan B was the Nathan you knew. Nathan C is Nathan's father's third specimen—Nathan's brother."

"Wait. So I could have another Nathan?" Angela said. Her eyes moved in quick steps, her thoughts indexed through the possibilities. "Would Nathan C have Nathan's light?" No answer came from the computers. "No," Angela said. "It would never be Nathan. I already know this."

"It would be his brother," Doc said, "with some recognizable traits: speech, personality, and physical features."

"It would make sense for me to want to have Nathan C here," she said. She paced back and forth. "Men. I don't know anything about them. Men did this to me, this whole thing—I know that much. Forsythe is a man."

"It would be a long time before Nathan C becomes a man," Doc said. "Lots of things determine the outcome of a person's nature. It is you who will be raising him, teaching him—not us."

183

"A woman cannot be a mother and, later, a wife," she said. "I could never be involved with any of these children after mothering them and watching them grow."

"You could become pregnant. We could transfer Nathan C," Doc said.

"Without ever knowing the father—another genius idea. Do you ever even *listen* to yourself, Doc?" She felt light-headed and reached for the bunk to steady herself. "Me, pregnant . . . It tortures me enough not to have known my own father. I hate it. I hate you two for this . . . this thing you are doing."

She listened to the sounds of mechanical motherhood. "How could you possibly ruin my life any further?" she said, gazing at the calliope of shiny mechanical things constructing future babies. She read the dish labels. One was turned so it was only partly visible. "Who is that one?" she asked.

"Let's see." Doc moved his lens closer. "The bar code says, 'Angel B.'"

"How many of me do you have?"

"Just one more," Doc said.

"I know it's difficult to stop you computers. But listen to me," she said. She recalled Forsythe's angry words carved on the wall of his ship, and pointed her finger at the glass. "I demand that you do not use that sample," she said. "I do not want anyone around me who is like me. I hate me."

Doc moved the container to the back. She stepped over the threshold and tended to the rabbit cages.

"Babies—what the hell?" she said. "Who the hell is going to help me with five babies? If Nathan was here, he would kick your computer asses! Five babies—why not ten? I have every bit of two good arms, you know, not just one. How am I going to handle five children?" She put her face in her hands.

"I can help."

She raised her head. "Oh, no." She picked up Nathan's bow and swung it at the air. "Didn't you get enough on the surface?" she said. She could not see him in this light.

"Yes, I did. I did get enough," he said.

The smell from his gangrenous wounds wafted over to her.

"I am just past the first bend of the creek. I am keeping my distance, and I want you to know where I am. These caverns can play tricks on voices—sometimes echoes, sometimes pillows, you know."

She looked toward the bend and located his shape. "What do you want?" she said. "No, wait, I have a better idea. You need to just leave me alone. Just get the hell away from me." She slammed the bow onto the ground. Her body was now looking muscular, strong, fierce. She heard him moving over pebbles to sit sadly on a rock, to listen to her.

"Just go away," she said, but with a slight degree less anger than a moment ago.

He closed his eyes. "Angela," he said softly over the damp walls dripping water. "I only want to help you."

"How can *you* possibly help *me*?" she said, punching out the words.

"Um-m . . . ah, I am quite smart, you know. Thirty years in a ship with nothing to do but learn. And I'm strong—I can lift stuff."

"Forsythe, I will never forgive you for Nathan," she said. "I hate you deep inside, where it can never be torn out or soothed away." She dropped the bow. "This kind of hurt is cancerous, and each day it grows and can never be removed." As moss covers a rock, grief covered her face.

Angela stepped into the ship, but she could still hear him wheezing and saying, "I know, and I can't expect anything overnight—maybe not ever. But we are kind of stuck with each other. Kind of like . . . like you said—like cancer."

After a moment, she heard him slosh away in the creek. She watched the flowing water from inside to see if any loose part of him floated past.

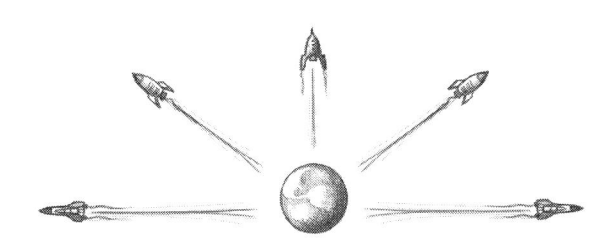

CHAPTER TWENTY-NINE

Angela sat at the table and worried. She thought about building warning traps or making a spear, to kill him once and for all. Mostly, she just wanted to pretend he wasn't there. She was tired of fighting him. She wanted this over.

With the nursery arms moving more slowly now, the blue fluid entered the five plastic balls surrounding the ceiling in the nursery. Doc tested the motor, and the fluid moved as the balls began to spin, and she looked up when she heard this. The sound was like an engine or a train.

She sat in the night and spoke to her rabbits by the fire. "They're going to know a simple life, that's for sure, these kids. No iPods, no crazy ships, no accidents. Having a bunch of kids actually might be a good thing. They can bug each other and not me. I am the queen, and that's how it's gonna be, and I won't take no crap from anybody." She stood. "Especially not you two." She pointed at the ship.

Doc's camera pulled back, and she pointed up the creek. "And especially, *especially* not you!" She paced the bank.

"Bring on the babies, Doc," she said. "Bring on the wrath of children!"

She walked over to the table. Exhaling, she closed her eyes and gingerly lifted the Bible out of the basket. She took a deep breath. The cover was pebbled and felt good in her hands—substantial.

"'The Holy Bible.'" She read the first page aloud. "'In the beginning, God created heaven and earth.'" She looked up at Doc's camera. "Where do you think I am in all this?"

"I think you are in the heaven part."

"Oh," she said. She loved turning a page. She loved it.

> Words are strong. Paper is like a place for knowledge to sit and rest. How can words be so strong yet so defenseless, thin, and fragile? One spark from the fire or even one drop of rain could wreck it all. I'd best keep myself from crying while I write.
>
> One word written in this diary, if I did not mean it, might ruin everything. If I said in my diary that I disliked this existence, would it end other lives? Would no one ever send out another ship or birth another child in this fashion again? Is what I write down real or pretend? Does it mean anything to anyone but me? Are people writing about me on Earth? How powerful would it be to read something from my father's pen? How wonderful?
>
> His family is gone. Would he love me just because I exist, just because I am? Perhaps if I had a sister on Earth, maybe he would write words for her. Maybe he would say he loves her. And if she is like me, well, he would have to love me then. Maybe he would say it and I could hear it, too, from the distance. If only I could hear him say it, that he loves me, then I might understand why I am here. I hope Nathan was wrong about our parents' not caring about us, but I don't know for sure. Nathan was pretty smart.

She thought of me at that moment so many years ago. That day in Georgetown, I was in my den, writing at my old wooden desk, with many dusty books on shelves behind me. She thought of me. She seemed to have some hope left, Angela did. I looked over my shoulder at my books, recalling their contents as I read each title.

She looked up just then. "Doc?"

"Yes, Angela," Doc responded.

"The first thing I want to do is build a library." She smiled. "I want to be a librarian." She sat up straight, and a small, colorful button she had made for her shirt popped off. "And secondly, Doc . . ."

"Yes, Angela."

"I want to be a better seamstress."

In the afternoon, she woke and stretched like a cat and opened the ship's door. She was greeted by less light than usual for this time of day. Just beyond the doorway, there was something out there, tall and dark, blocking the light.

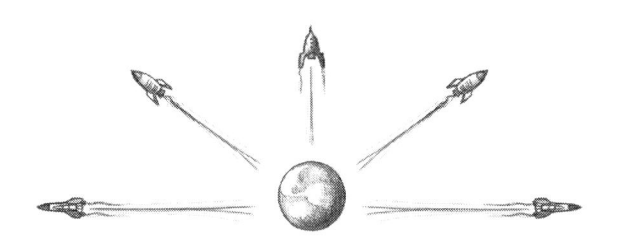

CHAPTER THIRTY

Outside the ship, standing before her, was a tall structure. She stepped back. It was daunting. She stood and watched it, but it didn't move. She studied it and approached it.

It was an apparatus built from evenly spaced stalks of dried vines. Ropes were artfully lashed through the stalks, and it was rigid and quite sturdy. Carvings were etched into the corners. It was made to hold something.

She stepped away and looked for Forsythe.

"It must have taken him a long time to make this," she whispered, stepping closer to it. Her fingers wrapped around the bars, and she ran her hand over a large framed drawing mounted to its side. It was an accurate chart of their solar system, made with colorful inks. On the opposite side was a topographically carved map of the planet's surface: the ocean, the plateau, the desert rock piles and dunes. The ceiling had a map of the stars made from round shells and rocks, and overall it was smeared with sand as apparent stars. There was a door and a very sturdy-looking latch.

"A cage," Doc said.

"I know," she said. "Like for monkeys and birds . . . for me."

Then a voice from the vines said, "For me." Forsythe approached her apprehensively.

She stepped back. He was in full light.

"Jesus!" she said. For the first time since his apparent death, she could now see him. The entire length of him was damaged. He was a deformed figure of a man, pelted and pussed, with unsplinted broken limbs, mutilated toes, and broad patches of hair and skin missing. He smelled like old sea mussels. She convulsed to vomit but swallowed it instead.

"I know," Forsythe said, mimicking Angela's disgusted expression with his own face.

"You zombie bastard," she said, half terrified but also half laughing because she had done this to him and he deserved every bit of it.

"So if you break something, you don't even bother to straighten it out? You just let it heal like that, with the bone sticking out?"

"Pretty much," he said. "Another drawback of being my own orthopedic surgeon is that . . . well, I'm missing a hand. I cauterized it on a hot rock after you left. That felt good." He held the stump up with a painful smile.

She gritted her teeth for Nathan.

Forsythe took a step forward, and she matched it with a step backward. He had little facial hair. What existed was spotty, and his face was slathered with scars like claw marks. There was a gap the size of a dime in the bridge of his nose, and the remaining portion of his wounded eye looked like a half-eaten egg white.

"So missing pieces don't grow back, either?" she asked him.

"No, no, no. Although my prior actions may contradict this statement, I am no reptile." He slurped a little. When moving his leg forward, his hip twisted with an audible pop. His torn pants revealed exposed leg muscle protruding through unsutured skin. Where it was once thin and emaciated, it was now bulbous and uncontained. His kneecap was broken in half, with a well-defined zigzag rift beneath the skin. She looked at the cage again, stepped forward, and pulled its door open.

"Who knows how long it will take for you to snap again?" she said. "You insane pirate."

As he stepped inside and she shut the door, the hinges squeaked like twisting bamboo. "Oil is scarce," he said, looking low and back toward her.

"I'm glad," she said, swinging the door shut and the latch down. "Most oil-based societies were faltering when we left."

Standing before him in his cage, she felt something she had not felt since Nathan was by her side: a sort of calm.

Forsythe stepped to the back of the cage and fumbled with something. It was a rickety one-legged stool. He sat down. He sat there balancing and creaking with the grace and poise of a miserable moray eel. She tested the bars again.

"Doc," she said, "can you examine this? See if he can get out—I don't want the undead wandering around the camp." Forsythe stared at the ground. She picked up her foraging basket and walked down the path.

Angela spent her days caring for the rabbits, making various recipes and medicinal concoctions, stirring things in pots and testing them on Forsythe. Months later, the first boy emerged from the nursery. Doc's nursery arms passed him through the hatch to Doc's main arms, and those arms set the boy down on the floor. Before her was a boy, a little gentleman of the smallest order and the greatest innocence and crystal clear, perfectly uncorrupt purpose in his tears.

"I hope you never know true sadness," she said as he cried. "I hope you never know grief as I have known it." She picked him up and carried him outside, whispering to him, "There truly has never been anything in the universe like a good companion." She did not look at Forsythe's cage even for a second.

She set the boy down in the sand and stood over him. She took in the cool creek-side air and said, "Although there is nothing here for you to hunt, I am going to name you Hunter. Since you are the fourth person on this world, I will call you Hunter Four when we are being formal or maybe if I am mad at you." Hunter Four rolled over and did a baby push-up with a funny smirk and then fell down and drooled on his fingers.

"He does look quite healthy," Forsythe said from inside his cage, and drew back.

"Yes, he does," she said. A long silence.

Forsythe said, "By the way, Angela, I wanted to—"

"Don't!" she barked. "Don't you dare apologize. Nathan's death is not a rude noise during a dinner party, or a slip of the tongue on a date. *Those* are things a person apologizes for." She turned her back to him. "I told you Nathan's death was—is—unforgivable. Keep that in mind. Keep your place in this world, *my world,* and I might barely tolerate your existence until I feel like tolerating it no more. And then I will end you. I will take your cage down to the waterfall and drop you over the edge." She ran into the ship.

Hunter Four stared at Forsythe.

"I do apologize," Forsythe said to him. Another long silence danced on the walls of the cavern and melted into the creek.

"I do apologize," Angela heard Forsythe say. She was holding back from weeping. She shook her head.

"I do," Forsythe said.

One tear silently touched her hand, and she tasted it.

Forsythe continued to speak. "Now, Hunter, what do you want to be when you grow up?" He looked at the silent child. "We'll need architects and wizards, balancing acts and zookeepers, mathematicians and librarians—"

"I'm going to be the librarian," Angela said, her voice soaked with muffled tears.

"Librarians' helpers, then," Forsythe said. He put his elbows on his legs and rested his face in his hands. "Mimes."

Angela smiled through her running tears and quietly puffed out a single laugh and mouthed the word "mimes" while crying and laughing by herself. Her gothness was washing away with the mix of laughter, water, sorrow, apologies, and new children contemplating an assortment of careers.

"Yes, let's practice the mime thing, Forsythe," she said. "Teach him how to do that for a while."

Forsythe quietly pretended to be in a glass box and then stuck out his mangled tongue—arguably the worst sight this boy was apt to see ever in his entire lifetime.

> It has been three months since the birth of Hunter. Three more children have been born since then. They are miraculous, children in this simple place. I have also become accustomed to Forsythe in his cage. Although I still see varying degrees of evil in him, he is the first thing I see when I wake and the last thing I see before I sleep. I have noticed many times that he has stayed up all night facing outward, almost standing guard for the camp. Although we have found nothing here to fear except for him, and the only life forms found so far are stinky mussels, he is watching outwardly, standing guard for Hunter, Emily, Cadence, Amelia, and me.
>
> I have begun to feel that I need to build a house. The babies are growing fast, and we will soon barely all fit in the ship at night. I thought it best to position the home downstream, away from the ship. Not only would this allow us more

daylight, as the cavern ceiling widens there, but I believe it would help the children learn to live a technology-free existence. I think I have found the perfect spot.

Although I do not intend ever to leave Echo Kingdom, Forsythe has been a great help in devising methodology for a relaunch. There is enough hard fuel and accelerant to lift off, and enough xenon all around us for a very long flight. This is now consuming much of my time. Tomorrow we are programming the actual trajectories for the launch, calculating the route to the atmosphere, and figuring out the physics. Many of these systems and processes, I admit, I could never do without Forsythe.

Most of the ship Amadeus's circuitry and systems are intact and in decent flight condition. The plan is to work on the programming in the Rhapsody and switch some of the drives with the Amadeus.

By the way, alien life forms are not at all what we expected. On Earth, people seem to think that aliens are extreme beings with high intelligence. These stinky mussels are not even good to eat. I don't really believe they can build or even steer a ship, but I will keep my eye on them and report any mischievous behavior I find.

Angela was in the ship, programming the hard drives, and Forsythe was instructing her from his cage. "Now engage the secondary retro rockets, precisely when the ship has broken free. This will be detected by Shepard. Once he gives the okay, then full throttle on those small jets—not the big one, not yet."

"Okay," Angela acknowledged.

Forsythe added, "Be sure to have Shepard simultaneously calculate and correct the trajectory, sense the depth of the water and any obstacles in the ship's path. We don't want this thing running aground; it would be near impossible to loosen it again if it gets wedged somewhere under this much thrust." She rapidly typed the code for these maneuvers.

"After the momentum from the water is fully realized, you must engage the abort motor. The fuel tanks were filled with hard fuel for an abort on earth and for secondary fuel, and the tanks should still have enough to propel this ship out of the atmosphere, piggybacking on these thrusters. We do need to disable the eject commands, so the thrusters do not fall off, and to make sure the output is programmed to face the right direction: downward and not sideways, as is the default."

"I think I got it," Angela said. This programming is going to take a while, though. Hey, I'm also going to copy all the video records onto this drive, in case somebody finds it."

"While you're doing that . . . ," he said. He tried to peer around the doorway to see her from the very corner around the very edge of the last bar. ". . . could you please bring me some vines and wood? Also, any flat bark you can find, as large as possible. I want to make something."

"Vines and wood . . ." She stuck her head out the doorway and looked at him.

"Don't worry, I won't make anything contraband. Just make sure the wood is soft, soft and green, so you won't be worried. Also, I need a rabbit skin and a little bit of the leftover guts."

"Just when I thought you were possibly approaching normal," she said.

She gathered the materials for him and put them within his reach, then went back into the ship. She created all the processes and checked them with simulations.

Eight days passed. Forsythe's back was to her most of this time, concealing his project. She noticed he had made a hat, brown with a wide brim.

"Pretty ugly," she said in passing. He took the hat off and stuffed it through the bars, and it floated down the creek.

She heard the sound of chiseling and, once in a while, the stretching and straining of wood. All was quiet one night. The flowers were still, the creek barely trickling, when she heard a sound, a whimsical *plunk*. She was mesmerized—such a sound from his cage! She heard it again. Then the sound was a bow moving across strings. It was wonderful. She peered around the corner to see what could have such a voice. He was facing the creek, and half hidden by his body was a rounded hollow box the height of a boy. Green with a tiger-striped grain, and a stout golden wooden neck. It was an amazing attempt at a cello.

He ran the bow across it three times.

The cello seemed more alive than she thought an inanimate object could be. Its voice was weighty and somber but at the same time gruff and tattered. The wavering vibrato under the pressure of Forsythe's quivering pinky hung in the air like leaves in autumn, dancing, touching down, and rising back up again.

He began to play a piece. To her, it was perfect, but she did not want to credit him with perfection, so she waited to find and point out the flaws in it, the mistakes. She was prepared to mutter a passive-aggressive little "oops" from inside the ship, but she could not—she heard nothing wrong. Nothing wrong existed . . . nothing.

He began to play a playful piece, and as she finished the programming, she heard the last notes of this song and stepped outside to stand close to his cage.

"Forsythe," she said.

His back was still turned. He stopped playing and looked slightly over his shoulder.

"Yes, Angela?" he said.

"I have decided that you should be our conductor."

"Ahh," he said with a hidden smile. "I would be honored to take such a position. And I will take payment in some of those fine mussels you prepare so well."

They both smiled, and he went back to playing. She gathered the children for the next meal and sat at the picnic table.

After dinner, she pulled the Bible from its basket and set it on the table. Forsythe saw this and stood up. She went to the fire to steep some tea.

"A Bible," he said. "What are you doing with that?"

"Reading it." She dropped the tea leaves into the pot.

"No, you mustn't," he said. "You must stop at once."

"Are you against religion, Forsythe?" She sat down on the bench and faced the fire.

"No, Angela, I promise you, that is not it. I insist. It is very important that you listen to me."

She blazed a look at him. "When I seek your advice, I will do just that: seek it." She spun around in her seat and faced the book.

"Angela, please," he said. "You have to listen to me. I have been good up until now for this long while. I am asking one simple thing."

She pretended not to hear him. She was the queen, the kids were loud, the freezer was leaking water, and she would have a big day tomorrow trying to fix it.

She turned a page in the book.

"Angela, look at me."

She looked.

"Inside that book is a poison. Not in the words—no, no, you mustn't believe I have anything against what is in that book. But I know for a fact, there is a jar of lethal poison in it."

"And how do you know this?" She stood up and stepped away from the bench. "Did you put it in there?"

"No. There was one in my ship as well. Just don't touch it."

She flipped the cover closed, stood, and spread her arms to keep her kids back.

He winced from pain. "While in *Amadeus,* I had this same type of book. I was suspicious when I found it, as you must have been as well—it being taped up in the freezer, suspiciously. But I analyzed it, the cover, the texture, and it came to me.

"As I read my Bible, I realized that the first pages of weight did not add up to the last pages of weight. I did not ever open it completely. I knew after reading twenty-two pages that this book contained something additional. I knew by the weight of it that something was wrong. You and I, being born in a weightless environment, can feel the slightest differences in weight. I flipped a few pages more, and I could see a round jar through the page, and an adhesive on the back of page thirty-two.

"I sat there for three days and stared at it. Being a schizophrenic paranoiac has its advantages. I surmised that if I turned the page, it would release a toxin. It was a test, some kind of test those NASA folks were putting me through. Or the Chinese snuck it in there. Something. If you are careful, you can go ahead; lift up the *whole* book."

She did.

"Doesn't it feel lighter than it should, if you were to add up the weight of the pages?"

"Yes. It feels hollow." She set it back down. "Now what do we do with it?" she asked, watching it . . . watching the kids watching it.

Forsythe answered, "I put mine in one of the centrifuge outriggers. There it will stay. So don't ever open up the port-side centrifuge on my ship. Don't ever go into the port centrifuge of the ark *Amadeus.*"

She held the book one more time and then wrapped it back in its plastic. The next day, she took it six miles into the desert and covered it with rocks as if it were a grave.

"Forgive me for burying this. I would have liked to finish it, but this world is different from Earth. I'm not sure these beliefs belong here anyway. I'm not sure that God made Echo. If he did, he would have saved my Adam." She headed back to camp.

CLIFF PARIS

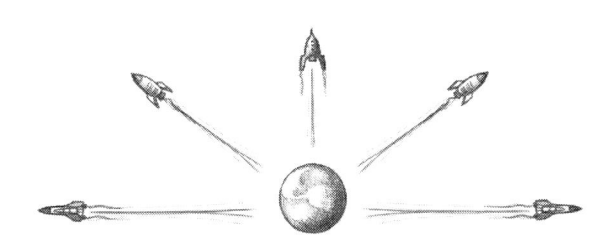

CHAPTER THIRTY-ONE

On the side of the creek with denser vines, she held her breath and hunkered beneath the heavy green tassels, beside a small pond where concentrations of xenon gas bubbled up every few seconds. It was Shepard's design to use the insulated baby breather as an extraction device. She attached the nursery suction hoses to the vines where they dangled over the water, and connected them to some transfer tubing that stretched to the ship's fuel cells. She went back to the ship and watched the computer screen.

"This is going to take forever," she said.

Doc moved his arms about, watching her, and said, "Angela, I understand why you want to perform this experiment. But if you are able to extract fuel and refill the tanks, what will you do then?"

As Doc's arm went to the ceiling pots and watered the plants, she said, "I have a plan."

"It is not in the mission to leave the planet, Angela."

She looked into Doc's camera. "Just let me know when I need to move the suction." She turned to find Emily Five, rubbing her eyes.

"Let's put you to bed, baby," she said, lifting Emily up and laying her down on the soft pillows of the tiny bed. Angela began a new drawing. "Although I want a modern city with streetlights and rows of buildings, arched bridges, and fields of electricity with a railway and a port full of three-masted ships, I never want us to go as far as Earth did," she said. "It is the future we need to keep contained. One advance always leads to another, until it's too late to turn back."

"Little one," she said. Her child's eyes widened. "Let's make nothing more than what we really need. A world of complexity can get ruined. Earth should never have gone so far as to need to send us out here."

On a new page, she drew a candle, a table, and a book.

"The first physical priority," she said as a corner broke off from her page, "is to make better paper." She smiled at the corner, in its place in the sand. Continuing to sketch, she walked around the fire, adding white pillars, marble steps, rows of shelves with books, and a chandelier with more candles. She held the page up for Forsythe to see. He stood.

She said to him, "It's a library. We have all the knowledge of our forefathers, with the wisdom of simplicity."

Forsythe replied, "Yeah, yeah, I hear ya." He paced back and forth in his cage. "But when is the concert hall going up?" he asked, and he sat back down and plunked his instrument—one sour note.

CHAPTER THIRTY-TWO

Years passed. The children grew, and the xenon gas collection was almost complete, and all the while, Forsythe remained in his cage. On more than one occasion, Angela offered to let him out if she needed help collecting, fixing, or moving something. But Forsythe would stay put and guide her in making the appropriate container, tool, fulcrum, or wheeled mechanism to help her perform her task.

One morning, she approached his cage. "We're going to the valley for the day," she said. "I want you to come." She hung a spool of heavy wire on the corner of the cage and slid a battery through the bars.

"I am at your service, Angela," Forsythe said, bowing as best he could. He looked at the wire curiously.

The children ran over to him. She slid a hand truck under him, and the cage tilted back with most of the weight on the axle.

"Now, push," she ordered the kids.

Hunter and Cadence grunted, helping Angela hold the weight, and Emily, Amelia, and Abigail all squealed. Cadence, the strongest boy, helped steady the cage whenever it tilted. Hunter would let go and run down the hill to clear away debris and fill in the potholes, with Emily directly behind him patting down the soil. Sometimes the wheels would get stuck in the softer sand. Then Forsythe would rock the cage, and all the kids helped push, and it always came free easily under the will and desire of so many.

"I do hate to be such a burden to you," Forsythe would say several times throughout the trip.

"Forsythe you are, and always will be, a *pain in the ass,*" Angela would reply, forcing a wheel over a rock, with a gasp and a grunt.

Upon arrival, they stood at the edge with closed mouths, casting small bits of fear down into the dark electrical valley.

"There it is." Angela looked at the footsteps coming from the mud. She looked at Forsythe with slightly surrendering eyes and pulled the spool down. Forsythe felt the scar on his neck where a bolt of electricity had hit him when he dragged Angela from the forest. He blinked repeatedly.

"I think we can use this power," she said. "I think we can use these thin metal rocks as materials—you know, to construct things." She handed him the drawing of the library.

He looked at the building on paper and then at the pile of rocks by the waterfall.

He raised his eyebrows and said, "We might need to tweak the design a little bit."

"Yes. Instead of old-style marble pillars, I am thinking angles made from steel plates."

Forsythe nodded, looking with one-eyed wide-eyed disbelief. "That is what I'm thinking." He rubbed his temple.

Angela lugged the spool of wire down the hill, careful not to enter the forest except in very short excursion. She set up the pair of cables to capture the arcs issuing from the black trees, then walked back up the hill.

"I hope this works," she said, out of breath.

"It will work. If I know static electricity, it will work. Look at my hair," he said.

No one looked. The children were gleefully collecting more rocks and stacking them in the pile.

"Cadence, you are in charge of making sure that the wires do not move from this position," she said.

Methodically, she screwed both ends down to the battery and brought out two shielded wires with bare ends. She wrapped the positive wire around a soft metal rod and clamped the other wire down against the metal rock, and an arc formed. Expertly, she moved the rod along the seam, and the rocks became tightly welded together.

"Brilliant!" Forsythe said. He sat back nodding, crossed his arms, and extended one foot out from the cage. "Why did you even need me?"

"I wanted to ask you what that is," she said, pointing into the water just before the fall. A bright glint in the stream bed caught his eye, and he smiled.

"That, my dear, is gold, a metal that has caused more trouble than anything on Earth."

"It's pretty," she said, bringing together two more pieces to weld.

"Yes. It's a problem with pretty things," he said, trying to bite off the last little bit of nail left on a finger.

Months passed, commuting with Forsythe to the building site and back. Often he would recite to the kids many things he had learned on the long journey to Echo.

As long as Forsythe was in this cage, it seemed that all his craziness was contained. He watched her build the building, and some nights he would ask to be left down there, on the hill, among the stars. The first building was almost complete, and the architecture reminded everyone of a house of cards, though the cards were of steel.

"It is quiet, with plenty of room for emptiness," Angela said, She stepped into the room.

"Yes, emptiness," Forsythe said, nodding sincerely.

While building the library, they often discussed the benefits of emptiness. To Angela, earth seemed to be compiled of many people trying to occupy the same area, infiltrating and overtaking one another's space, each trying to become a ruler, enslaving themselves and others for money. All the meaning of life seemed to become lost in such a system. She told Forsythe she viewed Earth as a spinning time bomb, and herself as the farthest-flung piece of shrapnel.

"You have your emptiness now," Forsythe said from outside the building. "What do you intend to fill it with?"

"Practically nothing," she said, her triumphant voice echoing inside. "I will fill it with practically nothing."

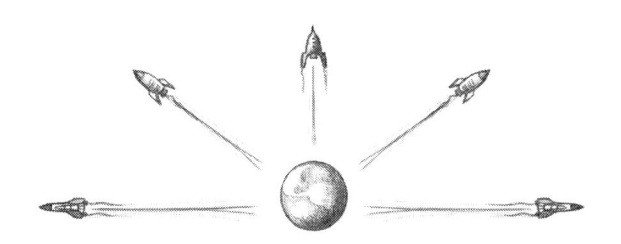

CHAPTER THIRTY-THREE

One bright day, fog moved from the cavern in quick waves, disappearing into the dryness of the desert. Angela and the kids climbed the ladder and emerged on the surface. They all were old enough, strong enough, and determined enough to make it up the ladder on their own. Forsythe was at the other end of the crevasse, hoisting up his own cage by a series of pulleys that he had devised and Angela had installed. Everyone watched him from a distance. Although they were never told about what he had done to Nathan, the kids all knew to wait until Forsythe went back in his cage to approach him. Angela followed them and said to Forsythe, "You could walk, you know."

"Then who would monitor the conditions inside the cage?" he replied.

She shrugged, leaned the cage back, and groaned, the children took their positions, and everyone pushed. The kids had collections of various containers of the xenon gas draped around their necks, along with trinkets and baubles to put in the ship for good luck. Forsythe closed his eyes and listened to the cacophony of clanking as the sun warmed his face.

When they reached the shore, the tide had just gone out, and she rolled the cage into the receding water. Everyone moved quickly, and Angela no longer walked in the pattern of eight steps and then a rest. There was simply no time for it, what with the kids, Forsythe, and the ship to take care of. Now her method was just to walk.

They reached the ledge where the ark *Amadeus* was lodged. Everyone had prepared for this, with chalkboard meetings, pop quizzes, recesses, and snack times.

Forsythe handed her the ready drives and preassembled components, and she put them inside while the kids scrubbed the interior of the ship.

Angela worked on the door. "This stuff is not bending very easily," she said, bashing at the dented door with the pry bar. The door bent to make an ugly but thorough seal. "Oh, there, I got it," she said.

Forsythe yelled from the ledge, "There's no question that you are strong for a girl."

She yelled back, "You're just saying that because I beat the crap out of you." She hit the door one last time with the bar, and it made a louder thud.

He muttered, "You're right."

She hooked her wire-and-rod welder to the bank of batteries and filled in the dent in the door, and everyone went inside except for Forsythe, who was timing the tide. The kids danced as if it were a ritual event.

Taking note of items needing attention, Angela went over the electronics and checked the nursery components. She caught Emily and Cadence drawing on the wall of the main cabin. It was a drawing of Forsythe in his cage. She looked at the kids and took the chalk from them and wrote, "My new ship!" With everyone laughing, Cadence mimicked

Forsythe with a hurrah fist in the air. "This is my new ship. Blast off in my cage. We're out of fuel—quick, get the handcart!"

Angela went back into the nursery and leaned against the main freezer. It was still cold. She twisted around and looked inside.

"The *Amadeus* has been underwater and stuck on this cliff side this whole time," she said, "but the freezer still works?" She squinted at the petri dishes. She read the label on the next one in queue and suddenly brought her hand to her mouth. When searching for other names in the Wombs Project, while programming the drives, she had found Forsythe's name. She had also found this one, one name down on the list.

"Sebastian A," she said. She quickly emptied the tool bag and located the ship's liquid nitrogen cartridge. With room for two samples in it, it was a little bigger than a lunch box. Reaching carefully into the freezer, she pulled the "Sebastian A" dish out. She felt an errant shiver jostle the lid, and quickly set the petri dish in the cartridge and looked deeper into the freezer for the other dish. There it was: "Sebastian A, mother eggs." After putting it in the cartridge, too, she secured the lid with the bolt-style closers and turned the valve to release the coolant around the samples, then fitted the container into her pack. Excited and nervous but also worried about the delicate status of this incipient person who was now her responsibility, she wanted to hurry back to the cavern, but she had one more thing to do while in this ship.

Angela swung out to the main cabin and knelt down to peer through the glass door and into the left centrifuge. At first she didn't see anything, but then there it was, the bottom half of its gilt-lettered cover peeking out from under the cushion. She sighed and cautiously inhaled a new breath of trust in Forsythe. Breathing out slowly, she connected her clamp to the centrifuge door frame and welded it shut, locking the treacherous Bible inside.

Angela had thought early on that Forsythe's evil behavior stemmed from his abusing the morphine. But since Nathan's death and the abandonment she felt until the children appeared, she concluded that Forsythe had been ruined by the isolation, the loneliness he existed in for so long, the emptiness he endured.

While the weld cooled, she again read Forsythe's graffiti on the wall: "Why would the world believe this could be done?"

She paused. "Why?" she said. "I guess we're finding that out, aren't we, Forsythe?"

She looked at the children. "Everyone, we are good to go," she said. "Now comes the test." Hunter took a seat at the control panel. "Ready," Angela said. She pulled back the control door, pushed some buttons, and touched Hunter's shoulder.

"Shepard?" Hunter queried and closed his eyes.

"Does anyone recognize that sound?" Angela said. A hard drive spun and scratched.

"That's Shep," said Abigail. They all looked toward the screen. Nothing.

"We can't have everything," said Angela. We'll get a monitor from the *Rhapsody*."

Amelia put her ear to the second computer case. "There's Doc," she said.

"Now let's see if the rest of Doc is working properly," Angela said to her children. "Doc, it's time for shots." Doc's arms moved around, and the kids screamed. "Just kidding—it's time for haircuts . . . gr-r-r-r." Doc started snipping at the air, and the kids screamed again.

Angela helped each child out of the ship with the utmost patience, for she had been in this sea, and it was not something she wanted anyone to experience again.

Everyone made it safely back down the vine ladder—tired and cranky, but safe. Adroitly entering the cramped nursery of her ship, Angela carefully removed the Sebastian A dish from the nitrogen cartridge and seated it in the foremost freezer slot, then aligned the mother egg dish into its access position. She swiveled Doc's arms to be certain they were operational, then climbed out and sat down with her head leaned back against the wall.

"Doc, I want you to begin the IVF process again," she said in a tender voice.

Doc awoke. "But, Angela, five kids—that is the protocol for the first batch."

"I really believe it is necessary to have this other child," she said, moving her hand through her hair. "Not for me—I think it is for the good of everyone."

An icy fog meandered over to the small centrifuge platform, which turned and lay flat. All around the tiny nursery, arms maneuvered, and the two dishes warmed under red lights, and a camera approached to document the specimens' thawing. A needle drew the sperm from the first warm dish and dived into the egg to inject it, in a process I watched closely through this microscopic lens. I pondered how carefully things touch one another, mix and blend, trade secrets, confide in one another, join, live. I felt myself begin to struggle as I watched this embryonic child's twitches and spasms. I felt as though I was observing not a growth so much as a once-empty silhouette now filling. I felt as if I were watching a soul squeezing itself into this life—a new being trying to force its way into this dimension.

When his size met each successive criterion, he was transferred from fluid-filled dishes to larger containers under the glow of the lamps, and soon he was lifted by his arms and passed from one robotic clamp to another, eventually to reach the top door of the plastic ball. The door opened, and he was plunged into the thick blue fluid, the door closing behind him.

The womb slowly spun on the track, one plastic ball rotating, the plastic connectors finding their way to him through the gel to feed him, the EAs reaching out and latching on to him to extract from him, the plastic clamps holding him steady, the wires observing him. He moved in harsh shudders. He struggled in silence in the womb I had made. This was so imperfect, I thought. What if, while Angela was carrying this child's essence across the desert, he sustained an injury? What if there was a tear or break in the process—a malfunction? I sensed how precarious this was. Although I had seen the other children and it had worked with such great success, I had the feeling something was wrong, something was incomplete here. I watched the child grow in the womb and worried for him.

                                    ◉ ◉ ◉

Angela sewed two dresses for a young girl: one blue and one yellow with a flowery pattern. She filled a lightbulb with ink and carved a nib from some of the green wood she had collected from the other side of the electric forest, where she had gotten the wood for Forsythe's cello.

While Angela worked on these things, Forsythe noticed that she was squinting, so one day a pair of wire glasses appeared on her desk, the optics ground from two of Shepard's navigational lenses, the frames formed from a band of braided wire.

She wore them on this day, eight months and fifteen days after the most recent birthing sequence began. On this day, she walked out of the ship with a blanketed bundle and headed toward Forsythe. In the blanket's folds, he could see pink skin.

Forsythe turned his back to her and sat motionless on his stool. He reached through the bars and pulled a blade of grass from the ground and chewed on it. "Who is that, anyway?" he said.

"Who, this?" she said, playing with the baby's fingers. "This is Sebastian . . . Sebastian Nine."

"I wondered what you were making in there," he said. "It has been very noisy for quite some time, all those arms rattling about. I thought that was over. I thought you had already completed the first protocol of children." He looked halfway over his shoulder. "'Sebastian'—that sounds familiar."

"It should." She brought him closer, crowding the bars with him.

"Why?" Forsythe asked.

"Take a closer look," she said.

Forsythe did not.

"C'mon, look."

He stood up and limped over and stared at the baby boy.

"Note the big, gangling feet," she said. "The ridiculously thin head."

"I get it. It's me," he said. "It's like I'm looking in a mirror." He gazed at her, quickly shaking his head. "I *don't* get it. Who is this?"

"He's your brother, dodo."

"My brother . . . how?"

"When I was repairing the *Amadeus*, the freezer was still working."

"Of Course, Angela," Forsythe said. "It's the most vital system, and any power at all coming from the photovoltaic cells goes straight to it, computer or no computer. Anything short of a complete annihilation of the craft, and these freezer systems—"

"Yes, yadda yadda, freezer, yadda yadda, annihilation . . . yadda, yadda, yadda . . . *Sebastian*." She pointed with her entire hand toward the child.

Forsythe surrendered. He peered at the child through each space between the different bars.

"Do you want to hold him?" She dangled the baby.

"No, no . . . not hold him," Forsythe said. "I would not know the first thing about holding a baby brother."

His eyes became confused, and she pulled the child back.

"Maybe someday," he added.

Angela stepped back into the ship.

"Maybe," Forsythe said quietly to himself.

He did not take his eyes off the baby as she took him inside, and he asked Angela to set his cage on the packed sand just outside the window of the ship, so he could look through to watch Sebastian sleep. Forsythe did not sleep for three days.

Angela lay curled in her bunk, concentrating on contacting me in her mind, as she had tried on many nights, but to no avail. Earlier that day, as she washed her hands in the creek and looked at her reflection, she could not see the splinter in her own eye—the one that, according to Yimosu's experiment, was supposed to be there by now. Inside her, there was no trace of the distance vision she had experienced during Maggie and Conner's accident—no trace of even the slightest vision of me, her father. Not anymore.

"Forsythe," she said to the wall of her bunk. She folded her glasses and set them on the blanket. "The children," she said. "I will never be alone enough to see my father. I will never see him again." She cried.

> Seeing Forsythe with his new baby brother, I realize that I have the power to help people, maybe even to help my father. I fear my father has lost all hope. Perhaps someday I will be able to hear his voice, to know that he is happy again and that he might love me. I have decided to do something drastic.
>
> I fear that the connection I once had is now lost, so tomorrow I am launching the Amadeus in hopes of helping this connection. I hope this will help me connect to my father. I want to help him. I hope I do not regret this decision I have made.

At the ocean's edge, Angela stood with her children and the caged Forsythe. When the tide was right, she shouldered the bag with the spare monitor and waded through the knee-deep water toward the *Amadeus*.

"Do you need my help?" Forsythe yelled to her. She kept moving. She pulled from her pack the plastic bag containing Forsythe's severed hand and stuck it under her jacket to warm it. The water disappeared, and she was soon able to jog across the wet, slippery plain to the Amadeus.

"What a perfect day for a launch," she said to the sky and the water.

Reaching the vessel, she checked the outside of the hull for further damage, pulled off some of the seaweed, and climbed in.

Inside, the ship was dry, proving that her door repair had held. She installed the replacement monitor and placed the dresses, the ink, the pen, and a single leaf of her finest paper under the blanket and tucked it all in.

"I wish I had had these things for my journey," she said.

Holding her nose, she pulled out the plastic bag with Forsythe's hand and squished it out as one would dispense toothpaste. It was warm. She placed it on the rocketry console, and everything lit, and she threw the hand out the door, into the sea. Then she set her bundle of books down in the corner with her diaries.

"Shepard, launch in twelve minutes," she said. The clock displayed on the new monitor.

She leaned into the nursery for a moment. Her back was toward me, so I couldn't see what she was doing, and a loose camera wire or something was making the sound on the video crackly, so I couldn't hear what she was saying. But she spent a moment in the nursery and then climbed out. Faint smile.

Shepard latched the ship's hatch, and she walked to the beach. With all the children linking hands, Forsythe on the end, she turned and faced the sea. The first sequence produced a roar, and the tip of the ship moved. A burst of flames pushed water and smoke into the air. Roots snapped, boulders fell into the water, and the *Amadeus* leaped into the air and curled into a dive, into the waves.

Watching this on the monitor, through the ship's fin camera view, I could tell the launch was a failure, ending disappointingly under the sea. But then the ocean turned shades of orange and the roiling tan of churned-up sand. My view then switched to the satellite camera, which showed swirls traveling beneath the water, moving faster and faster as, underwater, the ship speeded away from the shore.

217

I didn't know it could do that. *Perfect*—the water was acting as a launch mechanism.

The ship broke the surface of the sea and flew upward in a soft arc, toward space. The fin camera recorded the sound of a thirsty monster as the hull emitted billowing white exhaust.

On Earth on that day some thirty years ago, I recall having felt as though something heroic was happening—something unusual, albeit unknown to me at the time. I could, however, picture a shiny object, this gold, bright feature in the sky, which left an imprint on my retinas, as if I had stared directly into the sun.

As I heard the last crackle from the engine go silent, the satellite camera showed Angela and the children pushing Forsythe back to the crevice, with a tiny spot, Mendelbaum, zigzagging merrily behind them.

The camera in the cabin, the one that had given me so much information in my study of this whole thing, momentarily showed pink, then dark red, then only snow.

"Doc," I said, "rewind this. Do you have another view of Angela—the view of her when she put something in the nursery just before the launch? Do you have that?"

The screen showed the view from inside the nursery. Angela leaned in to open the freezer door. She placed a jar in the sequencer, resetting it to initiate a birth.

"Angel B," She said, reading the label on the dish, then peeling it off. "There should be only one Angel, I think," she said. "You can have any other name you want, though." She seated the jar in the first position, inserted the mother egg dish into the coinciding initialization chamber, and shut the freezer. Then she put her hand on the door and spoke.

"My sister, I set you to be born ten years before landing. Ten years is enough. Those last four years are awful. You will be able to handle things on Earth when you are ten. No younger, though, I think—children too small look so clumsy on Earth. I am sending you up alone in hopes that you will gain the attribute of the splinter. I have programmed the Yimosu experiment into the ship. Hopefully, it will work better for you than it did for me. Most of all, I hope you get to meet our father in real life . . . because I never will."

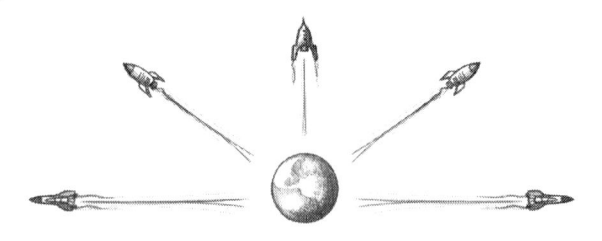

CHAPTER THIRTY-FOUR

"Where is this girl?" I said. I stood and ran into the ship, thinking I might not have checked the nursery close enough. I looked inside it again but found nothing. Where was Angela's sister? I looked in the freezer, and the petri dish was missing. The egg dish was also gone. There on the floor, wedged between the cabinet and the wall, were the two dishes, dry.

I was mortified that another life did not make it—another failure.

I carried them back to the table and sat down. "She didn't make it, Angela," I said. "Your sister did not make it. My daughter . . ."

There was no response, not that I expected any.

I had seen more than I ever dreamed about what happened in these ships, and I was grateful, for however unpleasant these things were, they were also awakening. I was grateful to know of my daughter, Angela, and her children, but now I had no further way to obtain information from planet Echo. The diaries, the videos—all that had been exhausted.

I rifled through the files one last, desperate time, and there, at the end of an obscure subfile, I found that the *Amadeus* hard drive had one more partition.

ACT III

CLIFF PARIS

On this mountaintop, the warm breeze, like a soft hand, comforted me. But then I heard loud thunder in the distance. I knew it wasn't thunder. The ache in my arm, the dull pain in my ankle, the sting of the deep gashes across my back—all this misery faded to nothing when I began touching the screen and opening this new file. The file contained the only remaining operational camera footage, from the fin of the hull. The monitor displayed the *Amadeus* flying through space—so far, nothing but years and years of darkness in time lapse. Then a small dot appeared. Shepard's readings in the bottom corner corroborated it: Earth. What a sight this was, the ark *Amadeus* returning home. As it neared North America, the clouds covering much of the continent seemed wrong somehow, humiliatingly marked with gray ash and floating black and brown debris. She was coming home, though. She was coming home to me. The *Amadeus*.

After decelerating, the ship entered the water and soon found the shore, beaching hard with the waves as if being newly born. She rolled three times under the last of Shepard's thrust and settled in the sand. The camera pointed down the desolate beach and caught a helicopter approaching in the distance. On the video, I could see not a soul standing on the beach admiring the spacecraft, not a soul in the water on this warm day, not even a bird sitting on a boardwalk lamppost or flying in the sky. Jets passed overhead.

The helicopter left my narrow view, but soon the rotor and tail reappeared, hovering just above the *Amadeus*. Arms and legs of men in dark green uniforms converged and lashed large straps and heavy chains around the hull. I would never have guessed a helicopter could lift one of these ships, but this was no ordinary chopper. It was a behemoth. The S-104 Air-Crane was the biggest-payload helicopter in existence. The cables soon tightened, fraying and threatening to snap, but the chopper managed to pull the ship from the sand and lumber along the shoreline, where it slowly gained altitude before turning inland.

The camera captured the Statue of Liberty. A wonderful sight, I thought. Then I noticed something faint on the top of her crown—something small, fluttering in the wind. It was red. What a horrific sight. Until that moment, I didn't know they had taken New York.

Here in my camp, sitting by the very ship I was watching, I felt as if I were watching the news of devastation. Communications had been down for weeks now, and I never knew to what extent my country was suffering, or how far this war had gone, until now. The ship rotated, displaying a fusion of decay—a charred city with the detail of melted buses, flattened cars, and pretzeled streetlights. Where this city was ordinarily warm with people, now entire streets were torn away, their blacktop lying in the trees of Central Park and across the mailboxes and benches and sidewalks. Some buildings remained standing, fragile, wounded with dark, sunken rectangular eyes, all of them looking out at sadness, all of them in agony and begging for mercy, for someone to end it, to topple them. White ash fell and floated, swirled and lifted like confetti on New Year's Eve. A series of sinister black craters meandered by—holes in the ground that were once lower Manhattan. Devastated, the city was hanging by hooks through its breasts and awaiting the crows.

Shepard showed readings on the recorded video: 87 roentgens per hour. *High fallout,* I thought. Temperature 99 degrees. *In May.*

The chopper crossed the highway to reveal fields of soldiers marching in columns, and I could almost smell the umber smoke, almost feel its sting in my eyes, the prickle in my throat. Another field had rows of jets and large guns, personnel carriers, and tanks in uncountable numbers.

The chopper approached a mountain and then, climbing and circling, hovered above a freshly laid heliport with Chinese flag waving tauntingly in the prop wash. I spat on the screen and went to take a leak. I looked in the chopper for something to eat but found only a bottle of

Kentucky rotgut. I poured a swash into a metal cup, took a swig, and sat back down.

"Shepard, start it back up," I said, wiping the screen off with my sleeve.

The ship's camera faced the greater part of the heliport. I heard voices approaching and tried to recall the little bit of Chinese I knew. A soldier ran his hand over the hull. "What have we here?" he said in a quick, choppy tone.

"*Amadeus,*" The other said with the same inflection, reading the metal identification plate embedded above the door.

A jeep pulled up. "General Katan," one said abruptly, and they stood at attention. Two other men got out with the general: a first lieutenant and a man in a black business suit.

"Chen Li Wu . . . so we meet again," I muttered. I studied his face. We all had the advantage of youth; we all looked forty-five when we were twice that. To me, he hadn't changed at all. I watched his every move.

"No worries, gentlemen," Chen said in refined American English, walking toward the ship. "It is no bomb or trick. This ship was part of a humanitarian mission sent into space sixty years ago. It is just like everything American: overpriced, useless junk—lots of bells and whistles but no purpose." They chuckled. The first lieutenant stood on his toes to look through the window at the graffiti on the walls, and the water-damaged monitors. The general received a call. Chen gazed long and assuredly at the ship, as if it were his.

The first lieutenant turned to him. "What is this thing? I have never seen anything like it."

Chen pinched his goatee and said, "This was an ill-conceived dream that we were able to quash. Only twelve got off the ground before the war. Those that did go, we were able to chemically sabotage. However, I am curious how this one ended up here. It probably got lost with that foolish guidance system they developed. Computers and babies—how far could it go?" He smiled.

A soldier walked up with a crowbar.

Chen stopped him. "We can't open it," he said. "There is anthrax in there. We put it in before they launched." He turned and walked away. He glanced over his shoulder for a brief moment, and the soldier put the bar down and pulled out a pack of cigarettes, rapping them sharply against his palm. The soldier leaned against the ship with one foot up.

I stood up from the makeshift table and again crawled into the *Amadeus*. I looked at the planters, the walls, the chairs, then down at the floor. The centrifuge hatches. I looked into the port centrifuge. Wedged behind the seat was the book, right where Forsythe had said he put it. I grabbed the crowbar, took a deep breath, and pried the glass hatch open. I waited for a lung-sucking, face-melting toxin, but nothing happened, so I pulled the Bible out. "Texas Bill Hawthorn," the inscription read.

"I'll be damned," I murmured. I turned the pages slowly, to page 31, as Forsythe had warned Angela against because page 32 had been tampered with. I could see through the thin page that there was, in fact, a cutout in the book. There was, in fact, a dish in this Bible.

I came from the ship and set the book down on the table, open to page 31.

I understood Tex maybe wanting to sneak this onto the ship. He had said more than once that he wanted to send Jesus into space. I knew back then that he was hiding something, concealing something foolish that he had done. No harm, though, but then that sneaky bastard Chen Li Wu must have gone in after Tex to do this, to poison the ships.

I took a knife and slid it beneath the page, to hold the dish lid down, and turned the page. The paper began to tear as the lid separated from it. There was the dish. I expected to see white powder in it—something a terrorist would conjure up, something depraved. What I found instead surprised me. It had traveled 4.97 light-years away and back: a perfectly preserved lotus flower, complete with points, round pink and yellow features . . . innocent features. I turned to the monitor and looked at the still frame of Chen Li Wu.

"Shepard, rewind," I said.

I watched Chen's face at the moment he turned back to make sure the soldier had put the crowbar down. If he knew it wasn't contaminated, why didn't he open the ship? His expression showed me subversion, corruption. He knew there was no anthrax, I realized. Perhaps he was working against orders.

The guy threatens to kill me. Plants a flower in the ships, telling everybody it's anthrax, sends me letters saying my death would be for the good of all. I took another swig of cheap bourbon. This guy had some seriously complicated motives.

On the video, Chen Li Wu went back to his jeep and talked on his phone. During the discussion, I saw my name cross his lips. I was sure of it. He looked suspiciously back at the ship.

As the video continued, an American jet speeded across the horizon, and the soldier handed a cigarette to another soldier, who stepped into view. They both ignored an explosion in the distance.

"The Americans spend their money—money they borrow from us—on babies in space, when we have all this hardware," said Chen. He exhaled smoke through his nose. "I remember my father telling me about these things. Our household cheered for this mission. We wanted these things to work. We wanted to know someone was making it, that someone could remain untouched by earth's problems."

I focused on the yellow fields and narrow dirt roads in the background. It started to rain on the fields and on these two men, and they tugged down their caps.

Those clouds had seen lots of wars, I mused. Rain only made war more miserable. Commendably, it was always trying to wash war away, but war was too heavy to move.

CLIFF PARIS

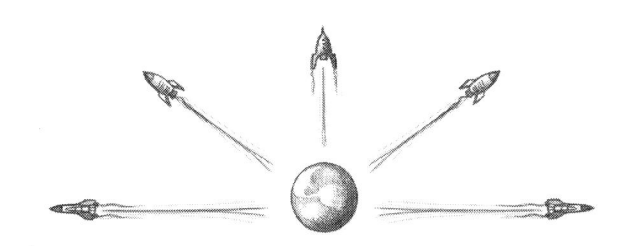

CHAPTER THIRTY-FIVE

Looking back, the day I knew of the war was two weeks and two days ago—two weeks before Tex landed this chopper in the woods. I was a month into my new job after moving from Georgetown to Dallas. I felt as though I was finally piecing my life back together since Maggie and Conner's death, twenty-two years earlier.

I was lead contract engineer for Humphrey and Dowd, designing for the big airlines. Sitting at my desk on the twelfth floor of a high-rise, I looked over my coffee cup and the variously shaped awards on the window ledge. My cell phone emitted a lost-signal tone, the television picture went to snow, and, seconds later, the power went out. I went to the window and leaned on the glass to look down on the perfectly even rows of streets. Between two buildings, I saw a tank.

"What?" I said.

Then another tank drove across and turned down the street, facing my building.

"A tank," I said. "A Chinese battle tank." My secretary ran past my door. I put my ear to the window.

On the tank's fenders, loudspeakers were shouting choppy English at the emptying buildings. "Remain calm . . . You must . . . ," I heard. I suddenly wished I hadn't left my gun at home.

I ran down the stairs to the crowded streets.

". . . You have four hours to leave the city . . ."

I thought about finding a gun store and shooting at the tanks, but they were not shooting at us. They were merely warning us. I followed the flow of people heading away from the center of the city—a frightened migration, divided by streets, heading through neighborhoods of brick row houses and funneling onto a two-lane road toward the desert.

We were about six miles outside town, in countless numbers: men and women in business suits, store clerks, cab drivers, cleaning ladies, mail carriers, chauffeurs. I recognized our building engineer, and we walked together and soon rested on the white brick wall in front of a gas station. Through the glass, we saw the proprietor inside, cradling a shotgun.

I felt the earth shake. Everyone looked back at the city. At first there was only the sound of rattling glass, a few frightened crows, and barking dogs. Then a thick white column rose from the buildings and pushed them away. The earth lifted into a formation resembling a wet pineapple being dropped onto a bedsheet: debris arcing away from its core, the ground swelling and wrinkling and lying back down. From the base of the monstrous white monolith, great curls of jetsam formed and rolled toward us.

Signs flew by, and telephone poles broke. A powerful wind shoved us all to the ground.

"Two hundred kil!" the engineer yelled over the burst. I looked at him. "Our flesh isn't burning. If it was a big one, we'd be gone."

Vaguely hearing the people screaming and crying around me, I watched the dirty cloud spill into the sky and thought of other wars.

Wars we started. The wind was still throwing things at us when I heard tank treads approach.

Within minutes, a convoy of shiny new troop transports arrived, each with a large red star on its canvas cover. The wheels and tires looked spotless, the faces of the infantrymen marching behind the trucks so young they seemed featureless—blank expressions under new hats. Aiming their rifles at us, they directed us to board the vehicles. We rode down our suburban streets while the drivers ignored the children on the roadsides, standing frightened amid the webs of telephone lines, the abandoned cars, the house fires. We were helpless to help them, and the soldiers' rifles rose when anyone stood up to try.

It was dusk when we pulled into the well-lit parking lot of the Home Depot, where several fires fueled by plastic bathtubs, area rugs, and cedar lattices produced an almost impenetrable black smoke. In the direction of the city, there was even more black smoke and jets. Soldiers in perfectly pressed uniforms and spit-shined boots directed us inside, where we found that our captors had turned the product racks into bunks by throwing rugs and cuts of carpet on them. They issued us plastic drop cloths as we moved down the aisles. Single-bulb lamps hung on long cords above us, swaying and blinking with the earth's rumbles. Intense shouting came from a back room, and our voices hushed.

A portly man with wire rimmed glasses—a cabbie, perhaps—whispered to our group. "Washington, D.C., was the first to fall."

"Georgetown," I whispered.

"Good thing you left, huh?" the engineer said. I nodded in agreement.

The cabby pushed his glasses up. "Everyone thought it was the work of terrorists, but it escalated by the minute. All at the same time, a massive coordinated attack—military base after base, gone, cities . . . gone . . . nuclear dirty bombs. San Diego, Los Angeles, probably more, and now us."

"How do you know all this?" I asked him.

"I gave a guard fifty bucks. He said it didn't matter what he told me—it was all over for us. He tore the bill up. He said the Chinese government voted unanimously for war—a vote to attack us and render us harmless to ever attack an innocent nation again."

I thought of Jing. Unanimous? She would have never voted for this. A few yards from me, a girl was being pushed around by a guard, and her mother was pleading with him. I started to walk toward them and grabbed the girl from the guard. They raised their rifles, eyes went back and forth, and they lowered their guns. Something was going on here.

Meanwhile, in Beijing, a towering glass apartment building overshadowed the terra-cotta roofs of historic homes hiding among the trees. Quickly moving clouds dramatically altered the light inside Jing's living room. The room was white. The carpet, the sofa, even the painting on the wall was pure white, with small traces of lesser white: birches in snow, in an ornate gold frame. General Yuan stood with his collar raised and two buttons open, holding a short glass of scotch in his stubby fingers. The ice clinking in the liquid was the only sound in the room until he spoke. Jing was near the glass doors of the balcony, looking down into her teacup.

"Is it not better . . . ," General Yaun's said. A scar on his throat ran straight across his neck and seemed to snare his remarks. ". . . to kill the snake *before* it bites you?"

Calmly, Jing answered, "America was not poised for war."

"What's done is done," he replied. "We made sure you had a vote."

"General," she said, eyeing him in disdain. She took a sip of tea and set the cup down, exhaling as if cocking a gun.

"You fabricated every justification you had for war. The people of China rallied behind misinformation. The wombs ships were never designed to carry nuclear weapons. You made it up, and I . . . ," she said, looking at the painting of snow. "I was brought into all this only for show. My real vote was ignored. All those against this were stifled."

General Yuan walked on the quiet carpet to stand beside her. They both looked out at the skyline, the new construction, all in a state of flux, of change. "We rarely count the votes against us," he said smugly.

Her face now wrinkled with anguish. "We were well on our way to becoming part of something greater, but now everything is lost," she said. "You have created an empty world."

"I admit, we did not plan to destroy cities," he said. "Well, perhaps a few, to emphasize our strength. With war, many things come that you do not expect, you do not want, but you must deal with them regardless."

"You act as though the world were yours to toy with," she said. "But it is like a chessboard—nothing is accomplished if all the pieces are knocked over." Her hands were shaking. The wind blew the curtain open, and she stepped onto the balcony. He put his hand on her back, caressing it. She moved closer to the railing.

"We are the same," he said. "We want China to live."

Jing said, "This is not ancient China—fight, conquer, control. Those houses in the trees, the houses of our grandfathers—they are shamed. They know that in this modern world, no country can live by killing. It is my destiny to help regain a livable world. It is what I must do."

The general laughed and stepped even closer to her, so close that her hair moved with his breath under the moving clouds. "Then you will be shot," he said, touching her hair with his fingers, trying to breathe in her fragrance. A fingernail touched her neck. She jerked away.

He threw the glass down and grabbed her, wrapping his arms around her body, holding her neck in his hands.

"No!" she screamed.

The front door burst open, and Yimosu entered, his pistol trained on the general.

"Where are my guards!" General Yuan shouted. "Guards!"

Yimosu waved the general toward the closet. Jing ran to Yimosu.

"They were coming to arrest you," Yimosu said to her, "Quick, this way!" He moved with her into the hallway, where the monk Gossum walked backward, keeping his old wooden-stocked rifle trained on the guards he had disarmed earlier. They found the exit door and all slipped into the back stairwell.

"It is futile," the general said. "We will find you. You will all be shot." He picked up the bottle and pulled another glass from the cupboard. "The balcony would have been easier for you."

They descended the stairs, stopping at the exit door. "How did you know something was happening to me?" Jing asked.

"A strong connection to Angela has developed within me," Yimosu explained. "It is through her that I can sometimes see you. I saw you today. Our splinters of light . . . it is like a feeling of unease, unrest. If all goes well, someday the experiment will sustain."

Jing smiled in relief. "I hope so," she said.

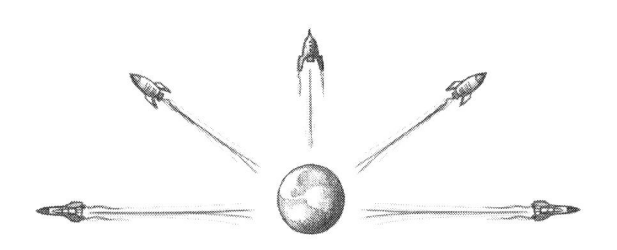

CHAPTER THIRTY-SIX

The doors to the monastery opened, and Yimosu, Jing, and Gossum entered.

"We must hurry," Yimosu said to the monks as they swung the doors shut and ran to him.

"We have news for you, Dr. Yimosu," the monk Plato said, following him and Jing up the stairs to the bell tower. "Something miraculous has happened."

"We don't have time," Yimosu said. "Not even for a miracle." He lifted a suitcase and set it on the bed. Above a short bookcase, he pulled a roll of money from behind a loose brick in the wall while, in the next room, Jing packed her things.

"It is important; you must listen," Plato insisted, bowing his head.

"What is it, then?" The three stopped. "Quickly, Plato—the police never take long to arrest someone."

Plato spoke. "Some soldiers returning from America brought us this news. A ship has landed."

"I know," Yimosu said. He put his hand on Plato's shoulder. "It *is* wonderful news."

"What do we do?" Gossum said.

"We need to find Jason," he replied. "The experiment cannot move any further forward until Jason Argenon has a solid connection with Angela."

"Chen Li Wu is still assigned to him," Gossum said.

"I will find out where Jason is," Yimosu said. A black car pulled up. "Quickly—Jing, you must go to Jason; help him find the ship."

"How will I know where Jason is?" she asked.

"I have a friend who will help us," he replied. "If only the connection worked between us, Jing . . ."

The opalescent splinter in her eye warmed. "Soon," she said.

She hugged Yimosu, nodded to Gossum and Plato, and ducked into the small passageway inside the church arch bridging the alley. Yimosu moved the bookcase in front of the opening as Jing emerged in an alley several doors down and melted into the crowd.

"A Wombs ship," Plato said.

"Isn't that wonderful!" Gossum said. Footsteps were coming up the stairs.

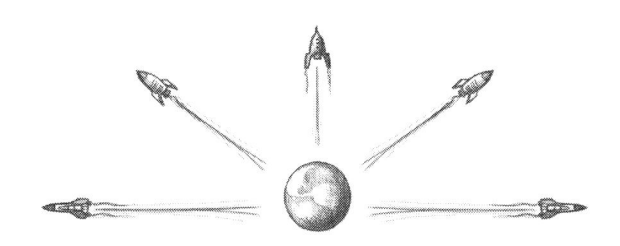

CHAPTER THIRTY-SEVEN

From the rafters of the room below the monastery's bell tower, Yimosu and Gossum watched as Plato spoke to the police. The policemen yelled and cursed at him, even slapped him, and it took all Yimosu's restraint not to pull his gun. Finally, after kicking over a Buddha and throwing some scrolls to the ground, they left to search the streets.

Meanwhile, Jing navigated Beijing's crowded streets and alleys. She knew the land and many of its humble people, and by walking the countryside trails and cowpaths, she reached the Laolangwo shore, where a small boat waited to take her to the Philippines. There, friends got her onto a private jet, posing as a stewardess, from Laog City to Australia. From there she caught a cargo plane, which stopped in Brazil before eventually landing in northeast Mexico.

Only four days after her escape from China, Jing was walking down a dirt runway outside Nuevo Laredo as the plain taxied away. Unfolding her sunglasses and pulling a scarf over her face, she approached a vendor's cart just outside the landing strip's chain-link fence. After buying a cheap local cotton dress, she ducked into a public toilet to put it on. Then she walked out onto the cobblestone street, where a boy no older than nine pulled up on an ugly, noisy moped.

"*¡Rápidamente!*" he said. "*Ven conmigo.*"

Jing stared blankly at him, but in the garble of incomprehensible words, she heard "Yimosu." She nodded and sat down on the torn backseat and put her arms around his waist.

As they roared away from the village, she watched people huddling in the doorways of their whitewashed houses, dogs and pigs and goats milling and running about with each distant boom and flash above the tile roofs.

"*Me llamo Joe.*"

"Joe," she said.

After a few miles, they stopped and the boy set the moped on its side. He flipped up his collar, and they walked together down a narrowing dirt road. A small woman with mocha skin, braided black hair, and a basket of bread in her arms emerged from a little adobe house. She smiled. "Camila," she said, and walked with them. From a vacant lot full of weeds and dry dirt clods, several children emerged to join them on their walk to the river. Camila taught Jing a few Spanish words and the names of the children.

"*José, Rosaura, Pilar, Maricela, y Faustino.*" Jing nodded to each as she spoke their names. In their colorful clothes and worn-out shoes, they smiled at her, and two of them held Jing's hands. As the group neared the fork in the road, they gave her a loaf of bread, and a hug from each. Then Joe clasped her hand and led her down to a concrete riverbed. The water was moving fast.

Jing shook her head. "I'll float away," she said, making hand gestures of waves. "The current—too strong!"

Smiling, the boy stepped into the waist-deep water. It barely rose above his shoe. Holding him up was a walkway of stones a few inches beneath the surface. Jing watched his progress and stepped in his steps.

On the other side, she and the boy climbed a concrete embankment, only to stop in the middle, where three rocks were oddly placed. He picked them up easily.

"Fake," he said.

"In Chinese, fake things are called 'bandit,'" Jing said as they ducked into a dark tunnel, where the air was cool and faintly musty.

The walk was over two hundred yards, and the walls tapered to a very tight fit at times. They encountered two Americans who wordlessly squeezed by them, going toward Mexico. At the end of the tunnel, they emerged from behind a thick growth of jimsonweed. The sunlight hit her, and when her eyes adjusted, she saw they were on the edge of a newly constructed suburban American community—an out-of-place subdivision of manicured lawns, curbs with stenciled address numbers, and matching gray mailboxes. The boy reached out his hand to shake hers, but she bowed to him instead.

"*Gracias,*" she said.

He bowed and, with an honest boy's grin, said, "*Adiós,*" and ducked back into the bushes. She pulled up her hem and began to walk.

From the grass, she stepped down on the newly laid street, where she smelled burning things, heard loose rain gutters flapping in the wind, and saw sprinklers watering toys, clothes, and other things left in the yards, including a couple of chained dogs, their barks squelched by their choke collars. She found a green and yellow lawn tractor, which she started and rode sidesaddle.

She rode past a lemon tree yanked out by a tank tread, a house with a hole blasted through the middle, a small mine disposal robot beeping across the street and turning the corner. She parked the tractor in front of a house, strolled up the sidewalk, and opened the door. The lights came on.

"Generator," she said.

In the living room, a mirror reflected a television screen that displayed only snow. When she crossed the room, a magnetically suspended chair bowed down and invited her to sit, then rose back up as she walked past. She ran her hand across the stone kitchen counter, and appliances rose smoothly up and hid away again as her hand passed.

"Americans," she said.

She waved her hand in front of the cabinet doors, and they opened. She looked for car keys. "Water," she said to the refrigerator, and a glass of water appeared in the door slot. She took it out and sipped it. Family photos lined a wall in the hallway: a man and a woman with kids, at the beach in colorful swimsuits, their bodies overweight and their hair a mess. The parents looked drunk. But then she stared.

"Smiles," she said. She touched their faces. She tried one of her own. She knew how to do it, and as it rose within her, it became barely evident in the picture frame's glass—delicate and simple, but true. The frame had a tiny oval sticker: "Made in China." Smiles were coming to China.

As she left the house, she could smell the thriving purple petunias and fresh mulch along the sidewalk. A tree had three plums on it, and the garden hose was wrapped neatly and hung on a decorative metal ring. Far off in the sky, Chinese fighter jets climbed with an unearthly roar. A flash, a preliminary concussion, then a *real* concussion, like a boulder being dropping into deep water. Just like that, mulch lifted, flowers ripped from the soil, and Jing's body flew across the lawn and fetched up against a parked car. Fires started.

She opened her eyes and touched her lips; she wiped blood from them. Raising herself up, she turned toward the sound of an engine and covered her face with her scarf. She crouched down to peer through the car's window and she saw a pickup truck with manhole covers strapped to its sides. Elvis's "Reach Out to Jesus" poured from the windows. She pulled her skirt in closer to the tire. The truck passed, its knobby tires humming on the road, the electric engine inaudible. It slowed and then stopped a few houses down.

"What *is* that?" Jing said to herself. A burly arm with a snake tattoo stuck out the driver's window and waved her to come on.

Cautiously, she started toward the vehicle. She looked down into the bed of the truck, at the old beer cans, the rimless tires, the spent shotgun shells. Continuing carefully and coughing on the road dust wafting by, she stepped to the window and peered in at the burly figure of a man. "I am headed toward northern Texas," she said.

"Me too . . . Jing," the man said in a deep west Texas twang.

She stared at him.

He stared back. "The little guy, Yimosu, sent me. Well, get in before those jets come around and flatten us for real this time."

She nodded and stepped into the truck. "Where did you come from?" she asked.

"Good ol' Mexico," he said.

"Me, too."

CLIFF PARIS

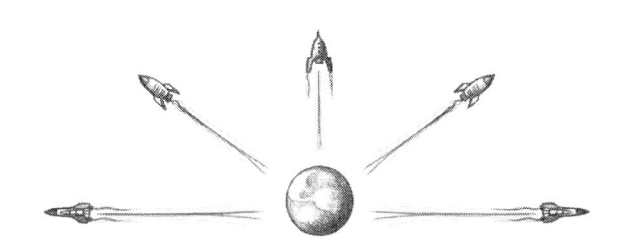

CHAPTER THIRTY-EIGHT

"How do you know him—Yimosu?" she asked, studying his scraggly face and sizable belly. He had binoculars on a strap around his neck, over a black T-shirt that read, "WWE Raw."

"Don't worry, it's my kid's," he said of the shirt. "Yimosu? I met him at the Wombs factory. Those were the days: free bed, free meals, all the overtime I wanted. I haven't had a decent job since." He eyed her and clenched his jaw. "I sure hope you did your part to keep this from goin' down."

The scarf fell from her face, and she had fear on her graceful lips.

"Don't worry," he said. "Yimosu vouched for ya." He looked at her face for a moment and noticed her tender features. He stared straight ahead and quietly said, "Jackpot." Then he turned the truck hard to the right and gunned it down a rough road. "Gotta stay on the two-lanes. Haven't seen any fightin' in this thing . . . really don't feel like it right now." He held out his big, heavy hand. "I'm Texas, ma'am; you can call me Tex." She shook his hand. "I do miss a good GPS," he said, peering ahead.

"Yes. The generals electropulsed the satellites," she said. "They thought if they took down your communications, your guidance systems, your military would crumble. China still relies on maps. It's funny how that should be their edge: old technology."

"You caught us by surprise, that's fer sure. I made a dash for Mexico." The truck jounced. "Did you know you flattened Vegas? I heard that. Now, I ask you, what good did it do anybody to blow up the Hound Dog Wedding Chapel? They had the dueling Elvis hitchin' package, where you get two different eras of Elvis for your money. I married Veronica there . . . didn't last, though. My fault, I s'pose. Still . . . what kind of fool flattens *Vegas,* man? My house is gone. I went by it. Dog's gone. Sad."

She looked at him and gave a closed-eyed one-nod condolence.

"Anyhow, I been in Mexico ever since. I found a note stuck to my door. It said *Jing* and had a longitude and latitude. It was signed Yim. I had to see what it led to—I hope you're worth it."

"A note . . . Do you have it?" she asked.

"Yeah, right here." He pulled it from the visor and handed it to her.

"I've been driving around this town for three days looking for somebody. Soon's I saw a Chinese woman in a Mexican outfit, I said, 'Bingo.'"

She pulled her hair back and started to braid it. "If it helps anything, I am working to fix this."

Tex slammed on the brakes, and Jing put her hands on the dash. Still braking hard, he turned the truck into a big parking lot. "What?" He looked through the windshield at a nearby field, where a decapitated oil pump hose was writhing on the ground, heaving oil into the air like a cut artery. "You can't fix this. The whole cotton-pickin' *world* can't fix this." He pointed his thumb at her and shook his head. "How *you* gonna fix this?"

"Let me explain," she said. She finished braiding her hair and let it go.

He sat back in his seat and tapped his foot.

"We can stop it," she said. "Everything can be different. I'm hoping we can find out where the ship has landed."

"The *ship*? Where you from—Mars?"

"No. A Wombs ship has landed here."

"Bullshit. You're speaking pure-dee bullshit, missy."

"There is a ship. It's true."

"A Wombs ship," he said. "On Earth? They weren't s'posed to do that."

"I know. We need to find out why it's here and what's inside it. Yimosu and I are hoping it holds some clues—perhaps some more secrets to the connection."

"The connection?" Tex said.

The cab was quiet except for Elvis, crooning "Love Me Tender." "Yes," she said. "A connection between people. Is it so absurd that we are connected? There is an invisible thread. Compassion, simplicity—many things are inside this connection . . . this connection of distance. I am here to help find it for all of us."

Tex was quiet.

She continued, "I know of this war's dirty secrets—the beginning of this war—and I am now wanted because I know too much."

Tex took a deep breath. "So we're in danger's what you're saying—more than just bein' sittin' ducks in a Walmart parking lot." He pulled a gun from a concealed holster inside his waistband—an old Glock nine from the desert war—and chambered a round. "That makes me feel so much better." Hitting the gas, he knocked several shopping carts out of the way, nicked a lamppost's concrete base, and got back on the road.

"By the way," he said, "the note had two other coordinates on it—on the back."

She turned it over and read aloud: "San Antonio, Home Depot on Fair Avenue; and Eagle Mountain, Pennsylvania."

After eight replays of the Elvis's greatest hits, the pickup slowed, and Jing opened her eyes. Tex turned down a service road and then into the thick woods. Climbing a hill, they weaved through the trees, crawling over down branches and humps of exposed limestone, and stopped just before the top.

"Come on," he said. He got out, and they both lay down on the dirt crest overlooking a big store parking lot. He handed her the binoculars.

Armed guards were standing around, looking bored.

A jet banked close by.

"See that fence next to the building?" Tex said. "They're only guarding the places with no fence. Before dawn we'll get you in down there." He pointed at the fence corner nearest the woods.

"Why Home Depot?" she said. "What's in there?"

"Jason. They gathered folks up and put 'em in there."

They went back to the truck and waited. From her pocketbook, Jing took out a folded piece of paper and placed it in the glove box. "I need to put this in here for safekeeping," she said. "I prefer that you not look at it."

He nodded.

Just before dawn, Tex used a pair of cutters to make a slice in the fence and helped her through.

"Now, find Jason and make it to the men's room," he said.

She looked at him curiously.

"All Home Depots use the same cookie cutter. The handicapped stall is along an outside wall." She ran toward the building and crouched down between two carts. As prisoners began to trickle out of the building, she rose, pulled the scarf across her face, and walked over to mix in with them.

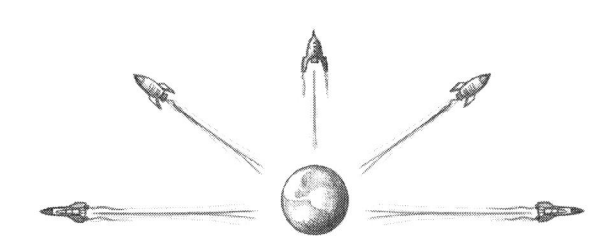

CHAPTER THIRTY-NINE

It was my sixth day in captivity. I was dirty from the day, laboring to haul more merchandise outside to make room for more prisoners. I was due for my B58 shot over three weeks ago and kept putting it off, so now I was well into the brutal withdrawal: twitching, cramping, vomiting nightly, falling into chronic deep exhaustion. I felt a lot older and was beginning to look it: too many missed shots, and time catches up with a vengeance. Organ after organ ages, almost overnight. You just die. My hands were shaking; my vision had bouts of blur and white spots.

Several new people were being shoved through the sliding doors. One man looked injured and disoriented. I walked up to him. "You okay?" I said, helping him up. He had bloodstained bandages around his head and face, and his arm was in a sling. Only his eyes and his black hair were exposed.

"Carl Wetherburn," he announced in a Midwestern farmer's way. He held out his hand.

We shook, and I told him we were just about to have dinner. I pointed him toward a group huddled around some big pots, shucking corn. A little later, after a captured priest said grace, we sat at some long tables and began to pass the corn around.

A guard approached—darker-skinned Chinese, twenty-something, hat strapped down tight, eyes peering closely at each of us. Everyone hushed. "Go about your food," he said, his boots crunching shattered lightbulb glass as he paced. "We want you all to know there is a place for you after all this," he said. This war is going to make things better, more uniform, less chaotic Chaotic America, spend, spend, spend—didn't you see it? Crazy times are over now." His shiny boots tapped loudly on the concrete floor. "All craziness is over." He slashed his hand through the air in finality and walked into the employees' lounge. "Sleep tight, my fellow Americans," he said.

I noticed a new woman at the end of the table. She had a scarf over her face and seemed to be shivering.

"It's okay, miss," I said. "They just like to scare us. I have seen no one seriously harmed yet."

"Yeah, except maybe for a blowed-up city," someone said.

She nodded at me with understanding eyes.

"Miss, what is your name. *¿Cómo se llama?*"

"Jason," she said. She pulled down her scarf.

"Jing . . . ?"

As she revealed her Chinese features, a hush went over everyone. Wetherburn's eyes went wild. I thought he was going to stand up and attack her right in front of all of us. I looked at him, and he calmed down just a notch.

She was still a stunning woman—as beautiful as when we met in college, when she was a feisty poetry-writing rebel publishing in the campus blog, bashing my robotics research with her overblown prose. She gained a following, trashing me. Yimosu was one year her senior. She would help translate for him, tagging along behind him, listening to whatever he said. In this place, though, she was the face of war, an enemy to the other prisoners in the Home Depot on Fair Avenue. She stood and walked over to me.

I loved her mischievous, girlish ways back then. We almost went out. She waited for me at the pub, but I couldn't make it. Years later I was indebted to her for her getting the Chinese government's financial support to launch my ships. But the news now circulating through the prison camp (albeit from the soldiers) was that the war began with a unanimous vote of the Committee of the National People's Congress, of which she was a voting member. I stared at her, crushed and questioning.

She must have seen the concern in my eyes, the mistrust, because she took me aside. "Jason, I did not want this," she said. "Women have no real power in China. We're only showpieces of change. I would never vote for war."

"China blamed my ships," I said to her.

"Yes, I know." She led me to a sparsely occupied aisle. "They believed your project was to acquire a strategic position in space. As financiers, they could watch you from the inside. But when those eight ships went missing, the Chinese government was furious. To them, missing ships meant nothing less than deception." She looked through the product racks at the guards nearby. She watched Wetherburn stand and walk casually past.

Lowering her voice, she said, "Too often I have seen them manufacture information to hang people with. The committee had a document they showed everyone. We do not have the technology to gain secret U.S. documents of this nature, so it had to be false." She looked away. "My father was killed when I was twelve. When they took him, they had such false documents. They manufacture things and use them to start things . . . like a war." Her eyes had one thread of hope, which swirled like a small, circling wind on a playground.

I touched her hand. "Jing, I believe you," I said. "I believe that you did your best."

The room became warm, and the guards became nonexistent to us. She looked into my eyes as she held my fingers. I looked at her lips and back into those eyes, and I saw no trap. We walked to sit down on a bench in a sparsely occupied aisle. She touched my cheek, and I kissed her.

She was the rest I needed, the one tenderness left on this earth for me in these ruins of mine. Amid all the devastation, this kiss was a note of such formidable silence that nothing else could be heard.

Laughter from somewhere made us both smile.

"There's something more," she whispered. Her lips drew close to my cheek; soft puffs of words reached my ear. "There is someone out there."

"Out where?" I said. My mind drew a rough sketch of a girl.

"I can't tell you anything more, but we share something . . . something wonderful." She smiled.

Jing turned away, wanting her shoulders to be touched, to confirm that I was speaking the truth. "I see her in you." She said. "She has your strength."

"Who?"

She turned to me with new eyes. "What is happening to us is more important than you know. All of us depend on this working. All of us." She tilted her head slightly. "Remember what I told you, in the monastery: that the whole ocean may come down on us? Well, the first raindrops are starting to fall."

I felt a chill. Her words reminded me of the threat on my life, that day in the monastery. Somehow, she was involved. I could see Wetherburn, pretending not to be listening to us through the racks of the plumbing department.

"You know, we will not be drones," Jing said.

"Drones . . . *what?*"

"We will still be individuals. I can't tell you more—you'll see," she said mysteriously. I let it go.

I lay on the plywood as people coughed and moved about to stake out their own personal space. We were enduring each other. Across on the next row of racks, I noticed a familiar face: a woman sleeping. I looked again, and yes, it was Mrs. Crumwell, Maggie's mom. She looked elegant—dressed expensively, her hair done, makeup, even the pearl bracelet and matching necklace she wore only on special occasions. She must have been visiting her family. They all were down here in the south; she was the only one who lived up north. The distance we put between us, Mrs. Crumwell and I, had grown to such a gulf, I was afraid she wouldn't want to talk to me, not even here. But she wasn't like that, not really one to hold a grudge. I imagined that she would open her eyes with honest, graceful surprise and welcome me with open arms and give me a kiss on the cheek, and then tell me to tie my shoes better and tuck in my shirt further. I had slept only a few hours since I got here; maybe she needed her rest, too. I could talk to her in the morning. I *wanted* to talk to her; I had a lot to say. She looked so like Maggie.

I lay back and rested my eyes, listening to people in pain, their moans and whispers and children crying, it all coming together in a familiar background noise of war. Feeling fabric brush against my arm, I opened my eyes to find Jing bending close to my ear.

"Jason," she whispered, "we must go. Now," she said, tugging on my shirt.

"Wait." I looked at Maggie's mother.

"There's no time. If we are successful, she will benefit, too. Leave her. Come."

I closed my teeth over the button on my sleeve, and the threads broke, releasing it into my mouth. I wiped it off and carefully placed it in Mrs. Crumwell's hand and folded her fingers around it, hoping she would wake, but she didn't. She breathed out in careful, worried, motherly breaths. She knew the story of Tex saving me in that high school fight. The button's lore, in that family, meant friendship.

I stepped down onto the floor, and Jing quietly guided me to the restroom. On the way, we encountered no guards. We went into the handicapped stall and found a hole sledgehammered into the cinder block wall.

"How did this get here?" I said. "How did you know this was here?"

"Sh-h-h!" she whispered.

Outside, we saw no guards, no spotlights, no obstacles of any kind while crossing the brown, dry grass to the hole in the fence.

I followed her up the hill, and as we reached the top, I looked back. Down below, standing in the grass, I saw the man with the bandages on his face—Wetherburn. He just stood there, looking. When I turned around, I was startled by a big, burly form standing in front of me.

"Tex . . . ? Hell, yes, it is!" I said. "Tex—I can't believe it." I patted him on the shoulder as he grabbed me in a crushing bear hug. Even in a whisper, I felt his deep baritone in my chest.

"Boy, you haven't changed," Tex said. "Still scrawnier'n a Meskin chicken." He went around the bed of the truck.

"You haven't changed, either, you big bastard," I said, opening the pickup door. Jing slid to the center.

Tex rolled the truck backward down the hill, with the engine and lights off. I pulled some prickly pear needles from my leg and rolled down the window. He handed me a nickel-plated handgun. It took me a moment to recognize it. It was my Colt Combat Commander.

"I hate fighting," I said, trying to hand it back.

Tex looked at me as if I had two heads.

"No, I've changed," I said. "I hate fighting."

"No, ya don't."

"Well, then I hate guns."

"No, ya don't."

"Well . . . I hate *this* one," I told him.

He reached out and took my nickel .45, my would-be suicide weapon. Then he pulled the black Glock from inside his pants and handed it to me.

He started the truck, and we drove fast through the woods, both Jing and me with our hands against the roof so our heads wouldn't hit. "Where ya been?" I yelled to him over the rustle and crack of tires over sticks.

"North side of hell and back, man," Tex said, using the wheel to keep from bouncing too high. "How's Maggie?"

"She's dead—car accident."

"*Day-umn* . . . I'm sorry, man."

We heard gunfire in the dark and saw two moving flashlights. He slowed the truck down and, with it still rolling, slipped out and disappeared into the woods. The lights got closer to us as they drifted farther apart.

Two gunshots lit the trees, and the two flashlights fell, one blinking off on impact. I reached over and steered the truck. A flashlight rose and aimed at the ground. A boot rolled a body over, and the flashlight turned off.

Tex reappeared at the driver's door. "Two are done," he said. "One was a goddamn American."

"Contractors," I said.

The big tires moved again and rolled over one of the downed guards' leg.

"Here's your money," Tex said to the dead man, and he punched it.

I took the shotgun from him, found more shells and slid them into the action, then pumped one into the chamber. "Got anything else?"

Tex smiled and pulled the roof lining down. Above us, secured with tidy brackets, was a row of pipe bombs and a crossbow with arrows. Just then a bullet clinked above the window. Two more shots came in quick succession, one pinging the door handle and the other breaking the side mirror.

"That was close," I said, looking around for the source of the attack.

"Bird," Tex said, looking in his mirror.

My blood went cold. In this war, the Chinese had a mean robotic helicopter. Not just quick and agile—it had an electric spray gun that could deliver a one-time shot of two hundred bullets, which would about vaporize truck like this.

"If they lock on, we'll only have a few seconds before it gets right over us," I said.

I repositioned myself with my back against the dash to keep the drone chopper in sight. A searchlight trained on us and panned back and forth. The roof was rusty, and I dug at the holes with my pistol and pulled down the crossbow.

"Don't let 'em get over us," I said.

I looked up at the arrows: two regular bolts, two more fitted with C-4 tips, and a single arrow with "Haymaker" scratched into it.

"What the hell's this?" I said, pulling it down. It had typical turkey feather fletching, but then the shaft widened at its notch, and at the tip it had a two-inch-long flat-ended cylinder. "That's a jet-propelled bolt with a pop tip," Tex said. "A little missile I made for blowing up shit like this."

I loaded it and pulled back the string, and with a soft click, the bow was cocked.

I slid the cylinder through the hole in the roof and held the weapon's stock hard against my shoulder. I hadn't looked down the sights of anything for many years, not since staring backward down the barrel of my own weapon. I kept thinking about the gun going off in my mouth, the blood and the mess and that god-awful racket. The vitamin withdrawal was going full bore. I shook my head. With the helicopter gaining on us and getting louder, Jing's eyes grew afraid.

I loved military hardware and aircraft and had always enjoyed locating engineering weak spots. Aviation design always involved tradeoffs of one sort or another—when agility was paramount, you made sacrifices in armor. I located the main rotor joint. I knew this model had no shielding over the lower quarter, left side. Waiting until the chopper drifted slightly right, I released the missile with a barely audible *pf-f-ft*.

"That'll do it," I said as I pulled the rig out of the hole and handed the crossbow to Jing.

I looked through the remaining shard of the right side mirror.

A soft *whump!* A crackling, then a crunching . . . a concussion of air.

Tex looked at me, grinned, and said, "How pleasant!" as fragments of chopper began blowing past us. A flaming piece landed in the bed.

Reaching the road, we stopped for a moment while Tex looked at the sky. We listened to the bedlam of frogs and chirring crickets.

"Cheap Chinese," Tex said. "Can only afford one chopper."

We headed east under a three-quarter moon. Mud flew from the tires, and lightning bugs smashed their little yellow-green lanterns on the windshield.

Jing lifted my arm and put it around her shoulders and fell asleep. The squeaky seat with the slightly damp foam, the smell of stale beer and pot—it all made me nostalgic for simpler days.

Tex and I were still talking about the Cowboys and old Camaros as the sun pushed up, but here the tan sky consumed all that was good about the sun, as if it were filtered through a dirty lampshade found at the dump. To our left was a mile-wide scorched crater, to our right a small lake with a stagnant white and brown film across the top and, poking out of it, a bus, two trailer homes, and the body of a black horse, soon to burst. We both made girlish faces of disgust and looked silently ahead.

Tex said, "They drove vans with dirty bombs into underground parking lots. One dead driver to kill a hundred thousand."

We listened to the road for a while. Then Tex whispered, "She put something in the glove box. . . . I promised I wouldn't look at it." He nodded for me to.

I opened the glove box, found the piece of paper, and unfolded it. Jing's eyes were closed, her porcelain face sealed in sleep.

It was a U.S. government document: a decoded transcript with standard-length encryption codes. It was signed by Colonel Bertrum. I remember the day of this order, when the eight ships went missing from the project and this colonel vanished with them.

I read it to Tex. "Priority Alpha: Relocate eight Wombs vessels to Biggs Army Airfield, El Paso, TX. Hulls to be retrofitted to internally accommodate four X-Fifty-one missiles armed with W-Eighty-seven."

The Chinese could not have forged this document. This was his signature. It was real. The U.S. was going to use the eight missing ships to carry nuclear weapons into space, and I had made it possible. I was to blame for this war. It was true. This war was my baby.

I looked at Jing, sound asleep.

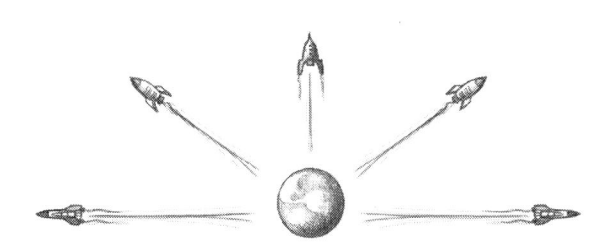

CHAPTER FORTY

I was mad and quiet, stewing in the news. I couldn't talk anymore; I was spent.

Tex said, "Well that's settled. You caused the war." He rolled his eyes. "You can't be that eat up with the dumb-ass! This crap would've happened anyhow. And just by the by, Jace, old buddy, there was a third location on the note from Yimosu." He pulled the note from the visor and handed it to me. "That's where we're headed."

I read the note. We rode in silence for a long time, but eventually, my curiosity won. "Eagle Mountain—what's that about?"

"Dunno."

Jing started to wake up, rubbing her eyes. "A ship," she said.

"We going in a boat?" I asked.

They both looked at me as if I were a little thick.

"You are in the dark, aren't you there, boy?" Tex said. He reached out and punched me in the chest. "One of your crazy ships came back. . . . Um, Jing told me, on the way up."

A *Wombs* ship? Come on," I said. "You gotta think of something better than that."

But they wore dead-serious expressions. "So you're saying a Wombs ship landed here—on Earth."

Tex nodded. I looked at Jing, and she nodded.

The math, the physics . . . the sheer impossibility. "It can't be," I said flatly.

"Maybe it's one of the eight missing ships—or a dud, a failed launch, or something," Tex said.

Jing shook her head slowly. "No. It's the *Amadeus*."

This was a lot to deal with: a rogue ship landing on Earth, the Wombs facility devastated, missing ships turned into nukes, a war instigated primarily because of my actions, my ships . . . a beautiful woman I kissed. These were all intensely complicated issues, coming at me all at once—rather a lot for a man my age. My face turned pale in the mirror, and I let myself fall asleep.

In the midafternoon, Tex pulled over, opened a black zipper case on the tailgate, and pulled a vial of yellow fluid from it. Jing and I stepped from the truck. He tapped the glass on the vial, and I grinned.

"Oh, yeah!" I said. "That's what I'm talking about."

"You first," he said. "You look like a half-dried apricot."

I rolled up my sleeve and felt the burn of the fluid entering my body. Life for almost everyone had changed with this invention. Just as we were attending to the final details for the first Wombs launch, Spanish scientists announced the creation of the B58 vitamin serum, made from a synthetic bone marrow extract, an enriched concentration of vitamins, an antiretroviral, and some type of elasticity component. This cocktail proved to stave off many illnesses, as well as having the happy side effect of slowing down the human body's aging process. It was later refined to make this the primary effect.

Tex changed the needle and vial, and Jing stepped forward. He poked her in the arm.

"Strong," Jing said through gritted teeth. Tex nodded, put away the syringe, and dabbed her arm with an alcohol swab.

"You know, lady," he said, "if it weren't for B58, we wouldn't be in this mess."

"I know. Too many people in China now, too little land. You do have some beautiful land here."

"You shoulda seen it before it had all these craters." He pushed a small circular bandage onto the spot.

"I gave you half doses so you don't get all woozy on me," he said.

He looked back down the road. "Good news: we're about two miles into Eagle Mountain Park. Bad news: coming in I saw hardware." He nodded toward the foothill's peak, where the tips of the trees were cut away and a chopper's main rotor protruded above. We drove up the winding road and pulled into the woods. I looked to see if dust was rising behind us, and patted Tex on the shoulder to slow down. We heard bombing in the distance.

I stepped out of the truck and reached for Jing's hand to help her out. "That document was real," I said as we stood there on the wooded hillside. "Those eight ships, the ones we were missing all along—they *were* being equipped with nuclear warheads."

She looked frightened and tearful, but as I watched, a new serenity came over her.

"It doesn't matter," she said. "Nothing like that does. We must reach our goal."

"What *is* this goal, Jing?" I demanded. "Why can't you just once be straight with me? Why is an assassin after me?"

I saw her eyes adore me, then turn complex. "The reason I cannot tell you is the very thing that will allow the event to function."

"The event . . . that's code for my death, I suppose."

"Yes." Her eyes changed again, now deep and longing and at odds with the meaning of "yes" when speaking of my death.

Tex came around the truck and said, "I don't know what you two are into, but we better go." We could hear a vehicle coming.

I put the Glock in my belt and loaded a bolt in the crossbow, and we headed up hill, through the woods.

"You know, Jace," Tex said as we walked, "In that old war, it wasn't the sound of chopper blades or gunfire that got to me. It was the sound of sand . . . sand pouring down on freshly starched uniforms. That sound will make you crazy when it's your buddy's uniform."

I understood.

We found a small path that kept us out of the poison ivy until the woods opened up. There on the edge of the helicopter pad was the ark *Amadeus*. She was battered and dented, her golden finish looking dull and faded against the lush grass, her glass cracked and fins bent . . . She was beautiful. This was the first time I had seen one of my babies in many decades. And in that moment, it came to me: I would fight for her. She needed rescuing. I put the crossbow down and retied my boot.

From where we stood in the trees, we saw heads and rifle tips over the wooden crates, and just beyond them, a tank turret. A huge Chinese dual-rotor crane helicopter sat on the pad, connected to the *Amadeus* by a heavy strap harness. Set back from the helipad was a guards' bunkhouse, with silhouettes of men with coffee cups in the windows.

"Well," I said to Tex, who was tucking his pant legs into his boots. "I guess they can afford two birds." I smeared my belt buckle with dirt and slung the bow over my shoulder.

"That's not their bird," he said, leaning forward to study the tank. "It's mine."

As we crouched down and worked our way forward, Tex and I stopped and stared at the same thing.

"Russians," Tex said. "Guarding Chinese hardware. Ain't that some weird shit!"

I checked the Glock: cocked and locked with a chambered round. *Enemy against friend,* I reminded myself, conjuring up a bit of that youthful courage I once had. I tapped him twice on his arm and motioned before working my way around the pad. Jing stayed crouched near the path.

From a dozen yards away, I watched Tex pull two pipe bombs from his jacket pocket, then suddenly start patting himself down. Shaking his head, he mimed scratching a flint and mouthed, "No lighter."

To my alarm, a black Hummer pulled onto the pad and stopped. But no one got out, and no gun barrels came from the ports. Tex headed for the tank, which had a mounted .50 caliber and whose commander was reading a newspaper.

I heard the familiar crack of my nickel Colt .45, and the tank commander slumped over. Tex unloaded four additional shots into him; his body jerked after the second round and then lay still. Two Russians scampered to positions behind the crates near me. They fired at him as he climbed onto the tank's engine louvers and yanked the dead commander out, using him as a shield.

I walked toward the soldiers at a steady pace. "Hey," I called out, and when they turned, I gave them two rounds each. From the shack came two Chinese soldiers, fumbling with uncocked weapons. I shot each of them twice, then put seven rounds through the door of the shack and watched two more soldiers fall. One looked like an officer.

Tex was busy with a stout little pistol-wielding Russian hiding behind the tank track. The guy would poke his head out long enough to fire one shot, then hide again. I took cover behind the *Amadeus,* and the next time his head came out, I shot him in the neck. He fell, and Tex climbed into the tank and shut the door. I trained my gun on the mysterious Hummer, which remained motionless, observing. I then heard a muffled shot from inside the tank.

Shit—he hadn't cleared it! All of a sudden, bullets began zipping past me, snapping splinters off the pallets and crates, pinging up off of the ground. I was pinned.

Amid all this, I looked down the mountain to the rolling farmland beyond: Chinese tanks rolling over fences and through cornfields; an American troop transport in flames, ribbons of black smoke reaching tentatively up, charred objects that looked like men scattered in the middle distance. A Mig dipped low and dropped its payload, obliterating a farmhouse and a pasture of cows.

A bullet sent a long splinter through my forearm. It felt like a bee sting at first, then more like a screwdriver, twisting and widening the wound. Removing the crossbow strap, I set the weapon down and wrapped the strap around my arm to stop the bleeding. An explosion sent the soldiers and me diving to the ground, a board cracked across my ankle, and wood or metal flew into my leg and back. Pistol out, I ran toward the chopper.

The soldiers regained their feet and trained their rifles on me, and I heard, through the tank's muzzle, the distinctive sound of the cannon door slamming shut. The turret turned toward the shack.

Now, fire, I said to myself. The shack disintegrated into splintered bits of wood and soldier.

I looked at the spacecraft, still intact.

Still no shots came from the Hummer. Tex aimed the turret at it, and the driver stepped out: a young Asian man in civilian clothes. He held his hands up.

The tank hatch flipped open, and Tex appeared, hunched over with one hand pressed against a bleeding abdominal wound, the other aiming his pistol at the Hummer driver.

I ran to the tank. "Are you okay?" I said. Tex climbed down and transferred his weight onto me. "Let's get out of here," I said.

With Tex on my shoulder and me wounded, out of the corner of my eye I saw a soldier moving. It was the little Russian, holding a rag on his neck, sitting up against the crates. He reached for a rifle and picked it up. I heard something metal hit the asphalt and looked down to find that Tex had dropped his gun. The soldier smiled. I would not be able to pull my gun from my belt fast enough. I saw triumph in this young man's face, saw that he thought himself worthy in his commanders' eyes.

These events then occurred in quick succession: The guard's eyes narrowed in concentration as he aimed his rifle at me. Then, in an instant, an odd speck appeared between two wrinkles in the center of his forehead. This, I realized, was the endwise view of the fletching feathers on a crossbow bolt, pinning his head to the crate. The eyes registered first astonishment, then nonexistence.

"Jing," I said. Moving across the pad with the crossbow, she reloaded—an explosive bolt this time—and aimed it at the Hummer. I put the Glock in Tex's hand and picked up my nickel Colt. Then Tex and I got in the front of the chopper, and Jing entered through the sliding door, leaving it cracked open to keep the crossbow aimed at the Hummer. Tex hit the switches, the engines wound, and the blades spun heavily.

"They're not doing anything," I said as the dust began to swirl. "Just watching us."

"They can damn well watch us take off, then," Tex said, coughing. A spatter of blood landed on the dash.

The rear passenger door of the Hummer opened, and a man in a black suit stepped out. He walked a few steps toward us. It was the man in the green car from outside the monastery so many years ago. Chen Li Wu. I aimed my pistol at him. One shot left. But why wasn't he drawing his weapon? Why didn't he try to kill me here and now, just get it over with? He had already had a few chances today—why didn't he take them?

He had something in his hand: a red and white rag. It was a large bandage. "I think we just met the real Carl Wetherburn," I said to Jing.

She looked at me and then looked down and slid the door open. "It's for the greater good," she said. The chopper blades had speed. "Chen Li Wu was assigned to you, Jason, long ago." She stepped out of the chopper. "But not by the government—by me." "Good-bye, Jason," Jing then said to me. "Take your ship. Find what you need to find. I'll be there for you when it's time."

I was speechless. Facing my assassin, the nightmare of my life, on the helipad with the woman I had kissed, the woman I was beginning to love. I watched her walk over to him and stand next to him.

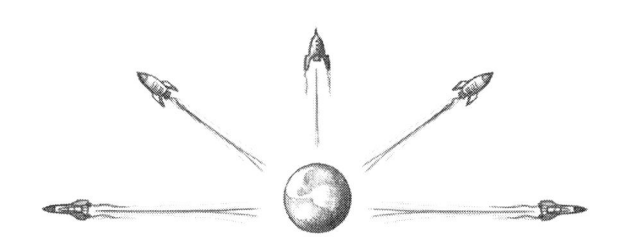

CHAPTER FORTY-ONE

As the helicopter lifted into the air, I thought of shooting him, but I couldn't. Why would she stay? I was stunned. Was she playing me all along?

The spacecraft's tethering cable tautened. The engine labored, rotors flogging the air, and the *Amadeus* broke free from the ground.

"That whole experiment thing was a load of crap, wasn't it?" Tex said. "Talking with people from far away—what a load! She just wanted to get near the project . . . to fuck it up."

We flew low and gained speed, as fast as Tex could push it, staying on the south side of the ridgeline to avoid the farmland battlefield below.

"This chopper's a monster," Tex said, rolling the rig into the contours of a pass.

"You're doing great," I said, trying to catch a glimpse of the swaying *Amadeus* while he fought the controls. As we lifted higher, the sky reminded me how much I loved to fly. In the sky, I felt closer to something—the truth, maybe. I sometimes felt as though I could almost touch it here, the truth, but today the sky seemed to let it slip away, let it fall into a lie.

An hour or so into flight, two blips appeared on the screen. Two green jets whipping by.

"That was close," I said. Tex banked north. I looked under the control panel and under the seats for the helicopter's transponder unit, but I couldn't find it, so I looked for more bandages. Instead, I found a cell phone and a map. The map was of the northern United States and southern Canada, just above the border. It was covered with handwritten X's and circles. The X-ed areas read, "Occupied," in English. Inside the hand-drawn circles, it read, "U.S." These marks seemed suspect, but we followed the circled areas regardless, flying above the mountains of northern Pennsylvania and into New York.

"This phone belongs to the pilot," I said to Tex. "It's got control tower numbers, some officers—government people." I scrolled down. "It has Chen Li Wu's number in it."

"Want me to call him for ya?" Tex drawled. "Say, 'Hey, buddy, when you think you might drop by and knock off Jason?' I kind of . . ." He struggle with the words. ". . . don't want to miss it."

I thumbed through the text messages and found one from Chen Li Wu, with attachments. Clicking on saved pictures, I found a photo of a vehicle. It was my white SUV.

"It's Maggie," I said. "Picture of Maggie walking into the grocery store. One of her coming out . . . one of her driving away. That was the dress she was wearing. That's the day she was using my car for groceries. That's the day she died. Tex . . . they have pictures in here of the day she died."

I clicked to the next photo. Taken through a car window, it was the outside of my house in Georgetown.

"They're the ones. Chen Li Wu was involved, Chen killed Maggie," I said, wishing I could replay the moment when I left him alive on the helipad. He was still alive only because I had let him go . . . only because Jing had walked to him—she contorted my reasoning by standing by his side. "I had him in my sights, Tex."

I looked out the window. I pictured Maggie sitting at the mirror that morning, getting ready, asking me what I wanted from the store. Asking me if I would be working late, or would I perhaps have time to watch her favorite show with her? It would be suicide to go back, though—suicide for both me and Tex.

Two more jets showed up on the radar. We watched the sky.

"They got us," Tex said.

"Maybe not."

"They got us. They're locking." A tone sounded from the panel.

Tex brought the chopper down lower into the valley but soon had to crest a hilltop. Treetops snapped and dragged at us as they brushed the hull of the tethered ship.

The jets were close. We had a visual on them feverishly winding untraceable patterns while maintaining missile lock. "Those are American," I said. I rapidly turned on the radio and dialed in 163.4625. The jets passed by in a wide arc and turned back toward us.

I triggered the microphone. "U.S. citizen and retired Army captain Jason Argenon flying enemy air crane."

I looked for them . . . There, high at our six. I saw the fierce underbelly of a stalking jet packed with weaponry.

"This is Romeo six," we heard. "Repeat."

I repeated, "U.S. citizen and retired Army captain Jason Argenon, flying enemy aircraft, over."

"What exactly are you doing out here? Over."

The chopper struggled to make it over a small mountain.

"I am a scientist. This is the last remaining Wombs ship. I intend to take it out of the country to safeguard it."

Silence, except for the missile lock alarm.

"I remember you, sir. My father worked for you. Damn, a Wombs ship! That's all my dad ever talked about. That ship is one definitive ID card, sir. You folks are free to go. I'd request an autograph, Mr. Argenon, but we have a mission." The missiles unlocked.

"Wait, I said."

"Yes, sir?" the pilot responded, already a mile out.

"We had an altercation back there." I looked at the map and noted the coordinates. "We escaped with one casualty but left enemies still standing." I took a deep swallow. "They had a hand in killing my family."

The radio crackled. "Yes, sir. Mr. Argenon. We will hurt these people for you. Do you have coordinates?"

It was this easy to have Chen Li Wu killed.

I looked at Tex. He saw my confusion: Jing.

"Jace, they *killed Maggie,*" Tex said. "I loved Maggie, too, God damn it. If you won't tell 'em, I will. Tell 'em the freakin' coordinates." He spasmed in pain, trying to keep the sticks steady.

"Tex . . . What if Jing is right?" I put my hand on his shoulder, and he sat back. "What if there is something out there . . . in the distance?"

"Don't ya think they played you about long enough?"

"I saw something in her eyes."

"The assassin—damn it, Jason, she *hired* the son of a bitch!"

"For the greater good."

"They've brainwashed ya, my man."

"Maybe."

"Then I'm callin' it in." Tex tried to wrestle the mike from me.

"No . . . no, we can't." I turned off the radio. "There's something more—there must be."

"You're a fool."

"I know."

"A crazy fuckin' fool."

"Jing is all I have."

"You don't have her, son."

I looked out directly into the guilty sun. "You should have told me what I was getting into with Jing," I said to the clouds, which cast confusing shadows across the wavering sky.

Tex wouldn't let me look at his wounds. What I could see through his torn shirt was raw muscle, gristle, and something oozing dark sludge. I found some morphine in the first-aid kit and gave him two shots. Insane, I know—he was driving—but all that blood . . . His heart could have been falling out of his chest, for all I knew.

Tex was not ordinarily talkative, but I could see the morphine giving him the feeling of invincibility.

"How long can this world last?" he said. "Russians and Chinese fighting together. Shit, I never knew a single Chinaman who could tolerate one single Russian." He convulsed in a short but violent spasm. I put my hand on the stick to steady it. He recovered and nodded. "The Christian way is dyin'," he said. "Some strange new mixture'll pop up from the burnt-up ground . . . Christ-less zombies, Jesus-less Krishnas. I'm gonna' puke." He vomited between his knees.

We moved into the low mountains of of Quebec. We were just below a broad wooded mountaintopwhen the chopper began to shudder and a spongy and alarming low vibration took over the ship.

"There's a clearing down there," I said. "Just over those trees . . . five, maybe six rotors wide." A burst of wind blew us sideways, I noticed my hands going numb from the cold, and the chopper's engine was sounding steadily rougher. Tex maneuvered to find the spot again.

"So that's your plan: to live down there," he said. We hovered over a knoll. He grinned painfully. "Beats the Safeway parking lot, I s'pose, but not by a lot." He coughed again. More blood.

ACT IV

My Last Day

It's been two and a half days since we landed, when I told you of Tex's death, the grave under the tree, the rifle marker to honor his service to our country, and of the button, of our friendship. I remain alone among the white birches and tamaracks, in a midafternoon fog that forms when the cool mountain breezes above meet the warm soil of this camp, where I have been searching, wading through the ark records and diaries, learning. This is where I learned that my life's work was surrounded by an underlying cover-up and that the U.S. government planned to use my project to put nukes in space, perhaps aiming them toward earth. I learned that the Chinese started this war because of it and that Yimosu—and, even worse, Jing—meant me harm.

So what was left? *My daughter,* I thought. *She is all that matters in this world—all I have left in* any *world.*

I put my hand on the diaries and decided to wrap them back up in their plastic, tie them with their twine, and set them back on the floor of the ship. I wondered about Angela and how she was holding up on that world, out there with those children . . . with that Forsythe in his cage . . . and Sebastian, who, I sensed, was bright—very bright. I warmed to the knowledge that they were out there. My mission gave me this firm, comforting warmth.

I knelt by the fire, my hands wet with sweat. "My last night," I said. From my pocket I pulled out the letter I had found in the chopper. I had kept it with me these three days, waiting for the proper time to read it. The stamp was faded, and the address ink had run. I tore the envelope's flap and pulled out the damp page.

The paper was elegant. The words were written by the same unwavering hand as the two letters before it, which haunted me—stalked me, even. How they and this one arrived to me no matter where I was—this was a great mystery to me.

But now we have met, Chen LiWu. Now I knew my assassin, whose eyes were so deceptively kind for a man of his occupation. Criminally gentle eyes, insanely off key in their innocence. I read the letter.

Jason Argenon:

I write this today to remind you that the time is almost here. I long to give you some details of myself, not with the agenda of having you absolve me of what I am about to do, but more to enable you to look into my eyes before it happens. I am the elite assassin with one purpose only. There are no others like me, and there will never be again.

I know about your mother and father, about your birth by the in vitro method. But what you do not know is that two children were born from this process: you and I. One of us was a mistake in this supposedly controlled system. Two instead of one, and it was because of this, I believe, that our parents never returned to claim us. We were alone in that cold, white facility. Do you remember?

The administration did not know what to do with you—or me. We were the stray cats everyone fed. The staff raised us, surrounded by their lab coats and sterile equipment. And in no time. I know you remember them.

When I was five years old, like an odd lot of merchandise pulled from torn boxes, I was adopted out, taken away. My adopted father was an American military man. He died in the Middle East. With his death, my adopted mother moved back to her home, China. I am not sure of the reason she left me, but the rest of my childhood was spent in the orphanage near the Psi Monastery.

As a child, you also never knew a real home. You have done so well. I look up to you, my brother. That is why I am so honored to perform the next part of this. Evolution is working, faster than ever before, than ever expected. Evolution itself is evolving. It is becoming stronger, quicker, and more concise. Some people may not follow. One race may adapt differently than others; some will grab hold while others are left behind. I hope this does not happen. I hope we are all included. But the selection process is still a mystery. I hope you and I are within it, because it will be wonderful.

Find Highway 812, one mile south of Ogdensburg, New York, at 3:46 P.M. I will be there.

*Very truly yours,
Chen Li Wu*

The fire crackled as I uncapped the bourbon bottle and took a swig and sat leaning against a tree. I read Chen's letter again: same outcome. Was I going to go down there? Was I going to meet him? Was he a liar like Jing? Another drink. What a thing to lie about—evolution. Earlier I had found a Marlboro cigarette in a crumpled pack shoved in the helicopter seat, and now I pulled it out of my shirt pocket and found my lighter in my pants pocket. The cigarette was bent in the middle, and a tear in the paper allowed some tobacco to tuft out. I lit it, and with the lighting of the paper, a soft gray ghost of smoke circled around me, and I felt as if I were in the quiet company of a hobo, one whose journey may have been quite like mine—one who listened and nodded, winked, and offered me a worn deck of cards from which I should pick a card, any card. I did not pick. He leaned back against the tree with me.

"Evolution," I said to the hobo ghost. "What a thing."

A twig broke behind me. "You mischievous squirrels," I said, taking a drag.

A deep voice gripped my attention. "A squirrel?" the voice said. "I can say I've been called worse." The cigarette fell from my mouth.

On the other side of the table was my pistol. I stood and looked at it. The man was a few yards away. He had a sidearm. He was an officer with a long face and gray hair under a gray Ushanka bearing the new Russian crest. He was tall, with a barrel chest bedecked with medals and badges on his outmoded uniform.

I started to move for my gun.

"Hold, please," he said in his thick Russian accent. His voice was low, breathy, and gruff, like an accordion full of dirt. He did not draw his weapon. I casually walked over and picked up my gun, with the barrel down.

He stared at the ship. "I am not to hurt you," he said, taking off his hat. "I come far . . . last journey . . . some sixty kilometers, walking. Please, water."

I nodded and tossed him my canteen. He caught it and then looked at me for permission to do something. I put my gun in my belt. When he moved, it was strong, his presence consuming space, as if his parents had conceived him in the inner workings of a tank track—deliberate, loud. He approached the ship and ran his hand over the hull.

"How many people are with you?" I asked. I noticed wild onion stems hanging from his jacket pockets, and he smelled of them.

"No. It is only me," he said. "The war has not come this far, and I would not bring it to you." He looked around and saw the branch-covered helicopter in the clearing.

"No, it hasn't been here yet," I said. I offered him a seat. "Where are you headed?"

"Here." He breathed out. "I am here . . . ah-h-h."

I put my hand back on my gun.

"No, no, it is not like this," he said. "Let us see, how to explain?" He put his hat under his arm and stepped to the fire. "That is the *Amadeus,* no?"

"How do you know that?"

"I know this ship very well, *Amadeus.*"

"But . . . how could you?"

He smiled.

"So, you are here for the ship," I said.

"No. Here for you, Jason Argenon. To help you understand."

"How did you know I was here?"

"Ah, now that big question, no? I show you answer," he said, rolling his "r." He walked over the dried pine needles to the ship.

Opening the door and stepping inside, he looked as though he had a certain familiarity with the cabin. I followed him carefully. Gently he pushed Doc's arms out of the way, opened the nursery hatch, and poked his head inside.

"It is okay," he said to the inside of the nursery.

"You can come out. I am here for you now," he said. "It is Stanislov. Come on. Come here, little one," he said, trying to coax something out.

I saw movement in the nursery.

From the corner, once hidden behind the machines and tubes, with arms almost as thin as a hinge pin and fingertips touching one another like clamps, was a girl with wide, bright eyes, in a zipped-up blue space suit.

"Oh, my God," I said.

"Be careful. She has never seen person before," he said. "Some functions of this ship, they failed on way here. Many lessons, physiological programs, not working so good. They did not reset from initial flight."

"How do you know all this?" I asked him.

The girl stood. Stanislov reached into the nursery and gingerly pulled her through to set her on her feet. "The computers did good job keeping her alive," he said. "You did good job, Doc, Shepard."

"How did you know she was here?" I asked.

He turned toward me, and deep in his eye was the movement—a swirling fluid compacted into an orange and red splinter of light. Like Yimosu . . . like Jing.

"This is my son's ship," Stanislov said.

"Your son?"

"My son. I am father," he said. "I am father of Forsythe . . . Forsythe of planet Echo."

His eyes, his disjointed gait, his voice. "You are," I said. This was a man like me: a man who had fathered a child born in space.

The girl stepped outside. She blinked rapidly at the sun, trying to look into it. She listened to the sounds in the woods, and when she walked she listened to her own footsteps. She tilted her head and gave me a subtle smile. The tips of her hair floated innocently in the wind, and with her arms spread wide, she spun in a circle and looked at the sky. A reflection of light caught her attention, and she stopped to stare at the gold and glass hull of the spacecraft. She walked over to it and touched her cheek to the warm metal. She hugged her ship.

Watching her, I leaned against the table. "I left her in there. I should have known. I should have searched the ship better."

Stanislov leaned against the table with me. "She is accustomed to living in there," he said. "You would never hurt any of them on purpose; we all know this." He smiled just a little. "She is your daughter, you know. She is Angela's sister."

"Yes," I said, recalling. I saw this in her—saw me. I saw Jing in her, and Angela.

"This can't be real," I said to Stanislov.

"It is," he said.

"I mean, she can't be real."

"She is real," he said, examining me, knowing of my story, how I was the one who created all this. I felt elevated when he nodded and said again, "She is."

"Earth," the girl said. Her eyes seemed so big to me. She spoke so slowly, "It is just . . . how I . . . imagined." She watched the squirrels. "It is just . . . like you said . . . Stanislov." She took long steps to walk over and hug him. "You described it perfectly," she said. She stepped back into the ship and looked over her shoulder.

Stanislov followed her. He pointed toward the bunk and handed her a blanket from the nursery. She lay down and covered herself completely. Doc's arm came close and watched her. Her eyes peeked out at us. At me.

The sun was now setting across the valley, hiding behind the trees.

Stanislov saw the bottle of liquor on the table. He hurriedly gulped the water from his cup and put his hat down. I smiled, nodding, and he poured the whiskey into two cups.

"I never thought I would ever need that second cup," I said to him. I never thought I would see anyone ever again."

"Da. Hope is good. Maybe it was this second cup. Brought me to you." We downed our drinks, and he poured again.

I waved my cup, like a drunken reveler. "So you are Forsythe's father?"

"I know—not the best child," he said.

"Yes, not the best," I said.

He looked at me, subtly searching for forgiveness. I could not give it.

"All stories . . . they need villain," he said. "My son, Forsythe . . ." Stanislov paused, a great dramatic pause, one of a father exhaling disappointment onto the earth. "Forsythe was cast for this role, it seems. Who is to blame, though? Am I, never having met him? Have I ever had opportunity to take him to church? Catch big fish with him? When baby, I have never held him, not shook his hand as grown man. He is product of your . . . how you say . . . *project*. But he is my son. There is much me in him. Chess. Music. Strength. Smartness." Stanislov clenched his fist with pride. "Yes, I am his father. No matter how far away he is. No matter how thin or distorted the vision," he said. "I say I am his father—from here, even."

My eyes started to well up, and with the conviction of a firm handshake, I nodded.

He set down his drink and put his fist to his chest, right over his heart. "I love him not-the-less." Feeling in his breast pocket, Stanislov pulled out a harmonica and slapped it against his palm a few times.

We had rummaged through the chopper and found another bottle, then sat near the fire, clanking our tin cups during unrecognizably Russian folk tunes. I rose and conducted them with my many drunken hands until he finally said, "An American title, for you, my American friend Jason Argenon."

From the crisp air and the fire's sparks and white smoke, he was able to tear down a melody from the elements, as singsongy a song as ever one sung.

I slurred, "It's Friday night on a Saturday . . . the regular cards shuffle in . . ."

He stopped playing; I continued. ". . . and the da-da smells like a beer."

"Ah, it's been a long time since I heard that one." Stanislov wore a blank stare.

"I don't think I have ever heard that one." He pointed the harmonica at me, and we burst out laughing.

I never looked at my watch, not the entire night. As the dew accumulated, I awoke on the bench. I found Stanislov at the other side of the table, with one of the diaries open. He had gone into the ship and unwrapped the diaries. He was writing in one.

I rubbed my eyes.

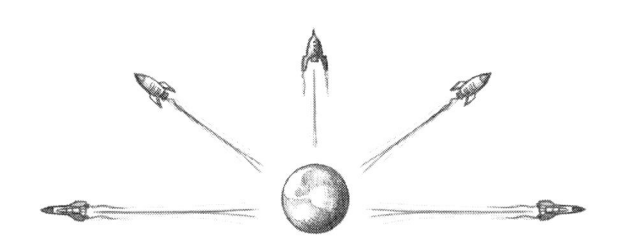

CHAPTER FORTY-TWO

"Good Morning," Stanislov said to me.

"What are you doing?" I said.

He pushed the diary toward me. The pages were filled with his writing. He opened another book and started to write again.

"Why are you writing in these books?" I glared at him. With his hat, his uniform, he appeared to be some sort of vandal or censor. He looked up at me. The red splinter swirled within his eye; its gold metallic reflections of the ship spun like glitter, like sand. I saw anguish.

"Look closer," he said. I lifted the book. I looked down at the words.

> *Every day Angela worked on her buildings, and only on her buildings. The large one reached ten feet high. I was pleased at such progress.*

Stanislov had written this. I sat down.

> *I watch the children when she works, tattle on them if they do wrong things, praise them for their good deeds, and pester them when I am bored. One day Angela said I was a good teacher. She said I had the most succinct method of discussing things and that my thoughts were well organized and well labeled for her to see. She also said that in addition to the cage around me, I had a cage within me. She truly understands me, I think.*

"So this is Forsythe," I said to Stanislov while he continued to write in the other diary. "He is telling you these things?"

"The thing about the distance," Stanislov said, writing fast and not looking up, "is what I hear. His voice, his words—I write them as if he live in head." He patted his forehead. "I could never write perfect English as this. I hear and see him as clear as vodka, but is painful that we cannot tell when these things are happening. Could be same time, could be condensed version which we view later. We just don't know."

I now admired the quality of the newly penned words in the book, as I admired Angela's own words. I admired Stanislov—not the vandal or the censor, but Stanislov the communicator, the interpreter.

Stanislov wrote with Forsythe's voice,

> *Through these bars I watch each movement, of each child. I appreciate the art in their simple and honest ways. Most of all, and most unusually to Earth, would be that I admire the flaws in the children. I love their flaws. I know they are flaws only because of Earth's standards. Here they are not flaws at all. Here there is no basis for a flaw, no comparison.*
>
> *Sebastian, my brother, now 16, has proved himself to be a fine example of an Echo Kingdom citizen. Angela and I agreed to allow him to perform the most difficult and hazardous job*

invented, but with it comes the most prestige. He is the locator of charged rocks.

Each night after dinner, he stands, pulls his pack from a particular place on the wall, and walks into the darkness. As he goes, everyone, young and old, says his name together: "Sebastian," we say. He follows the sound of the creek down the path, descending the hillside beside the waterfall to walk fearlessly into the electric forest, where no one else can pass.

Instinctively he evades the snapping bolts of electricity. He wears rabbit fur gloves, and without guidance of any form, he locates and digs out the fist-size charged rocks from beneath the surface. When he arrives back at camp, dirty and covered with oil, he has a whole satchel of them. Each individual rises from the table and touches his shoulder in thanks. The rocks light the camp for days, I place one under my cage to keep the floor warm, and everyone places one under their bed. He is the one who could do this. He is the one who can find things in the dark, because Sebastian is without eyesight. Not a flaw at all—a gift, as useful as sight itself.

I sat picking my teeth with a root and resting from dinner on my one-legged stool. I took out my pipe and filled it. I lit it with a match Cadence made for me. He has become quite the chemist. On this night, Sebastian approached me after all the others had gone to bed. On my one-legged stool—this is where people knew to find me if I should be needed.

Sebastian said in his tender voice, "I know you say my blindness is not a fault. But I feel alone because of it."

"I understand. Alone, my little brother," I said. "That is one thing I know all too well." I reached out and put my hand on my brother's shoulder.

"I am not sure how long I should stay like this," Sebastian said.

"Ah-h, yes," I said to him. "This idea of keeping people going on and on like a rechargeable batteries is moronic, if you ask me. If someone has lived, they have lived long enough. This is how life really works. On earth, a fly's life is only a few days, but did the fly not live a full life? Time is not like us," I told him. "We are better than time. Time leaves you, runs out, but once we are alive, we are alive forever. I have learned this much.

"I could never have accepted the demise of my earlier unborn companions, my fellow cosmonauts while in the ship, if I did not truly believe this. They lived for an instant. But it is, in fact, a lifetime, maybe longer—I don't know." I then caught a cough and strained to speak through it. Sebastian reached for my hand.

"I feel like my agony is diluting you somehow, Sebastian," I said to him. Someday I will be gone. When I go, will you be my effort in this world, my chess piece in this game?" I then said, with a tear in my eye, "Sebastian, grow and become who you want everyone after you to be."

Sebastian started to sing, but it was not his magnificent voice reverberating across the rooftops that brought everyone out to listen, not his superb command of his tone and notes. It was the words that made Angela's skin bump, her brow rise in wonder. He sang the first part of each verse with a straight, solid note, and at the end of each line, the last four words, he sang them, as an aria:

"Sunflowers try to reach the sky, but they are never tall enough.
They remind us of how small we are.
Angela caught the melody and sang along softly.
"Maybe our sight to see great distances

*So we will try to go that far.
Try to reach everything,
Try to grow that tall."*

Stanislov handed me the last diary and, with three thick fingers, pointed at the last few pages he had written:

The children are all grown. All have homes of welded metal, twisting and conforming to the topography in complex rows among the roots and rocks along the creek, like a rendition of the alleyways of Sicily I had once seen in a photograph. Each night, the combination of moons lit the cavern, scattering different shades of gray and purple over us. With this light, Angela formed a calendar from the colors cast down and reflections on rooftops casting up. Light calculates with noncliché math. She invites this and revels in it.

The view from the sky upon this village, I imagine, is surreal. I imagine myself above it all, floating uncontained, looking down onto the moss-coated roofs, through the ripples in the glass. Angela's houses have formed an earthlike embodiment into the soil, and if they never existed, if they were never here, they would surely be sorely missed by this cavern. The sky would miss the reflection of the light from the metal, and the ground would miss the weight of peopled homes.

On a night with a soft breeze, scents like those of rose and tulip flowed through the room. In the library, writing at her desk, was Angela, beneath a singular glass window. This window bent starlight and held the sky aloft. Her window protected her, displayed her—glass, from engine heat, metal and sand, ingenuity and desire.

"Nathan," she said softly, casually attempting contact. "Can you see me?"

I heard hope. Hope that Nathan could see her, see the candle and see that she was writing about him. Four volumes stood on the shelf, each leaning on the next.

Through the doorway behind her was a large room. I was in my cage, facing all the children as they sat impatiently tuning their instruments. I was dressed in my same old shirt, but with the addition of a bow tie Emily had folded from something green and purple and still wet. Sebastian sat in the second row.

I held my cello, which was now a mature dark orange. All the pits were buffed out, and each night I pressed its body using a device of rods, ropes, and rocks to keep the instrument's delicate timbre in place. The sides were now smooth, the fingerboard now perfectly curved, and the strings in excellent tune. All this, I believe, was to act as my connection to the air.

Cadence was handing out the sheet music I had copied by hand for each child.

"Careful," I told him. "Oh . . . no . . . watch bending . . . be easy." Cadence glanced over his shoulder. "Don't . . . rip . . ."

I had also written down the most difficult parts for my own use and put them before me. Sometimes one score of music can mix with another and exit from me at an improper time. I needed to be careful with certain demisemiquavers in the first piece, which sounded like semiquavers from the fourth piece. Although it has happened only once, long ago, during practice, I could not afford to make a mistake—not tonight.

I tapped on my bars, and everyone sat up straight. "All right, everyone, let us begin," I said. Emily poised her flute made from a hollowed vine once packed with clay, the body thickened, drilled, and dried. Abigail, Hunter, and Amelia raised their violins. Roger stood in front of a large bass drum of bent steel, a cymbal polished and thinly honed, and three forged triangles.

Under the guidance of my bow, the violins let soft notes swim into the room. Emily stood. She played her flute with a breathy, entertaining, and overly dramatic presence.

Sebastian put the most complex instrument to his lips. Its sound was warming, like that of a boxcar running over railroad tracks combined with the rough ramble of pulleys and anchors working their magical tasks. Sebastian's efforts carving the wood so accurately, his positioning of the individual reeds, and the foundry and machining of the ornate miniature screws paid off in the hard and bending, peppery crunch of his harmonica when he played his solo. Roger and Hunter looked on with a tinge of jealousy.

Cadence smashed two cymbals together, and the violins returned, even stronger, eagerly filling each written note with life.

You could not compare the sound of what was occurring here on Echo to anything else in the universe. To label music is to rinse it of its protective coating of originality, to cram it unwilling into a block with sides, a floor, and a roof, rendering it ordinary. But here and now was this music; here it was escaping to swing acrobatically on the vines, to roll through the desert with tumbleweed wheels, its reaching arms grasping at the low-flying planets and its lips blowing kisses to the stars. This music was quietly setting a rebellion, a resistance, starting a fight, like a single drummer leading an army into battle. Survival for Angela and her family was now imminent. Progress was taking hold, gaining traction. Tonight was relieved of gravity's heavy load; tonight touched every existent thing, and the music inside the night lived the life of a song, the life of a voice dying to be heard, and the life of soft skin dying to be touched, moving celestially through everyone. The entity of the Distance parallels this, Father. The Distance is like music.

When we finished playing, we clapped for one another. Angela laid down her glass pen and clapped the longest. A tear hit her delicate page, and the letters she had written wicked up the wetness. "Forsythe." She had written my name. My name was now on her page. My name was written in admiration, as she had never done before today. It was written, yet distorted by a tear in her book.

Angela walked into the room, looking at the children with smiles and then to me. She said, "Forsythe, that was wonderful." She sighed. "Would you like to say anything about your first performance in the hall?"

I cleared my throat and said, "Well, in most symphonies the players don't need to manufacture their own instruments, and the hall is rarely acoustically enhanced by dirt, but I believe"—I pulled my head back and nodded with crossed arms—"that everyone performed well, including the dirt."

Angela looked over, and for the first time in a very long time, she looked directly into my eye. I felt as though I was a person again—a complete, real person.

She said, "Thank you, everyone. I so enjoyed my evening listening to you tonight."

The children all stood and left to go to their homes and to bed. Hunter approached me with the handcart, but I shook my head.

"Not tonight, Hunter. Thank you," I said to him.

Angela blew out the candle, and the smoke waltzed to the lingering recollection of the music. Angela stepped through the arched doorway and down the three white steps. Above her, carved in the archivolt, were large bold letters filled with gold: "Library and Symphony Hall 2091."

The moonlight found its way onto me. It was applying blue light. Father—Leytenant Stanislov—I thought of you and how much it has meant to me to be able to speak with you in this way, to be able to know you from so far. This trip has been worth it; however, this life has been far too long. If it were not for meeting Angela and the children—if not for meeting you—I would have preferred to be a fly. Then this body should have died in only days. I believe that time has come for me. It must have heard me speak poorly about it on more than one occasion.

Forsythe's words stopped. I looked at Stanislov, and his features turned red. A thick, clear wash ran over his eyes and cheeks, but he did not release one full tear. Although vast wells of them existed somewhere inside him, they did not venture outside, did not go beyond the edges of him.

"Stanislov?" I said. "Are you okay? What happened?"

He lowered his head. It was then that it happened. My own eye blazed. A light—a stunning brightness, the impression of the splinter white and brilliant and intensifying—it overcame my view of the ship, the woods, the mountains and the sky. It nullified and wrote over all this. The splinter overran reality and demanded my full attention. Inside this light, in crystal clarity, I could see Angela, but then, just as suddenly, I could see through her eyes as if they were my own, and there before me was Forsythe. His head was back, his mouth was open, his cello leaning against his knee. His arms were limp, and his lacerated skin was cold and exhausted. Forsythe was dead.

Angela's eyes were watering. She had lost him, her enemy . . . her friend. She touched his fingertips. She touched his hand and the long scar across his face. She felt the ridge around his missing eye and moved the backs of her fingers down his scruffy beard. She encountered a depression in the bone of his jaw, where a meteorite from the planetary ring had flown through and chipped away pieces of him. Turning, she went back into the library and put her head down on her arm, on the table. She was alone inside. I could see her. I could see alone. The connection was made. Yimosu was right. And Jing. Uninterrupted. Angela was real and illuminated here.

I forced the light in my mind to dim. I was disoriented. I could see Stanislov. He raised his head. His splinter was flowing with a river's strength.

"She loved him," Stanislov said. "We both see her now, you and I. It was Forsythe holding her back from you. Although they fought—*and he had one mean streak*—she owned a form of love for him. She loved him. He's gone."

Stanislov took the diary from me, closed it, and set it down to stare into the woods. "We learned from him, no?" I gripped his shoulder and nodded. My daughter stepped through the doorway of the ship, rubbing her eyes.

"Your sister is here," I said to Angela in the Distance. I felt something warm respond. "She is here," I said again.

Angela heard my voice. On Echo, she lifted her head. She stood and walked to stare upward and through the window in the ceiling.

"Your sister is here, and she is well," I said.

"Father?" Angela said. "Is that you, Father?"

"Yes, it's me, and I can hear you. I can here you!" I yelled to the sky.

"I never thought," Angela said. "I never thought you would become real. Then Earth is real, too. All the lessons are real, aren't they?"

"Yes." I smiled and laughed. "But I am not really sure I know what real is anymore."

"There is something bothering you, Father. A great weight."

"Yes, Today is a day marked for an unusual event to occur to me . . . but forget about that," I said. I needed to conceal things. I struggled to think of the assassin only as a man in a black suit on a street, not real to me at all. I made him unobtainable to her. Stanislov slowly looked at me with dark eyes. I looked away.

"Did you hear me tell you, your sister made it here safely?" I said to Angela.

"Yes, yes. That is so wonderful. Angel B," Angela said.

"Let's find her a different name," I said. I knew Angela wanted this. We then said, in unison, "Far."

The girl in the flowery dress looked at me. "That is my name, isn't it?" she said. "'Far' is my name." She gave me a big hug.

"I felt her hug you," Angela said. I looked at Stanislov. He nodded and smiled. "Father, I am so glad to see you," Angela said. "I knew you would come for me. I knew it."

Angela heard a footstep behind her and turned to find Sebastian lighting a candle in the concert hall. Sebastian touched Forsythe's still, cool hand.

"He is gone," Angela said.

The wind was blowing her hair across her face. Rain started to fall into the cavern—rain she had never seen before. Sebastian turned toward Angela. Carefully, he reached out and touched her face.

"No, Angela," Sebastian said, reading her lost smile with his fingertips. "Forsythe is not gone." Sebastian's splinter moved in a way like no others, like water forcing itself upward. She was struck by the depth of his expression. It was fear and something toxic. She stepped away from him.

"I am alone," Sebastian said. "Without my brother . . . therefore, I see."

The other children stood in the doorway, each with a glassy-glowing splinter embedded in the left pupil. They said in unison, "Sebastian." I felt them going somewhere. I felt all of them searching. They found a thread of a connection.

"What do you see, Sebastian?" Angela said. "What can you see?"

"I can see more," he answered. "I see many people walking where things are destroyed." He stepped over to Forsythe's cage and gripped a bar. He stared straight at the dead body of Forsythe. Sebastian turned to face the other children. "I see a metal fence among concrete ruins," he said. "And . . ." He paused. ". . . I see my mother."

"Forsythe's mother, our mother, she is suffering; she is barely breathing. My father, Stanislov, is holding her and weeping. He is kneeling in the Moscow snow, and passersby are ignoring them." A tear fell to Sebastian's lip.

Stanislov stood. "I need to borrow your helicopter," he said. I nodded to him. "Sometimes these things we see, they ignore time," he said, walking with stern boot steps toward the chopper. I heard him say, "Sometimes they are not real at all."

I sensed denial. Far and I stood in silence and watched the chopper fly over the mountain's shoulder.

"Angela, she is great," Far said, and looked up at me. I saw that her fingers were unusually straight and touching at their tips. Reaching down and looking into her eyes, I carefully separated them and held my hand up for her to see me clench my fingers tight, then opened them wide. She tried this, and I was relieved to see her hands no longer functioning like robotic clamps. Giggling, she ran inside the ship. "I miss Forsythe," I heard her say.

I whispered, "You weren't alone in that ship at all, were you?"

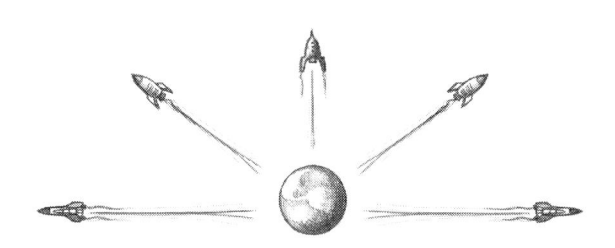

CHAPTER FORTY-THREE

In the afternoon, I came to the door of the ship, and Far stepped out. She had on another pretty dress, blue and simple, and Doc brushed her long brown hair, which, I noticed, was almost the same color as my own but with natural black steaks. We stood there smiling, existing.

The light in my eye pulsed like buildings in an earthquake, shifting. I felt like an architect who is trying to redesign a city as it falls into ruins. I anticipated the blank page—a clean slate. Even a rockslide forms a new surface to build on. But without careful thought and consideration of the past, and remembering what history teaches us, the things we do are senseless; the wind covers old sand only with other old sand.

My splinter showed to me Stanislov, landing the chopper a hundred fifty miles south, on a two-lane road near a strip mall and a bank. In his path, as he walked, were men, tattered and bandaged, lying near their rifles with their bootlaces untied. A voice blasted from the speaker on the fender of a Russian tank. "Two American platoons are heading toward our position," the voice said. "Use the September assault route...."

Stanislov reached the top of the hill, where hundreds of Russian soldiers were beginning to march. Standing above them all, he unsnapped his holster and threw his pistol into the dirt. Then he took off his medals, his ribbons, his bars, tightened his fist around them, and dropped the bent pieces to the ground.

One by one, the soldiers' faces turned up. Each man saw real life for the first time.

Stanislov smiled. "These are your new orders," he said.

They saw no rank, no age, no deception, no ego. They saw no reason to fight another minute. And so they set their weapons down. In the valley, tanks halted, and men climbed out of them. Jets banked back. This army was going home.

"Do you feel it, Jason?" he asked me from so far away. "Instantaneous," Stanislov said. "The web of people is colliding together, and the world is beginning to connect like a virus. It is invigorating, my friend. Invigorating!"

The soldiers felt no rank, no rage, no deception. They felt no will to fight another second.

"You, my friend, Jason, you must go where you know you are needed. Go where we all know you must. I know it is difficult to be the first of anything—a pioneer—but I salute you, comrade," he said. "Death does not mean death."

I felt footsteps in my own heartbeat. Angela's mind listened. Another mind connected to me: a woman holding a child. She was wading in the ruins of their war-torn home, broken white-spoked kitchen chairs and vegetable cans strewn about, photographs—any photograph of her husband—not to be found. A man connected. He was in a shelter, bombs shaking the dirt floor, babies loudly protesting, and mothers reading aloud from old schoolbooks. She could see her husband, the woman in the ruins could. I felt her find him. More visions stacked and organized themselves like glass blocks placed by invisible hands, each one making room for another, shrinking and shaping and establishing themselves within my mind. The ocean was coming down on us all. I felt thousands of people multiplying into me. I saw a woman and placed her in priority. It was Jing, standing beside Yimosu. This ocean was good. The visions were contained and controlled. Jing was right, in the prison, when she said we would not be drones. I did not feel like a drone. I felt freer than I ever felt before.

I pulled my view back. I wanted to see the monastery. But pulling back, I did not see the bamboo or the pond, nor did I see the young servant boy scurrying about. Instead, my view was of a palace. This was the emperor's palace, with everything removed. Condensation rolled down the side of a glass of water that sat on the floor in front of Jing and Yimosu. The water gathered more droplets, combining, collecting.

Yimosu lifted the glass. I heard him speak.

"Jason and Angela have enabled us to forge a new beginning and a new ending in the stream of unseen matter. Angela and Jason have connected, and the in-between is filling in. One distant mind connected to another, and now we are harmlessly occupying the emptiness and multiplying into it like muscle mass. Mankind will become a stronger species, more alive than anything ever known. However, survival is the reason behind evolution, and this new beginning may be only a sign, it may be only an occurrence in preparation for a threat greater than we have ever known.

Yimosu said, "There is, however, a degree of cloudiness steeping in the Distance. I can feel another type of war coming. It is a clash between the world of material things and those of us who are evolving. Hatred hinders our work. But hatred exists nonetheless. Can you feel it?"

I felt him walk to the door, Jing following close behind. "Jason, my friend," he said, "we must become even stronger. And you must be the first to gain this strength."

The hinges to the tall and ancient doors of the palace moaned as monks pushed the doors open. The crowd outside cheered, and Jing unearthed her subtle smile. It was a vote in the minds of all. They could hear him. They could hear Yimosu's wisdom, his good, and in his wisdom—even better—he could hear them.

The guards from the Home Depot prison walked into the oak-wooded hills, toward their aircraft carriers anchored in the Gulf. I could see the evil ones remaining disconnected, perhaps banished until remorse prevailed over their guilty minds. Crime all but stopped. Bad deeds slid away like wrinkles on a bedsheet brought tight and tucked in. Jails began to empty, and even the jailers went home. People yearned to be better. I could feel them yearning to grow away from the madness of the past. I felt companionship flourishing like fresh vines and blossoming, connecting. I felt the warmth that meant someone was close by. In contrast, I could feel the moment they thought of abandoning me, and others stepped in gently to help resolve the issue with me, with them, within me, within them.

It is a struggle we endure in these dilapidating bodies: the adversarial conditions, the self-built quandaries of monetary survival, of physical fulfillment, of material gratification. We come to find out that this struggle was removable, like an inflamed and unnecessary organ. This struggle was discardable like an appendix.

I felt as if I owed the world something because of my project, because the Wombs project spawned the war and I failed to act to bring to justice those who stole the missing ships for the wrong purpose. I see them here now, and I bring them forward to all of you. Colonel Bertrum stands before you.

On Echo, Sebastian climbed out of the cavern and onto the desert and stared into the sky. He could see the Kremlin. Just as Yimosu was in the palace in China, the honorable stepped forward, and the dishonorable walked away, unknowing of the connection, not yet able to understand. They needed remorse. If they did not feel sorry, they could not join us . . . not yet.

Chen Li Wu stood beside his Hummer, in his black suit, rifle over his shoulder, pacing by the railroad tracks. He looked at his watch and searched the road to the border gates.

He sensed that I could see him. He became joyous.

With Far in the forest collecting acorns, I went into the ship and stacked the diaries back up, put the monitor back inside, patted Doc's camera arm, and closed up the ship.

Far looked up at me, and I stopped. She reached to my stomach for my gun, and I pushed her hand away. She looked at me disapprovingly, turned, and shuffled her feet through the deep leaves, and I followed her. She stopped. I smiled when she curled down into a ball and rested, then rose and walked ahead eight more steps, then rested.

I adjusted my sling and held Far's hand as we moved down the hill, and when we reached the bottom and followed the crumbled road, I started to feel people near us. Over one last hill, people lined the road. I focused on a singular woman who held a child. In my splinter were her ambitions to own a bakery. We heard thunder. Everyone thought it was another bomb.

"Jason, we thank you," I heard people say. "We appreciate what you have done and what you are about to do." A group of Russian soldiers rested near the corn stalks. They stood and saluted me.

I heard a familiar voice. "This thing is greater than you and I," Jing said. "You are the most capable to do this honorable movement." The crowd thickened and began to split as the man in the black suit walked through it.

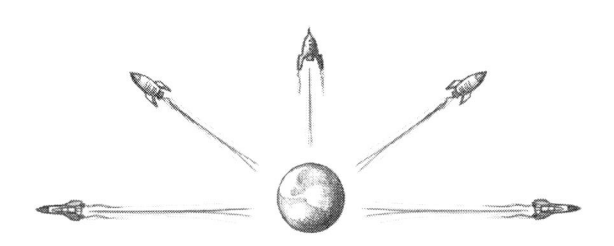

CHAPTER FORTY-FOUR

Chen Li Wu went down into the berm and back up, heading toward me on the road and bringing the rifle down from his shoulder. Only one thing was keeping me from drawing my weapon, shooting him dead, and walking back home. That one thing was my mind.

He is my brother, I thought. *Everyone seemed to believe in this.*

I stopped and hugged Far, and she held on tight. She did not cry when she let go. The baker-to-be stepped forward, and Far stepped back with her. I walked on. Far tried to reach me. I walked on, and she let go.

There he was, with a red tie and perfectly polished shoes. He reached out for a handshake. I did not.

"Jason," he said. "I knew you would come. You are blazing a trail for all of us. You and Angela have opened a new realm, and now you will be opening an even larger realm—a universe, an ungraspable entity. Ungraspable. But with you, the invisible will now turn visible. We'll be able to touch it, to exist in it," he said.

"Why me?" I asked.

"It is your project. You have conquered distance. You know of great loss. You will certainly survive beyond this physical life. You will . . . be," he said.

"By dying, I will be?"

"Yes, by dying you will be," he said, pulling back the rifle's bolt and offering a bullet into the chamber. He aimed for my heart. Two local men ran toward him, but instead of stopping him, instead of grabbing at the rifle, they stood beside him.

I began to reach for the barrel of the gun myself, but something stopped my hand from moving the final inch to touch it. He waited. It was the people around me and the people far away. They were holding their breath. They wanted him to kill me.

I felt a sense of honor filtering through the wide green fields and coming down from spun-cotton clouds.

Everyone was looking upon my murder with great hope. One woman nodded to me. I saw anticipation in another man's eyes. I saw the love of a child.

The gun barrel wavered. I must have displayed a look of consent, surrendering my life. I think I gave in.

"Let the simplicity grow upon you, Father," Far said. More weapons across the world fell. Orderlies ran to the ailing in the fields, and only one more act of aggression occurred in this war. It was a single shot of a bullet through my heart. Everyone could see me gasp for my last breath. With this air, I spoke only one word: "Angela."

She answered, "Yes, Father." She saw me fall. "Dad, I love you!" She struggled with what she had seen. I should have warned her. "Dad, I love you," she said, weeping. "I thought we had time," she said, screaming now. "NO!" she cried. Through others, she saw my body fall to the ground. My body now useless . . . my body now dead.

What is death like? Imagine the expression of a baby who sees a stranger with a beard. It's that simple.

I felt the race stop. I felt the rain of summer become pretend. Death is the life within the motion of your hand on the downward throw before you strum a string. Forward and deliberate, it is within this unstoppable intention, the instance before the sound, that death joins life. Death joins life; it does not replace life. I pour a glass of water into another, which was once only half full.

I was yanked from my worn physicality and cast into the distance. "I love you, Angela," I said. She smiled. The people smiled.

"I love you," I heard Angela say with smiling tears, her hands reaching out.

Heat lightning played quietly in the sky on this summer's night, and the wind moved a porch swing. *I would like to sit there,* I thought. *Sit down and rest.* The chains felt as solid as the earth. I was a newborn today, quietly initiating the formal commencement of a new sense. The bouquet of a magnolia tree wafted by me as I watched people through imaginary eyes and Forsythe sat next to me. He began to play the cello for me. He wore a bow tie, a real one—black, tight, its tufts carefully tugged.

"Space suspends us with wires," I said to him. "It suspends our words." I looked at Forsythe. I realized the look of someone born in space. *It is different,* I thought.

"Death and miles exist only in our minds," Nathan said. Angela heard him. "We *all* now live in a city of transparent thought. Life, even more so, is in our minds, too."

Angela asked, "What of America?" Amelia's violin joined Forsythe's cello, soft in its caress of each tender note. Amelia fell behind to turn a page and then regained perfect time in the duet.

I shared an image with everyone. The president of the United States stood on the steps of an old farmhouse. Very few belongings were inside. His wife stood under his arm; they were glowing with pride. "We have endured it; we have conquered the difficulties of physical life," he said. "But we need to prepare for what is next," he said to me and to everyone. And he closed the door to his home.

With Forsythe and Amelia, Sebastian began to sing. They were singing the arias of Echo, lofting above the peaceful chants of Plato and Gossum and all the other monks on Earth.

Angela's grandchildren played in the sandy desert with the bright purple passing quickly above them. Everyone could see their joy. Angela hung Nathan's scroll on the wall. When the last tap of her hammer landed on the head of the nail, we heard Nathan say, "Thank you." He then began to play a piano. "How would we ever have made a piano?" he said.

I watched Mrs. Crumwell walking beside Mendelbaum down a wooded path. She was humming.

I warmed my hands on this music.

Maggie found me. She was here. She was walking alone by a circular pond. She sat down on its concrete edge. A koi's tail broke the surface and stirred the light. "Where is Conner?" I asked. "Where is our son?"

She shook her head. "I am not sure," she said. "I don't think everyone makes it here."

I felt people become sad for me. I said, "I will find him. I will find our son."

At this very moment, Jing is at her desk, writing under a single candle's light, with many pages filled, though many pages are yet empty.

You want me to tell you what the experience is like, what it is like in the Distance.

I will. It is within all of us. We create it on our own. I am inside it. If you really want to know what it is like, you can live in it, even in your physical being at present. You can join me and all the others right now. Anyone can. Open your eyes.

Think of someone you truly love and dearly miss. A person who makes you feel alone because they are not with you. Picture not what they look like, their physical appearance, but try to imagine what they are doing, how they are feeling, what they are thinking, but most of all, why *they* might feel alone. Picture them picturing you. Do something they like to do, and think how they would think while doing it.

Look for the splinter within your own eye. Look closely. Although this may take some time, you must never give up. It is like a wordless story being told. It is a dive from a cliff, with no ground to fear. It is a waterless ocean floating us. The light will form within you, and with practice, solitude will never be seen or heard from again. A funny thing—children's fingers can almost touch us here, and no matter how far we walk in any direction, we are not alone.

Now you ask the important question: how is it that I, Jason Argenon, am telling you all this from what is known to mankind before these events occur as "the afterlife"? Let me explain. One person is just like the other in her or his core being. Our physical traits manipulate our perception of events, but in the pure essence of people, we are all built the same. We are all matterless formations whose intangible ingredients are precious. These are qualities we share, and they are timeless.

I am here. I am experiencing it. The bullet from my brother only began my life. Matter does not matter anymore. I can only speculate that our great technological advances of electronic person-to-person connection helped our minds adapt, explore, and develop, but now as we look back, we realize the need to lose the hindrances of the mechanical, the electronic, the manmade, if we are to grow. Like the first steps of an ancient organism willing itself to walk out of the sea and breathe the air, our minds are adapting, to lose the crutches of systems and infrastructure and, ultimately and thoughtfully, shed our primitive bodies as well.

As I have no physical apparatus to manage the motion of a pen for those of you not yet connected into the Distance, Jing has chosen to write these words for me. She is my documentarian, connected to me.

She has been infinitely generous in catering to me through these years. Together we will continue to document the events of the other arks, the people within them, their lives, their worlds and what the future holds for the planet Earth.

Signed,

Jason Argenon,

Through the pen of Jing Emerald

These works were transferred to the written word through dictation to Jing Emerald, who received this story in all its detail through the Distance.

Cliff Paris was born in Pasadena, California in 1963.
He is a member of the Screen Actors Guild, Mensa, ASCAP and
The Recording Academy.
His favorite place is Griffith Park Observatory in Los Angeles,
California, where he remembers Saturday trips with his parents,
Henry and Charlotte, to enjoy looking through the large telescope.

His spoken word piece "Watersound." Played before the live
audience at the 2002 Winter Olympics.
"Keskare' Floats" Directed by Cliff Paris:
Won the Best Music Video Award NYIIFilm and Video Festival in
LA 2007
and Official Selection into the Chicago Short Film Festival and the
San Francisco Short Film Festival 2007

In 2011 He is Producing and Directing Wombs as an
Independent Film

He Lives in Northern Virginia with his wife Karen and nearby to his grown son CJ
This is where he plans to write the rest of the Wombs stories…